As a child, **Fiona Harper** was constantly teased for either having her nose in a book or living in a dream world. Things haven't changed much since then, but at least in writing she's found a use for her runaway imagination. After studying dance at university, Fiona worked as a dancer, teacher and choreographer, before trading in that career for video editing and production. When she became a mother, she cut back on her working hours to spend time with her children and, when her littlest one started pre-school, she found a few spare moments to rediscover an old but not forgotten love—writing.

Fiona lives in London, but her other favourite places to be are the Highlands of Scotland and the Kent countryside on a summer's afternoon. She loves cooking, good food and anything cinnamon-flavoured. Of course, she still can't keep away from a good book or a good movie—especially romances—but only if she's stocked up with tissues, because she knows she will need them by the end, be it happy or sad. Her favourite things in the world are her wonderful husband, who has learned to decipher her incoherent ramblings, and her two daughters.

Kiss me Under the Mistletoe

FIONA HARPER

MILLS & BOON

First published in Great Britain 2012
Mills & Boon, an imprint of Harlequin (UK) Limited,
Eton House, 18-24 Paradise Road, Richmond, Surrey TW9 1SR

KISS ME UNDER THE MISTLETOE © Fiona Harper 2008
Revised text © Fiona Harper 2012

This is the expanded text of *Christmas Wishes, Mistletoe Kisses*, which was first published by Harlequin Enterprises Limited in 2008.

ISBN: 978 0 263 90251 8

013-1112

Harlequin (UK) policy is to use papers that are natural, renewable and recyclable products and made from wood grown in sustainable forests. The logging and manufacturing processes conform to the legal environmental regulations of the country of origin.

Printed and bound
by CPI Group (UK) Ltd, Croydon, CR0 4YY

For Mum again. Still love you.

CHAPTER ONE

Most women would have given at least one kidney to be in Louise's shoes—both literally and figuratively. The shoes in question were hot off the Paris catwalk, impossibly high heels held to her foot by delicately interwoven silver straps. The main attraction, however, was the man sitting across the dinner table from her. The very same hunk of gorgeousness that had topped a magazine poll of 'Hollywood's Hottest' only last Thursday.

Louise stared at her cutlery, intent on tracing a figure of eight pattern with her dessert spoon, and eavesdropped on conversations in the busy restaurant. Other people's conversations. Other people's lives.

Her dinner companion shifted in his seat and the heel of his boot made jarring contact with the little toe of her right foot. She jerked away and leaned over to rub it.

'Thanks a bunch, Toby!' she said, glaring at him from half under the table.

Toby stopped grinning at a pair of bleached blonde socialites who were in the process of wafting past their table and turned to face her, eyebrows raised.

'What?'

'Never mind,' she muttered and sat up straight again, carefully crossing her ankles and tucking them under her chair. Her little toe was still warm and pulsing.

The waiter appeared with their exquisite-looking entrées and Toby's eyebrows relaxed back into their normal sexily brooding position as he started tearing into his guinea fowl. Louise's knife and fork stayed on the tablecloth.

He hadn't even bothered with his normal comments about the carbs on her plate. She was supposed to be getting rid of that baby weight, remember? Never mind that Jack had just turned eight. His father was still living in a dream world if he thought she was going to be able to squeeze back into those size zero designer frocks hanging in the back of her wardrobe.

But then Toby had emotionally checked out of their marriage some time ago. She kept up the pretence for Jack's sake, posed and smiled for the press and celebrity magazines and fiercely denied any gossip about a rift. He hadn't ever said he'd stopped loving her, but it was evident in the things he *didn't* do, the things he *didn't* say. And then there was the latest rumour…

She picked up her cutlery and attacked her pasta.

'Slow down, Lulu! Good food like this is meant to be enjoyed, not inhaled.' Toby said, eyes still on his plate.

Lulu. When they'd first met, she'd thought it had

been cute that he'd picked up on, and used, her younger brother's attempts at pronouncing her name. Lulu was exotic, exciting…and a heck of a lot more interesting than plain old Louise. She'd liked being Lulu back then.

Now she just wanted him to see Louise again.

She stopped eating and looked at him, waiting for him to raise his head, give her a smile, his trademark cheeky wink—anything.

He waved for the waiter and asked for another bottle of wine. Then she saw him glance across and nod at the two blondes, now seated a few tables away. Not once in the next ten minutes did he look at her. Her seat might as well have been empty.

'Toby?'

'What?' Finally he glanced in her direction. But where once she had been able to see her dreams coming to life, there was only a vacancy.

He rubbed his front tooth with his forefinger and it made a horrible squeaking noise. 'Why are you looking at me like that? Do I have spinach in my teeth?'

She shook her head. What spinach leaf would dare sully the picture of masculine perfection sitting opposite her? The thought was almost sacrilegious. She was tempted to laugh.

The words wouldn't come. How could she ask what she wanted to ask? And how could she stand the answer when it came?

She tried to say it with her eyes instead. When she'd

been modelling, photographers had always raved about the 'intensity' in her eyes. She tried to show it all—the emptiness inside her, the magnetic force that kept the pair of them revolving around each other, the small spark of hope that hadn't quite been extinguished yet. If he'd just do it once…really connect with her…

'Jeez, Lulu. Cheer up, will—'

A chime from the phone in his pocket interrupted him. He slid it out and held it shielded in his hand, slightly under the table. The only change in his features was a slight curve of his bottom lip. Now he made eye contact. He searched her face for a reaction, and then returned the mobile to his jacket pocket and his gaze to his plate.

She waited.

He shrugged. 'Work stuff. You know…'

Unfortunately, she had the feeling she did know. And she kept on knowing all the way through dinner as she shoved one forkful after another into her mouth, tasting nothing.

The rumour was true.

All afternoon, since she'd spoken to Tara on the phone, she'd hoped it was all silly speculation, someone putting two and two together and coming up with five. Six years ago, when the tabloids had been jumping with the stories of Toby's 'secret love trysts' with his leading lady, she'd refused to believe it. She had given interview after interview denying there had been any truth in it. During the second 'incident' she'd done the same but while her outward performance had been just as impassioned, inside she'd been counting all the things that hadn't added up: the hushed phone calls, the extra meetings with his agent. Never enough to pin him down, but just enough to make her die a little more each time she shook her head for the reporters and dismissed it as nonsense.

She blocked out the busy restaurant with her eyelids. No way could she go through that again. And no way could she put Jack through it. He'd been too young to understand before, but he was reading so well now. What if he saw something on the front of a newspaper? She squeezed her jaw together. What kind of message was she giving to her son by lying to the world and letting Toby use her as a doormat? What kind of man would he become if this was his example?

'Oh, my God! It's Tobias Thornton! Can I have your autograph?'

Louise's eyes snapped open and she stared at two women hovering—no, make that *drooling*—next to Toby's chair. Toby smiled and did the gracious but smouldering thing his fans loved as he put his ostentatious squiggle on the woman's napkin. Louise just tapped her foot.

Only when they'd finished gushing and jiggling on the spot did they glance at her. And a split-second scowl was obviously all she was worth. They didn't even bother keeping their voices down as they walked away. Huddled over her new treasure, she clearly heard one say, 'He is *so* hot!'

Toby opened his mouth so speak but, once again, his phone got the first word in. He glanced at the display, stifled a smile, then gestured to Louise that he was going to have to take this one. 'My agent,' he mouthed as he walked off to stand near the bar.

My foot, thought Louise, as the waiter cleared her half-eaten pasta.

She watched him out the corner of her eye as he talked. Her husband smiled and laughed and absent-mindedly preened himself in the mirror behind the bar. His agent was male, over fifty, and as wide as he was tall. No, Louise could do the maths. And the number she kept coming up with was *four*.

Even as something withered inside her, she sat up straighter in her chair. She demanded eye contact from Toby as he finished his call and sauntered back towards her. Now she got her smile—warm, bright, his eyes telling her she was the most wonderful thing in the world.

As he sat down at the table, he reached for her hand and brushed her knuckle with the tip of his thumb. Louise leaned forward and smiled back at him, turning on the wattage as only a former model knew how to do. Toby leaned in, clearly hoping he was going to have his cake and eat it too this evening. She should have thanked him for that; it just made what she was about to do easier.

She let the grin slide from her face and spoke in a low, scratchy whisper. 'Toby…' She paused, mentally adding all the names she wasn't about call him out loud. 'I want a divorce.'

'What charity is this thing tonight for again?' Tara asked as she slid into the limousine beside Louise and flicked a coil of artfully tonged blonde hair over her shoulder.

'Relief,' Louise said quietly. 'They support carers— especially children.'

Tara scrunched up her pretty face. Five years younger. Three sizes thinner. She had none of the tell- tale lines on her forehead that Louise had, the ones that refused to disappear completely when she stopped frowning. Not that she did that much these days.

'Isn't child slavery illegal?'

'It is,' Louise said. 'But there are tons of kids whose parents are sick and they have to take on the role of looking after them. Sometimes they have no choice.'

A different form of child slavery. One Louise knew all about. But she wasn't going to tell Tara that. The younger woman might be the closest thing she had to a best friend in this shark-infested world she lived in, but she didn't tell anyone about her childhood. They had enough ammunition for looking down at her as it was.

At least she could support Relief in some small way. At the end of the charity benefit she'd be writing a ridiculously large cheque. Since that dinner a week ago, spending Toby's money had become an act of revenge.

'You're so good to remember all of that stuff they put on the invite,' Tara said, fluffing her hair and looking out of the window as they sped through central London. 'All I do is turn up and drink champagne at these things. One benefit just seems to merge into the next.'

Which was a pity, Louise thought. Relief could use someone like Tara championing them. She might play the dumb blonde, but she was nothing of the sort. She'd been to a good private school, got a university degree—in other words, had the education that Louise had only been able to dream about. Tara knew words that Louise couldn't even spell, let alone understand, but she chose to hide that side of herself away. Didn't serve her purpose, she said. Degrees didn't get you much these days. Certainly not a footballer husband who earned more in ten minutes than most people made in six months.

The limo pulled up outside an exclusive Park Lane hotel. She and Tara slid out and walked down the red carpet together. Louise heard her name called repeatedly, but she practised the vague and ethereal smile she wore for these occasions, never really focusing on one person or one thing.

She wanted to rush inside as quickly as possible, but

that wouldn't do. She needed to look calm and poised as always. While she wasn't going to cover up for Toby about this latest story, she knew that if she gave a hint of a twitch or a frown a lens somewhere would catch it and she'd see it blown up in the morning editions, with a caption reading 'Louise's private hell', or some other rubbish. She wouldn't give Toby—or his pre-schooler of a girlfriend—the satisfaction.

Oh, she'd fall apart at some point. Just not tonight, especially as this was her last public engagement before she announced her split from Toby and her retirement into private life. She was going to make it count.

But as she and Tara ran the gauntlet of the red carpet, stopping to pose for the cameras, Louise's smile began to take on a frozen quality. Nowadays, this kind of thing was as common to her as walking down the aisles of a supermarket once had been, but Toby's shenanigans seemed to have hurled her into a time warp, back to the days when she'd been terrified of all the noise and popping lights, when she'd half-expected to hear a lone accusatory voice above the crowd. 'Fake…! Imposter!'

'Let's get out of here,' she whispered to Tara, who was taking far too long. But she'd just had her boobs done again, so Louise supposed she was happy to have the excuse to show them off. The lime-green halter-neck dress she was wearing had been deliberately chosen to showcase their new gravity-defying properties.

Tara frowned at her request, and Louise thought she

was going to pout and moan, but she took one look at Louise's flushed face and furrowed brow and gave in. Only when they were in the lobby, once they were out of earshot and camera range, did she turn to her friend and whisper, 'I thought you were just letting off steam when you ranted to me about Toby down the phone the other day, but you're really going to go through with it, aren't you?'

Louise gave her a hooded look. 'He's cheating on me. Why would I *not* go through with it?' For an intelligent woman, Tara could be really thick sometimes.

'He loves you really, you know,' she said, smiling brightly as they entered the ballroom. She paused to waggle her fingers in reply to someone on the other side of the room. 'Can't *stand* her,' she said out of the corner of her mouth, and then switched seamlessly into the one subject Louise was hoping she'd drop. 'Husbands like ours… There are some big perks, but there's a price to pay too.' She gave Louise a sideways look. 'It never bothered you before.'

Louise snorted. 'I never had anything truly concrete before, just suspicions, and my darling husband would just deny everything convincingly and make me feel stupid and disloyal for asking in the first place.' If Toby's on-screen performances had been as good as his private ones, he'd have had an Oscar or three by now.

Tara's eyes widened. 'You have actual proof? Really?'

Louise nodded. She'd got up early the next morning after their dinner and had checked Toby's phone and email account. Plenty of proof. All sickeningly graphic. He'd got lazy about hiding it from her. She really didn't want to think about what that said about the state of their relationship.

Tara sighed as she plucked two glasses of champagne from a passing waiter's tray and handed one to Louise. 'But divorce… it's such a big step. Are you sure?'

Louise nodded.

Around them the glitzy party continued. People swanned past, greeting each other loudly, air-kissing each other even more loudly, all the while their eyes moving, gauging just how many others they'd impressed with their entrance.

It *was* a big step. This was the only life she'd known for more than a decade. And the only security she'd ever known in her thirty years. Until her late teens she'd been an outsider, someone who only got to look on while other girls her age were young and silly and care-free. She'd felt like a ghost. Someone not real. Someone who didn't count.

And then Toby had come along and swept her off her feet. He'd not only seen her, but he'd liked what he saw. It had been nectar to Louise's neglected soul. She must be worth something if a man like him wanted her, right? For so long she'd hung on to that thought, used it to give her inner strength when she felt out of her depth or that everyone could see past the designer clothes and make-up to the lanky, shy teenager still hiding beneath.

But now everything had gone wrong. Toby didn't want her any more.

Not really. Oh, he might say he didn't want the marriage to end, that he wanted to work on it with her, but she'd lost hope he'd ever change. Even if he wanted to—which was a big *if*—she wasn't sure he was capable of it.

So, big step or not, it was time to go.

And no one thought being with Toby made her special any more, anyway. Even though she knew for a fact that half the newspaper reports hadn't been true, Toby had not behaved well the last few years. The rest of the world thought she was a fool. And she was finally ready to agree with them. Staying with Toby was making her an object of scorn—or worse, pity.

'I'm going to buy a big house in the country somewhere,' she told Tara, 'Maybe Devon or Somerset. And Jack and I are going to have long, healthy walks in the fresh air and enjoy the community spirit of village life.'

'Devon!' Tara almost choked on her champagne. 'Nobody lives in Devon!'

Louise blinked. She knew for a fact they did. The county had been the location of some of her favourite family holidays as a girl, before her mother died. 'Well you'd better phone up the police and report all those people in the houses down there for breaking and entering then,' she said.

Tara rolled her eyes. 'You know what I mean. God, I'm so lucky that Gareth is the sort who'd never stray. I'd hate to have to do what you're doing. But do you really have to go to the lengths of burying yourself alive in the back of beyond?' She turned to Louise with a genuinely sincere expression on her face, so Tara's next words astonished her completely. 'Couldn't you just, you know, have a hot fling with some young stud to get Toby back and then forget about it all? Tit for tat and all that…'

Louise shook her head again. 'I can't.'

She had to think of Jack. What would seeing an I-can-shag-more-people-than-you-can contest between his parents in the tabloids teach him? It was precisely *because* she didn't want him to grow up and think that was normal behaviour that she was leaving.

'Pity,' Tara said. 'There's going to be a complete lack of eligible men in Dorset…'

'Devon,' Louise reminded her.

Tara waved a hand. 'Wherever. The geography's irrelevant. You're going to become a dried-up old prune with no sex life.'

'Thanks for the encouragement,' Louise said dryly. 'Nice to know you're on my side.'

Tara's brows arched. 'I *am* on your side. I'm trying to get you to think this through properly, Lou. I don't think you've really considered what you'll be giving up.'

Ah, the one time Tara liked to play the clever card was when she was instructing Louise on how to live her life. She did it very well. It got right up Louise's nose.

'Perhaps I'll meet a hot surfer dude or a nice young farmer,' she told Tara in silky voice, going for shock effect and knowing she'd succeeded from the look of horror on the other woman's face. Unlike Tara, Louise didn't need guarantees of Porsches in the garage or Rolexes on a man's wrist before she dropped her knickers.

'Maybe I'll have a hot fling after all,' Louise said airily, then swigged back a mouthful of her warming champagne. 'All men are rats, anyway. There's not a good one out there. I don't want or need their money. I might as well use them for sex. That's what they do to us, and it's about time someone turned the tables.'

Tara's expertise also extended to her vast vocabulary of swear words. She let a choice phrase out now. 'I seriously don't know what's wrong with you tonight, Lou. I've got half a mind to bundle you into a cab and take you to The Priory.'

Louise just laughed. 'What for? Regaining my sanity? Taking control of my life? I don't think they make a pill or a detox treatment for that.'

Tara's brows lowered as she looked at her friend. 'They *should*.' And then she pouted. 'I'm going to miss you if you move away from London. What are you going to do with yourself?' She looked her up and down. 'I suppose you could try plus size modelling.'

Louise closed her eyes briefly and swallowed. *Thanks for that, Tara,* she muttered silently in her head. *You know just how to cheer a girl up.*

And she wasn't plus size, really. She was a normal thirty-year-old woman, with a normal, post-pregnancy, thirty-year-old body. Why was that such a crime? So what if she was the only one amongst her peers not to have shrunk back to beanpole proportions within ten minutes of giving birth?

That was the problem with the kind of life she led: her current version of 'normal'. Everything was distorted: body image, priorities, people, marriages… children. What some of her older acquaintances were shelling out in rehab fees for their teenage children was shocking. She didn't want that to be Jack's fate in a few years' time. Some of those kids were only thirteen, fourteen…

No, she didn't want to have a get-you-back fling and carry on like nothing had happened. She wanted out of this life. For her and for Jack. She wanted to find a way to be normal again, to feel like a proper person again. But Tara wouldn't understand that. All she was interested in was climbing the bling-encrusted ladder of WAGdom until she was Queen Bee. And Louise was quite happy to step out her way and let her.

The time came for speeches and donations, and Louise wrote an eye-watering cheque for the charity. But even that only gave a momentary lift in her spirits. All evening she'd talked and sipped champagne and watched the other people congratulating themselves on having made it onto the exclusive guest list, and all she'd been able to think was: *is this all there is? Is this all I was made for?*

That couldn't be true. It couldn't. She wanted more from life. Needed more. There was a great gaping hole inside her that demanded it.

And once she'd thought she could get that elusive something by being Toby's wife. It hadn't worked. Not even one little bit, because Louise felt more of a *nothing* now than she'd ever done.

So this new life for her and Jack would all be about finding out how she could be *something* without him. A strange quivering feeling started up in her chest as that thought floated through her brain. She squashed it down. She could be something without Tobias Thornton by her side. She *would*.

CHAPTER TWO

15th May, 1952

Finally I have something worthwhile to write in my diary, something more than screen tests and script learning and rehearsals.

I've fallen in love.

I knew it from the very first moment. Never, ever have I felt anything like this before. I've found my soul mate. Pity it's a house and not a man. However, I could never imagine a man being as perfect as Whitehaven. I envy the owners so much it hurts.

Still, for the next two months I can pretend it's my home. That's the beauty of being an actress. I can step into another reality for a while. Alexander isn't coming with me to film on location, so I can pretend I'm not married too, just for a bit. He always says his travels do him good, so maybe this will be my holiday away from him.

The house sits on a wooded hill high above the River Dart in Devon, farther upstream than the busy town of Dartmouth, just before a bend where the green waters widen. I spotted the whitewashed exterior and columns from the river as we crossed over in the local ferry from the little village of Lower Hadwell. Just a glimpse. Even then the house seemed to be calling to me, tempting me...

Alex would scoff if he heard me talking this way out loud. He'd call me sentimental and a romantic fool. He hasn't got time for my impractical mental meanderings, he says. But maybe they've done me some good.

I know that the script for this latest film is marvellous, that we've got the best director in the business, and that the cast is top-notch, but for the first time since my agent signed me up for it I've got excited about this project. Finally, like everyone else has for months, I feel this summer will be magical.

CHAPTER THREE

A hefty gust of wind blew up the river and ruffled the tips of the waves. The small dinghy rocked as Ben tied it to an ancient, blackened mooring ring on the stone jetty. He stared at the knot and did an extra half-hitch, just to be sure, then climbed out, walked along the jetty and headed up a narrow, stony path that traversed the steep and wooded hill.

He whistled as he walked, stopping every now and then just to smell the clean, slightly salty air and listen to the nagging seagulls that swooped over the river. At first glance it seemed as if he was walking through traditional English countryside, but every now and then he would pass a reminder that this wasn't a wilderness, but a once-loved, slightly exotic garden. Bamboo hid among the oaks, and palms stood shoulder to shoulder with willows and birches.

After only ten minutes the woods thinned and faded away until he was standing in a grassy clearing that was dominated by a majestic, if slightly crumbling, white Georgian mansion.

Each time he saw this beautiful building now, he felt a little sadder. Even if he hadn't known its history, hadn't known that the last owner had been dead for more than two years, he would have been able to tell Whitehaven was empty. There was something eerily vacant about those tall windows that stared unblinking out over the treetops to the river below and the rolling countryside of the far bank.

He ambled up to the front porch and tugged at a trail of ivy that had wound itself up the base of one of the thick white pillars. It had been nearly a month since his last visit and the grounds were so huge there was no way he could single-handedly keep the advancing weeds at bay. Too many vines and brambles were sneaking up to the house, reclaiming the land as their own.

Laura would have hated to see her beloved garden's gradual surrender. He could imagine her reaction if she could have seen it now—the sharp shake of her snowy-white head, the determined glint in those cloudy eyes. Laura would have flexed her knobbly knuckles and reached for the secateurs in a shot. Not that her arthritic hands could have done much good.

At eighty-eight, she'd been a feisty old bird, one worthy of such a demanding and magical place as Whitehaven. Perhaps that's why he came up here on the Sundays when it was his ex-wife's turn to have Jasmine for the weekend. Perhaps that was why he tended to the lilies and carnivorous plants in the greenhouses and mowed the top and bottom lawns. He stuffed his hands in his pockets and shook his head as he crunched across the gravel driveway and made his way round the house and past the old stable block. He was keeping it all in trust on Laura's behalf until the new owner came. Then he'd be able to spend his Sunday afternoons dozing in front of the rugby on TV and trying not to notice how still the house was without his whirlwind of a daughter.

He ducked through an arch and entered the walled garden. The whole grassy area was enclosed by a red brick wall dotted with moss, and sloping greenhouses filled one side. It was the time of year that some of the insect-eating plants were starting to hibernate and he needed to check on them, make sure the temperature in the old glasshouses was warm enough.

And so he pottered away for a good ten minutes, checking pots and inspecting leaves until he heard a crash behind him. He swung round, knocking a couple of tall pitcher plants off the bench.

The first thing he saw were the eyes—large, dark and stormy.

'Get out! Get off my property at once!'

She was standing hands on hips and her legs apart, radiating annoyance but managing to look haughty at the same time. But then he noticed that she kept well back and her fingers worried the flaps of her pockets.

His hands shot up in surrender and he backed away slightly, just to show he wasn't a threat.

'Sorry! I didn't realise…I didn't know anybody had—'

'You're trespassing!'

He nodded. Technically, he was. Only up until a few seconds ago he hadn't known anybody had cared—save a dead film star who'd loved this place as if it were her only child.

'I made a promise to the previous owner, when she was ill, that I would look after the garden until the house was sold.'

She just stared at him. Now his heart rate was starting to return to normal, he had time to look a little more closely at her. She was dressed entirely in black: black boots, black trousers and a long black coat. She even had long, almost-black hair with a heavy fringe. But beneath that dark curtain her face was pale, her eyes large. Ben thought he'd seen beautiful women before, but this one was in another league altogether.

'Well, the house has been sold,' she said as her chin tipped up. 'To me. So you can clear off now. You won't be required any longer.'

He pressed his lips together. There wasn't much he could say to that. But the thought of leaving Whitehaven and never coming back shadowed him like a rain cloud. Funny, he hadn't realised that he'd grown so personally attached to the old place or how

much he cared about its future. This new woman—
striking as she was—didn't look like the sort to pot-
ter around a greenhouse or dead-head flower borders.

But that really wasn't his business. He picked up his
coat from where it lay on the bench and turned to go.
'Sorry to disturb you. I won't come again.' There was
a door at each end of the long narrow greenhouse and
he headed for the one at the other end from where she
stood, the one that would lead him back into the woods
and back down to his boat.

'Wait!'

He'd almost reached the door before she called
out. He stopped, but didn't turn round straight away.
Slowly, and with a spark of matching defiance in his
eyes, he circled round to face her.

She took a few steps forward, then stopped, her
hands clasped in front of her. 'The estate agent told me
the place has been empty for a couple of years. Why do
you still come?'

He shrugged. 'A promise is a promise.'

Her brows crinkled and she nodded. A long silence
stretched between them. He didn't move, because he
had the oddest feeling she was on the verge of saying
something. Finally, when she knotted her hands further
and looked away, he took his signal to depart.

This time, he had his hand on the door knob before
she spoke.

'Did you really know her? Laura Hastings?'

He let his hand drop to his side and looked over his shoulder. 'Yes.' A flash of irritation shot through him. For some unfathomable reason, he'd not expected this of her. He'd thought her better than one of those busybodies who craved gossip about celebrities.

'What was she like?' Her voice was quiet, not gushing and over-inquisitive, but her question still irritated him.

He stared at her blankly. 'I really must be going. I meant what I said. I won't trespass here again.'

She followed him as he swung the greenhouse door open and stepped out into the chilly October air. He could hear the heels of her boots clopping on the iron grates in the greenhouse floor. The noise echoed and magnified and he let the door swing shut behind him to muffle it.

'Hey! You're going the wrong way!'

No, he wasn't. And he wasn't in the mood to chitchat, either.

She didn't give up, though. Even though it must have been hell to stride after him in her high-heeled boots, she kept pace. Something to do with those long legs, probably.

Either the changeable riverside weather had turned milder, or he could feel the warmth of her anger radiating towards him as she closed the gap. He left the garden through an arched gate in the brick wall and started off on the path that took him back down the hill and to his boat.

'I asked you to get off my land!'

He stopped and turned in one motion, and was surprised to find himself almost nose to nose with her. She just about matched his height at six foot two, but then she had the advantage of heels and was standing on a slope.

She stepped back but her eyes lost none of their ferocity.

He didn't have time for mood swings and tantrums. He had more than he could handle of those from his ex at the moment. That was why coming to Whitehaven was such a good distraction on a Sunday afternoon. It soothed him.

He looked Miss High-and-Mighty right back in the eyes. 'And I'm getting off your land as fast as I can.' Even though he had a strange sense that *she* was the trespasser. *She* was the one spoiling the peace and quiet of this perfect spot.

Her lips pressed together in a pout. One that might have been quite appealing if he weren't so angry with her for being here. 'The road is that way.' She jerked a thumb in the direction of the drive.

'I know.' He deliberately didn't elaborate for a few seconds. Just because he was feeling unusually awkward, although, in the back of his mind, he knew she was bearing the brunt of his frustration with someone else. But the woman in front of him was cut from the same cloth—expensive designer cloth, by the look of it—and he just couldn't seem to stem his reaction. He took a deep breath. 'My boat is tied up down by the boathouse.'

He blinked, waiting for more of her frosty words.

'I have a boathouse?' Once again, the tide had changed and she was suddenly back to being wistful and dreamy and far too beautiful to be real. That just got his goat even more. When she spoke again she was staring off into the bare treetops above his head. 'It's real? It wasn't just a film set?'

He shrugged and set off down the path and his features hardened as he heard her following him.

'Now what? I'm going, okay?' he called out, only half-turning to let the words drift over his shoulder.

'I want to see my boathouse.'

Ben normally loved the walk back down the hill on an autumn afternoon, but today it was totally ruined for him. He couldn't appreciate the beauty of the leaves ranging from pale yellow to deep crimson. He didn't even stop to watch the trails of smoke snaking from the cottages of Lower Hadwell, just across the river. All he could hear were the footsteps behind him. All he could see—even though she was directly behind him and completely out of sight—was a pair of intense, dark eyes looking scornfully at him. It wasn't a moment too soon when he spotted the uneven stone steps that led down to the jetty.

As he reached the top step he heard a loud gasp behind him. Instinctively, he turned and put out a hand to steady her. But she hadn't stumbled; she hadn't even registered his impulsive offer of help. She stood with her hands over her mouth and her eyes shining. Great. Now it was time for the waterworks. He was out of here.

As quickly as he could, he made his way to where his boat was tied and started untying the rope, busily ignoring her slow descent of all the steps behind him. Just as he was about to step off the jetty and into the dinghy his mobile phone chimed in his back pocket. He would have ignored it, but it was Megan's ring tone. Something might have happened to their daughter.

And, since she was standing within reaching distance, not doing much but staring at the old stone boathouse, he slapped the end of the rope into the frosty woman's hands and dug around in his jeans pocket for his phone.

'Dad?' Not Megan, but Jasmine.

'What's up, Jellybean?'

There was a snort on the other end of the line. 'Do you have to keep calling me that? I'm almost twelve. It's hardly dignified.'

Ben's brows lowered over his eyes. Less than

twenty-four hours out of his custody and she was already starting to sound like her mother. 'What's up, Jas?'

'Mum says she can't drop me off this evening. She's got something on. Can you come and get me?'

Ben looked at his watch. Jasmine had been due back at five. It was past three now. 'What time?' Maybe it was just as well he'd had to leave Whitehaven early. It would take all of that time to cross the river, walk back to the cottage and drive the ten miles to Totnes.

He waited while his daughter had a muffled conference with her mother.

'Mum says she has to be out by four.'

Ben found himself striding along the jetty in front of the boathouse. 'I can't do it, Jas.' He kept walking while Jasmine relayed the information back to Megan. And when he reached the end of the jetty he turned and went back the way he'd come.

'Mum says she wants to talk to you.'

There was a clattering while the phone changed hands. Ben steeled himself.

'Ben? I can't believe you're being difficult about this! I know you're still angry with me for moving on, but this kind of behaviour is just childish.'

He opened his mouth to explain there was nothing *difficult* about not doing the physically impossible, but Megan didn't give him a chance.

'Everything always has to be on your terms, doesn't

it?' she said in that weary, self-righteous tone she seemed to have adopted recently. 'You'd do just about anything to sabotage my new life, wouldn't you? But I'm not coming back, Ben. I can't.'

It had taken a while to get there, but Ben really didn't want her back any more. Not that Megan was ever going to believe that. Her ego had puffed up far too much since she'd found her 'freedom' to allow that.

His voice was more of a growl than he'd intended when it emerged from his mouth. 'I do hope you are not letting our daughter overhear this. She doesn't need to witness any more arguments.'

Megan gave a heavy sigh. 'That's right. Change the subject, as always!' Still, he got the distinct impression she had moved into the hallway as her voice suddenly got more echoey.

'Megan, I'm at Whitehaven. This has nothing to do with sabotage and everything to do with being too far away to get there by four o'clock.'

He waited. He could almost see the pout on his ex's face. And, as he found himself back by his boat, he noticed a similar expression on the woman standing there watching him. He abruptly turned again and carried on pacing. Not *exactly* the same expression. The lips were fuller, softer.

'Fine! Well, if you're not going to make the effort to come and get her, I'll just have to take her with me.

I'm having supper with…a friend. I'll drop her back at eight.'

And with that, Megan ended the call. He was tempted to hurl his phone into the slate-grey waves. This is what that woman did to him—riled him up until he couldn't think straight, until he was tempted to do foolish things. And he never did foolish things.

He jabbed at a button to lock the keypad then stuffed his phone back in his pocket. Then he marched back to his boat.

'Thanks a lot for giving me some privacy,' he said dryly as he got within a few feet of the glowering woman on the jetty.

She gave him what his grandmother had used to call an 'old-fashioned look' and waggled the end of the rope from side to side. Incredible! How did the woman manage to make a *gesture* sarcastic?

'You didn't give me much choice, did you?' she said.

Ben ran his hands through his wind-tousled hair and made himself breathe out for a count of five. He had to remember that this wasn't the woman he was angry with, not really. 'Sorry.'

He'd expected the pout to make a reappearance, but instead her lips curved into the faintest of smiles. 'Divorced?'

He nodded.

'Me too,' she said quietly. 'Well, almost. That conversation gave me *déjà vu*. I bet I could fill in the blanks if I thought hard about it.'

Against his will, he gave half a smile back. 'You've got kids?'

'A boy,' she said, her voice suddenly lower and huskier. When she caught him glancing up towards the house, eyebrows raised, she added, 'he's staying with his father while I move in down here.' She turned away quickly and stood perfectly still, staring at the woods on the hillside for a few long seconds.

She turned back to him, a smile stretching her face. 'What do you know about the history of the boat-house?'

He played along. The same smile had been part of his wardrobe in the last two years. Thankfully, he was resorting to it less and less often. 'As far as I know, it was built long before the house. Some people say it's sixteenth century. And, of course, it featured promi-nently in the film *A Summer Affair*, but you know that already.'

The defiant stare vanished altogether and she now just looked a little sheepish as she stared at the glossy seaweed washed up on the rocks nearby. 'Busted,' she said, looking at him from beneath her long fringe. 'It was a favourite when I was younger and when I saw the details of the house, I knew I had to view it.' She turned to look back at the two-storey brick and wood structure. 'I didn't realise this place was real. I suppose I thought it was just fibreglass and *papier maché*, or whatever they build those sets out of…'

'It's real enough. Take a look. But I ought to…' Ben looked at the rope in his hand. '…get going.'

She nodded. 'I'm going to explore.'

Ben stood for a few moments and watched her climb the steps up to a door on the upper level. It hadn't been used for years. Laura hadn't been steady enough on her feet to make the journey down the hill for quite some time before she died.

He climbed into the dinghy because it felt like a safe distance but carried on watching. The wooden floor could be beetle-infested, rotten. He'd just stay here a few moments to make sure the new owner didn't go through it.

His hand hovered above the outboard motor. Any moment now, he'd be on his way. He readied his shoulder muscles and brushed his fingertips against the rubber pull on the end of the cord. He gripped the loosened rope lightly in his other hand.

The boathouse was on two levels. The bottom storey, level with the jetty, had large arched, panelled doors and had been used for storing small boats. The upper level was a single room with a balcony that stretched the width of the building. He was waiting for her to walk out onto it, spread her hands wide on the railing and lean forward to inhale the glorious salty, slightly seaweedy air. Her glossy, dark hair would swing forward and the wind would muss it gently.

A minute passed and she didn't appear. He began to feel twitchy.

With a sigh, he climbed out of the boat and planted his boots on the solid concrete of the jetty. 'Are you okay back there?'

No response. Just as he was readying his lungs to call again, she appeared back on the jetty and shrugged. 'No key,' she yelled back, looking unduly crestfallen.

All his alarm bells rang, told him to get the hell back in the boat and keep his nose out of it. Whitehaven wasn't his responsibility any more. Only, the message obviously hadn't travelled the length of his arm to his fingertips, because he suddenly found himself retying the boat and walking back up the jetty to the steep steps that climbed up to the boathouse door.

As he reached the bottom step, she turned and looked down at him, one hand on the metal railing, one hand bracing herself against the wall. Her thick hair swung forwards as she leaned towards him.

'The door's locked. Any ideas?'

With his fingernails, already dark-rimmed from the rich compost of the glasshouse plants, he scraped at a slightly protruding brick in the wall near the base of the stairs. At first, he thought he'd remembered it wrong, but after a couple of seconds the block of stone moved and came away in his hand. In the recess left behind, he could see the dull black glint of metal. Laura had told him about the secret nook, just in case.

He supposed he could have just told the woman about it, yelled the vital information from the safety of the dinghy. He needn't get involved. Even now his lips remained closed and his mouth silent as he climbed the mossy stairs and pressed the key into the soft flesh of her palm.

There. Job done.

For a couple of seconds, they stayed like that. Then he pulled his hand away and rubbed it on the back of his jeans.

'Thank you,' she said, then shook her long fringe so it covered her eyes a little more.

She slid the key into the lock and turned it. He'd half-expected to door to fall off its hinges, but it swung in a graceful arc, opening wide and welcoming them in. Well, welcoming *her* in. But his curiosity got the better of him and he couldn't resist getting a glimpse.

'Wow.'

He'd expected shelves and oars and tins of varnish. Decades-old grime clung to the windows, and the filmy-grey light revealed a very different scene. A cane sofa and chairs huddled round a small Victorian fireplace, decorated with white and blue tiles, and a small desk and chair occupied a corner in front of one of the arched windows.

She walked over to the desk and touched it reverently, leaving four little smudges in the thick dust, then pulled her fingers back and gently blew the dirt off them with a sigh.

'Did she come here often, do you know? Ms Hastings?' she asked, still staring at the desk.

Why exactly he was still here, keeping guard like some sentry, he wasn't sure. He should just go. He'd kept his promise to Laura. He wasn't required. And yet…he couldn't seem to make his feet move.

She turned to look at him and he shrugged. 'Not when I knew her. She was too frail to manage the path down, but she talked of it fondly.'

She blinked and continued to stare at him, expressionless. He wasn't normally the sort who had the urge to babble on, but most women he knew didn't leave huge gaping gaps in the conversation. He stuffed his hands in his pockets and kicked at the dust on the bare floorboards with the toe of his boot. Everything was too still.

'Not really your sort of place, is it?' he muttered, taking in the shabby furniture, the broken leg on the desk chair, held together with string. The place was nowhere near elegant enough to match her. This woman was used to the finer things in life. Finer than a dilapidated old boathouse like this, anyway.

Her chin rose just a notch. 'What makes you think you know anything about what sort of woman I am?'

Just like that, the sadness that seemed to cloak her

hardened into a shell. Now the room wasn't still any more. Every molecule in the air danced and shimmered. She strode over to the large arched door in the centre of the opposite wall, unbolted it, threw the two door panels open and stepped out onto the wide balcony.

He was dismissed.

He took a step towards her and opened his mouth. Probably not a great idea, since during his last attempt at small talk he'd planted a great muddy boot in it, but he couldn't leave things like this—taut with tension, unresolved. Messy.

Her hands were spread wide as she rested them on the low wall and looked out over the river, just as he'd imagined. The hair hung halfway down her back, shining, untouchable. The wind didn't dare tease even a strand out of place. He saw her back rise and fall as she let out a sigh.

'I thought I'd asked you to get off my property.' There was no anger in her tone now, just deep weariness.

He turned and walked out of the boathouse and down the stairs to the jetty with even steps. She didn't need him. She'd made that abundantly clear. But, as he climbed back into the dinghy, he couldn't help feeling that part of his promise was still unfulfilled.

This time there were no interruptions as he untied the rope and started the motor. He turned the small boat round and set off in the direction of Lower Hadwell, a few minutes' journey upstream and across the river.

When he passed the Anchor Stone that rose, proud and unmoving, out of the murky green waters, he risked a look back. She was still standing there on the balcony, her hands wide and her chin tilted up, refusing to acknowledge his existence.

CHAPTER FOUR

21st May, 1952

  We started filming almost a week ago now, but today was my co-star's first day on set. Sam Harman might be a very talented director, but he has some very strange methods. Very strange. Up until now he has insisted that Dominic and I rehearse separately. Ridiculous. I mean, instead of building the rapport I should have had with my leading man—in a love story, for goodness' sake— I've been getting acquainted with an assistant producer who reads the lines off a crumpled script like a robot.

  The plot's a simple one, I suppose. Dashing son of the wealthy family falls for the gardener's daughter, and she for him, but the snobbery of both families conspires to keep them apart. I'm sure there are a thousand stories like it on library shelves. But what makes this one different is the characters, the chemistry. In the script, it just leaps off the page, and I didn't understand why Sam had stopped Dominic and me meeting until we shot our very first scene together—coincidentally, Charity and Richard's first meeting too. (She's come back from uni-

versity, aged 22, having always been in love with him, and he suddenly sees her with new eyes.)

I wish I could write in an American accent, because I'd so love to reproduce Sam's blunt instructions accurately. I can't remember his exact words, but I do remember that he told us the scene had to pulse with unspoken longing, with electricity.

If I'd had more time to think, I probably would have panicked awfully. That was just what I'd been afraid of, having read the script—that I wouldn't be able to do that 'instant connection' thing Sam has been drumming into me since we started rehearsals. I tried to explain this, why it had been such a bad idea keeping Dominic and me apart, but he just kept talking about it being important, about only getting one chance to capture that sweet awkwardness of a first meeting.

To be honest, I thought he was barking up the wrong tree completely. Or maybe just barking mad. Still, he's the director and I'm no diva. I need to work. I have to work. It keeps me sane.

So we all tramped down to the darling boathouse at the bottom of the hill and I went out onto the balcony overlooking the river. (Richard finds Charity there. She isn't supposed to be there really, but she goes to the boathouse to think, to breathe. It's her sanctuary.) I suppose Sam is quite clever as a director. He likes his actors being 'real', he says.

Anyway, I didn't enjoy it much at the time, because he

left me standing there, facing away from the door, hands wide on the balcony railing for what felt like an age. By the time Dominic (as Richard) actually did arrive, I'd been waiting so long, all worked up, that I actually did jump when the door crashed open. Didn't have to act that reaction one bit.

And then I turned round and saw him.

'Breathless,' Sam had said to me. 'That's all I want from you, Laura. Breathless.'

And breathless I was.

I'd seen him before, of course, on a cinema screen like everyone else. I knew he was good-looking, with that sandy thick hair and those startling blue eyes. I always thought it was something about the colouring process that made them look that way, but they really are that blue. And he came striding across the room to confront me...I mean, Charity...and I found I literally had to suck the oxygen into my lungs. I seemed to have forgotten how to do it automatically.

What was worse was that at first I could tell he was just in character, ready to put a flea in the ear of some- one he thought was a trespasser, but the then he reached the door to the balcony and he just...stopped. Stopped dead. I couldn't tell if he was still acting at first, or if he'd forgotten his lines. I'd certainly forgotten mine.

And then I realised that he felt it too—the thing I'd hardly realised I'd been feeling myself. It was the strangest thing...

I knew I wasn't Charity any more, and he wasn't Richard. I was me and he was Dominic, and yet something just...fell into place. Instant connection. The only words I have to describe it are Sam's. How ironic. And it still seems like a poor reflection of what it felt like.

I knew.

Knew I loved him. Right from that moment.

So now I'm not just a sentimental, romantic fool; I'm obviously ready for the nuthouse too. And possibly the divorce courts.

I also knew that he was married, as I am. But, unlike me, he loves his wife. He's one of the few film actors who has a good reputation in that department. Another man might act on whatever weird 'electricity' of Sam's passed between us, but I know Dominic won't. Even if he felt what I felt.

But now, alone in my hotel room away from Whitehaven, the more I recall the moment, the more I think I was maybe kidding myself. He's an actor, after all. A very good one. Much better than me.

He's probably not worrying about the upcoming scenes, the ones when he'll have to take me in his arms and kiss me. But I can hardly sleep for thinking about it. I haven't resorted to marking the calendar with big red crosses yet, but I'm close.

I can't wait. But I also know it'll be just a few, snatched moments of perfection and then they'll never come again. Which would be worse: to kiss or not to kiss?

And it might mean nothing at all to him. Like shaking hands with a stranger...

And, even if it did, it can only mean something for two glorious months, and then only when the cameras are rolling and Sam is barking his orders at us. Maybe that would be worse.

Come to think of it, Sam was very quiet today. The last couple of days, when I've been shooting scenes involving Charity and her parents, he's been interrupting all the time, making us do things over and over again. But today I hardly heard a squeak out of him. He watched Dominic and me play the scene, his arms folded, and when Dominic had left and I was just staring at the open door, finally able to heave in a breath, Sam just said, very quietly, 'Cut'.

One take, that was all, and then he packed up and said he was done for the day. Most unusual.

CHAPTER FIVE

Louise had been staring so long at the field of sheep on the other side of the river that the little white dots had blurred and melted together. She refused to unlock her gaze until the dark smudge on the river in her peripheral vision motored out of sight.

Eventually, when it didn't seem like defeat, she sighed and turned to rest her bottom on the railing of the balcony and stared back into the boathouse.

He couldn't have known who he'd looked like standing there below her on the steps as he offered her the long, black key. It had been one of her favourite scenes in *A Summer Affair*—when Richard came to meet Charity secretly in the boathouse. Not that anything really *happened* between them. It was the undercurrents, the unspoken passion that had made it one of the most romantic scenes in any film she'd ever seen.

The trespasser had looked at her with his warm brown eyes and, somehow, had offered her more than a key as he stood there. For the first time in years, she'd blushed, then hurried to hide the evidence with her hair.

And then he'd had to go and spoil that delicious feeling—the feeling that, maybe, not all men were utter rats—by reminding her of who she was.

Louise stood up, brushed the dirt off of her bottom and walked back into the little sitting room. Of course, she wasn't interested in getting involved with anyone just now—despite what Tara said about the therapeutic nature of a hot and heavy fling—so she didn't know why she'd got so upset with the gardener. Slowly, she closed and fastened the balcony doors, then exited the boathouse, locking the door and returning the key to its hiding place.

The light was starting to fade and she hurried back up the steep hill, careful to retrace her steps and not get lost, mulling things over as she went. No, it wasn't that she was developing a fancy for slightly scruffy men in waxy overcoats; it was just that, for a moment, she'd believed there was a possibility of something *more* in her future. Something she'd always yearned for, and now believed was only real between the covers of a novel or in the darkness of a cinema.

She shook her hair out of her face to shoo away the sense of disappointment. The gardener had done her a favour. He'd reminded her that her life wasn't a fairy tale.

She snorted out loud at the very thought, scaring a small bird out of a bush. She was probably just feeling emotional because she wouldn't see Jack for two weeks. Toby had kicked up a stink, but had finally agreed that, once she was settled at Whitehaven, their son could live with her and go to the local school. She and Jack would be together again at last.

Toby had been difficult every step of the way about the divorce. Surprising that he would lavish so much time and energy on her, really. If he'd paid her that much attention in the last five years, they might not be in the mess they were in at present. But that was Toby all over.

She pulled her coat tighter around her as she reached the clearing just in front of the house. The river seemed grey and troubled at the foot of the hill and dark, woolly clouds were lying in ambush to the west. She ignored the dark speck travelling upstream, even though the noise of an outboard motor hummed on the fringes of her consciousness.

Not one stick of furniture occupied the pale, grand entrance hall to Whitehaven, but, as Louise crossed the threshold, she smiled. Only two rooms on the ground floor, two bedrooms and one bathroom had been in a liveable state when she'd bought the house. All they needed was a lick of paint and a good scrub so she could move into them. The furniture would arrive on Wednesday but, until then, she had a blow-up mattress and a sleeping bag in the bedroom, a squashy velvet sofa she'd found in a local junk shop for the living room, and a couple of suitcases to keep her going.

She'd let Toby keep all the furniture, disappointing him completely. He'd been itching for a fight about something, but she just wasn't going to give him the satisfaction. Let *him* be the one waiting for an emotional response of some kind for a change. She didn't want his furniture, anyway. Nothing that was a link to her old life. Nothing but Jack.

None of that ultra-modern, minimalist designer stuff would fit here, anyway. She smiled again. *She* fitted here. Whitehaven wasn't the first property she'd owned, but it was the first place she'd felt comfortable in since she'd left the shabby maisonette she'd shared with her father and siblings. She knew—just as surely as the first time she'd slid her foot into an exquisitely crafted designer shoe—that this was a perfect fit. She and this house understood each other.

The kitchen clock said it was twenty past eight. Ben sat at the old oak table, a lukewarm cup of instant coffee between his palms, and attempted to concentrate on the sports section of the paper instead of the second hand of the clock.

Megan had never been like this when they'd been married. Yes, she'd been a little self-absorbed at times, but she'd never shown this flagrant disregard for other people's schedules, or boundaries, or…feelings. He wasn't sure he liked the version of Megan that she'd gone in search of when she'd left him. Or this new boyfriend of hers that he wasn't supposed to know about.

Twenty minutes later, just as his fingers were really itching to pick up the phone and yell at someone, he heard a car door slam. Jas bounced in through the back door and, before he could ask if her mother was going to make an appearance—and an apology—tyres squealed in the lane and an engine revved then faded.

'Nice dinner?' he asked, flicking a page of the paper over and trying not to think about the gallon of beef casserole still sitting in the oven, slowly going cold. Eating a portion on his own hadn't had the comfort factor that casserole, by rights, ought to have.

Jas shrugged her shoulders as he looked up.

'Just dinner, you know…' she said. And, since she was eleven-going-on-seventeen, he supposed that was as verbose as she was going to get.

'Have you done your homework?'

'Mostly.'

This was quality conversation, this was. But he was better off sticking to neutral subjects while he was feeling like this. In the last couple of years as a single dad, he'd learned that transitions—picking-up and dropping-off times—were difficult, and it was his job to smooth the ripples, create stability. Being steady, normal, was what was required.

'Define mostly,' he said, smoothing the paper closed and standing up.

Jas dropped the envelope assorted junk she was clutching to her chest onto the table and threw her coat over the back of a chair. 'Two more maths questions, and before you say anything…'

Ben closed his mouth.

'…it doesn't have to be in until Thursday. Can I just do it tomorrow? Please, Dad?'

She stared at him with those big brown eyes and blinked, just once. She looked so cute with her wavy blonde hair not quite sitting right in its shoulder-length style. His memory rewound a handful of years and he could hear her begging for just one more push on the swing.

'Okay. Tomorrow it is.'

'Thanks, Dad.' Jas skirted the table and gave him a hug by just throwing her arms around him and squeezing, then she lifted a brightly coloured magazine out of the pile of junk on the table. 'Recreational reading,' she said, brandishing it and attempting to escape before he could inspect it more closely.

He wasn't so old that his reflexes had gone into retirement. The magazine was out of her fingers and in front of his face before she'd fully disentangled herself from the hug.

'What's this trash?'

Jas made a feeble attempt at snatching it back. 'It was Mum's. She'd finished it and she said I could have it.'

Ben frowned. *Buzz* magazine. He'd never read it himself, but he knew enough from the bright slogans on the cover that it was the lowest form of celebrity gossip rag. The lead story seemed to be 'Celebrity Cellulite'. Nice. What was Megan thinking of giving Jasmine a publication like this? Didn't his ex know how impressionable young girls were at Jas's age?

'I don't think this is appropriate.'

Jas rolled her eyes. 'It's interesting. All my friends read it.'

He raised his eyebrows. 'All of them?'

The nod that followed couldn't have convinced even Jas herself.

'That's what I thought,' he said. 'I mean, there's no substance in here. It's just rubbish…' He flicked through the pages, hoping his daughter would see what he saw. 'It's the worst kind of gossip. I—'

But then he stopped leafing idly through the pages, his whole frame frozen. His mouth worked while his brain searched for an appropriate sound. He placed the magazine on the table and stood, arms braced either side of it, as he stared again at one particular grainy photograph.

'Told you it was interesting,' Jas said with a smirk.

'But that's…'

Jas turned so she was side-by-side with him and leaned against his bunched-up arm muscles, looking down at the magazine too. 'Lulu Thornton,' she informed him, in an astoundingly matter-of-fact voice. 'Or *Louise* as she now likes to be called. Mum thinks she's a waste of space. Most people do.'

'Lulu *who*?' he whispered hoarsely.

Jas punched him on the arm. 'Da-ad! You're stuck in the Stone Age! You know… She married Tobias Thornton, the actor.'

Again…*who?*

'We watched him in that action movie last weekend. The one with the bomb on the private jet?'

Oh. *Him.*

The picture was dull and not very clear—the product of a telephoto lens the size of a space shuttle, no doubt. But there was no doubting the fierce glare in those eyes as she squared up to the paparazzo, her son clutched protectively to her, his face hidden. He'd been on the receiving end of that very same look just a few hours ago and it still gave him the shivers thinking about it.

'And she's famous?' he asked Jas, trying to sound as uninvolved as he actually was, but less involved than he felt.

Jas nodded. 'Well, famous for being married to somebody famous. That's all.'

Married. He should shut the magazine right now and condemn it to the recycling bin. Only…she'd said she was divorced. Almost divorced. And, in the few moments that she'd let her icy guard down, he'd known she was telling the truth. The gaudy headline splashed across the top of the feature seemed to confirm his gut instinct: 'Louise's Private Hell Since Split!'

He took one last look at her image and felt a twinge of sympathy. Going through a divorce was bad enough, but having every spat reported for the world to see? More like public execution than private hell. No wonder she'd freaked out when she'd found some strange man in her greenhouse.

He closed the magazine and looked at Jas. 'Sorry, Jas. I think these sorts of magazines are a gross invasion of privacy. I'd rather you didn't read it.'

She chewed her lip and her fingers twitched. He could tell she was torn between doing the right thing and insatiable curiosity. Thankfully, when she gave him a rueful smile and a one-shouldered shrug he knew he'd been doing an okay job of counteracting all the psycho-babble her mother had been subjecting her to since their separation.

He grinned. 'Good girl.'

Jas's smile grew and changed. 'Since I've earned a gold star, can I have fifteen pounds for a trip to the theatre with school?'

Ben looked heavenward. What was it with women and money? Any good deed seemed to need a reward— preferably in the form of shoes. Perhaps he should be glad that at least this was something educational. But the shoes would come later. Oh, he had no doubt the shoes would come later. 'Give me a second while I find my wallet. What are you going to see, again?'

'*The Taming of the Shrew.*'

Ben nodded approvingly while he searched the kitchen worktops for his battered leather wallet. He hunted through the junk drawer. Where had he put the darn thing when he'd come in this evening? 'Jas, I'll come and give you the cash when I've found my wallet, okay?' he said slamming the drawer in an effort to get it to close in spite of the disturbed odds and ends inside.

'Cool.'

'And Jas…?'

She turned at the doorway to the lounge.

'This Louise Thornton woman. Do *you* think she's a waste of space?'

She looked up at the corner of the ceiling and then back at him. 'Mum says any woman who finds her identity in a man, or puts up with the…rubbish…she did, is TSTL.'

From the way Jas paused before she'd said 'rubbish', Ben guessed his ex-wife's version had been a little more earthy.

But TSTL?

'Too stupid to live,' Jas elaborated and scooted off to watch the TV.

The sounds of her programme floated in from the adjoining room as Ben searched for his wallet for a full ten minutes. He checked his coat, the car, the kitchen again… Just as he was racking his brains and replaying the day in his head, it struck him. He knew exactly where he'd left it. He could see it so clearly in his mind's eye, he could almost reach out and touch it.

A rough wooden bench, long rays of the afternoon sun slanting through uneven Victorian glass. A black, soft leather square with cards and ancient till receipts poking out of it sitting next to a pot containing a rather spectacular pitcher plant.

He sat back down on a chair and frowned. His wallet had been too bulky in the back pocket of his jeans and he'd taken it out and put it on one of the shelves in the greenhouse this afternoon. And then, with all the scowling and marching back down to the boat, he'd forgotten it.

He blew out a breath. If it had been just the cards and the few notes that were in there, he might have just left it. There was no way his face was going to be welcome back at Whitehaven any time this century. But the wallet contained one of his favourite photos of Jas and him together, taken in a time when she'd had ringlets and no front teeth and when he didn't seem to have permanent frown lines etched on his forehead.

There was nothing for it. He was going to have to go back.

Ben knocked on the door twice. Hard enough to be

heard, but not hard enough to seem impatient. And then he waited. The clear, pale skies of yesterday were gone and a foggy dampness dulled every colour on the riverbank. He turned his collar up as the mist rallied and became drizzle.

He raised his fist to knock again, but was distracted by a hint of movement in his peripheral vision. He turned quickly and stared at the study window, just to the right of the porch. Everything was still.

He grimaced and shoved his hands in his pockets. At least he and Louise Thornton were both singing from the same hymn sheet. Neither of them was pleased he was here.

Knowing she was probably hovering in the hallway, he knocked again, just loud enough to make a dull noise against the glossy wooden doors.

'Hello? I'm sorry for the intrusion—' He'd been going to say *Mrs Thornton*, but it seemed odd to use her name when she hadn't revealed it to him herself.

'I really didn't want to disturb you again,' he called out as he pressed his ear to the door, trying to detect a hint of movement inside, 'but I left something behind and I—'

There was a soft click on the door opened enough for him to see half of her face. She didn't have the heels on today—not that he ever noticed women's shoes—but instead of being almost level with him, she was looking up at him, her face hard and unreadable.

'I left my wallet in the greenhouse,' he said with an attempt at a self-deprecating smile.

She just stared.

He should have looked away, ended the awkwardness, but she had the most amazing eyes. Well, eye—he could only see one at present. It wasn't the make-up, because this morning there was none of that black stuff. It wasn't even the hazel and olive-green of her irises, which reminded him of the changing colours of autumn leaves. No, it was the sense that, even though she seemed to be doing her best to shield herself, that he recognised something in them. Not a familiarity or a similarity to anybody else. More like a reflection.

He shook his head and stared at his boots. This was not the time to descend into poetry. He had come here for one reason and one reason only.

'I'll just pop up and get it quickly,' he said. 'Then I'll be out of your hair as soon as possible. Promise.'

She looked him up and down and then the door inched wider. 'Wait here and I'll get the key.'

The key? It had never been locked before. But he supposed if he'd have found a stranger lurking in his greenhouse, he'd have been tempted to lock it too.

A couple of minutes passed and Ben stepped out of the porch and onto the gravel drive, the crunch underneath his boots deafening in the still of the autumn morning. Louise Thornton reappeared just as he'd managed to find himself a spot where the pebbles didn't shift underneath him. Her long, dark hair was scooped back into a ponytail, but the ever-present fringe left her face half-hidden. In her jeans and a pullover she *should* have looked like any other of the young mothers who stood outside the school gates.

He followed her up the hill, round the house to the top lawn. When she moved, her actions were small, precise, as if she didn't want to be accused of taking up too much space. Megan and all her friends had reached an age where their body language spoke of a certain confidence, a certain comfort in their own skin. This woman had none of that, despite her high-gloss lifestyle and multi-million pound bank account.

Once again he felt an unwelcome twinge. He fought the urge to catch up with her, to tell her that it would get better one day, that there was life after divorce. But, since he'd become a cliché by burying himself in his work and, therefore, wasn't a glowing example of man with an active social life, he thought it was better if he kept his mouth shut.

She unlocked the greenhouse door, then stood well back, giving him plenty of room to pass through. She didn't stay outside, though. He heard her footsteps on the tiled floor of the greenhouse behind him and, when he looked over his shoulder, she was watching him suspiciously.

The wallet was right where he'd remembered it was, tucked slightly out of sight next to a plant pot. He picked it up, jammed it into his jacket pocket, then stooped to pick up the plant that had been a casualty of yesterday's meeting. He'd forgotten all about it after Louise Thornton had appeared.

Carefully, he placed it back on the shelf and pressed the compost down with his fingertips. Despite his ministrations, the slender pitchers pointed at an odd angle. He would have to bring a cane from home and…

No. There would be no canes from home. Not any more.

He stepped back and indicated the listing plant. 'This needs a cane. There might be one around here somewhere—' Down the other end was a likely place. He started to walk in that direction, checking behind pots and peering under the bench as he went.

'Why should you care?'

That kind of question didn't even warrant turning round to answer it. He carried on searching. 'It's a beautiful plant. It would be a shame to leave it to die.'

Once again he heard footsteps. Just a handful, enough for her to have stepped further into the greenhouse. He found what he was looking for—a small green cane—hidden between the window sill and a row of pots. He picked it up, careful not to send anything else flying, and turned to find her fingering the delicate cream and purple foliage of the ailing Sarracenia.

'Then you really are a gardener?'

He moved past her, retrieved a roll of garden wire

from a hook near the door and returned to the plant, unwinding a length as he walked. 'You think I like to play in the dirt for fun?'

She remained silent, watching him fashion a loop of wire wide enough to help the plant stand up without pinching it to the cane. When he'd finished, and the little plant was straining heavenwards once again, she took a few steps backwards.

'Most men are big kids. So it's entirely possible you play in the dirt for fun.' There was a dry humour behind her words that took the edge off them.

His lips didn't actually curve but there was a hint of a smile in his voice when he answered. 'It is fun. The earth feels good beneath my fingertips.' She raised an eyebrow, clearly unconvinced. He'd bet she'd never hadn't had dirt underneath fingernails in her life. And he'd bet her life was poorer for it.

'Gardening brings a sense of achievement.' He fiddled with the stake and wire loop around the Sarracenia until it was just so. 'You can't control the plants. You just tend them, give them what they need until they become what they should.'

She broke eye contact and let her gaze wander over the plants nearest to her. 'These don't look like they're *becoming* much. Aren't you a very good gardener?'

He fought back the urge to laugh out loud. 'They're in their dormant phase. They'll perk up again, when the conditions are right.' He stood looking at her for a few seconds as she stared out into the gardens. 'Well, I've got what I came for. I'll be going now—as promised. I did say I was one not to break a promise, didn't I?'

He took a few long strides past her, breathed out and opened the greenhouse door. He was halfway across the lawn before she shouted after him.

'Then promise to come again.'

Ben didn't want to turn round. He'd told himself he wouldn't respond this time. After all, he'd had enough of high-maintenance women. But...

She stood on the lawn watching him, her hair whipped across her face by another surly gust of wind. Once again, her eyes held him captive. Not for their dark beauty, but because something deep inside them seemed to be pleading with him. His friends had told him he was a sucker for a damsel in distress, and he'd always denied it, but he had the awful feeling they might be right. Hadn't he tried—unsuccessfully—to rescue Megan?

Louise tugged a strand of chocolate-brown hair out of her mouth. 'The garden. It does need looking after. You're right. It would be a shame to...'

Once again, the eyes pleaded. He should have a sign made, reading 'sucker', and just slap it on his forehead.

He'd do it. But not for her. For Laura. Just until he was sure this new owner was going to care for the place properly. And then he'd pass it on to one of his landscaping teams and charge her handsomely for the privilege. After all, he reminded himself, life was complicated enough already without looking after somebody else's garden.

Or somebody else's wife.

CHAPTER SIX

11th June, 1952

It was both better and worse than I'd feared.

Today we finally shot the scene in the boathouse—the one I'd both been anticipating and dreading. The basic story was this...

Charity had realised she was utterly in love with Richard, but his parents announce his engagement to the highly suitable Margaret. Heartbroken, she runs through the woods on a glorious summer afternoon and hides away in the cool of the boathouse, the one place she can be alone and think of him.

He comes to find her.

She's on the balcony, crying, and he pulls her into his arms and kisses her tears away. It's the first time she knows he feels the same. Before then he's been trying to keep the peace with his parents, despite their growing attraction, but when they push the engagement issue, it makes him realise what he really wants. Who he really wants.

Thank goodness for incompetent sound recordists, that's all I can say.

Just like that first time, we might have only needed one take otherwise. I forgot to fake it totally, thereby giving Sam exactly what he wanted. Dominic came towards me. I could hardly see him through the glycerine the make-up woman had put round my eyes, but I didn't need to see much. Just the look in his eyes.

Whether it was Richard's eyes or Dominic's I wasn't sure at first.

I shook. Literally felt myself rattle in my shoes when his lips first touched mine. It was what I'd always thought kissing should be like.

When I kiss Alex, it's different. At first it was nice. Warm. Comforting. Now I do it because I think I ought to, because it's what husbands and wives are supposed to do. I'm not even sure Alex notices the difference. Maybe that's because he always seems to be in such a rush.

Dominic wasn't in a rush.

He was soft, gentle. Patient. I know it was all supposed to be about Richard and how he felt about Charity, but I couldn't help feeling as if he was gently reaching inside me to see what no one else has ever seen before. All the bits I hide. All the bits that are too precious to let anyone see. It was utterly, utterly bewitching.

I fluffed the next three takes on purpose.

But then I think Sam got wise to me. He gave me one of his looks. The ones I've learned to pay attention to. It doesn't do to cheese the great Samuel Harman off, not if you want a career that lasts longer than a fortnight, so I steeled myself to make the last take count.

Dominic walked onto the balcony, placed his hands on my shoulders and turned me to face him. The shaking started again. I couldn't help it. This was going to be it—the take Sam wanted, and my very last kiss with a man who felt like my perfect match. It was almost too much. I nearly fluffed it for real.

He stared down at me, looked deep into my eyes in a way that made my insides both churn and come to rest at the same time. I felt as if I was flying. And then he pressed the softest of kisses to my eyelids. I hung onto him, taking all I could. Giving everything back.

And then his lips were on mine. Sweet, sweet heaven. I started crying for real. No need for the glycerine.

And then something wonderful happened. Dominic had been leaning against the balcony, pulling me close against him, and he lost his balance, stumbled slightly because of the way he'd turned his body to kiss me more deeply. I knew the camera was in really close on us, and I heard Sam swear when we both lurched out of shot.

'Cut!' he yelled, and Dominic and I broke apart.

I looked up at him and I thought my heart was going to pop right out of my chest.

'Sorry,' he said, but there was a glimmer of humour

in his eyes, a sense of being co-conspirators in some wonderful secret.

And that's when I realised that Dominic Blake had messed up on purpose.

CHAPTER SEVEN

Louise watched Ben go. She kept watching until long after his tall frame disappeared round the side of the house into a tangle of grass and shrubs and trees that were now, technically, her back garden. Not that she'd had the courage to explore it fully yet.

She forced herself to turn away and look back at the greenhouse.

Was she mad? Quite possibly.

In all seriousness, she'd just given a man she knew nothing about permission to invade her territory on a regular basis. Yet…there'd been something so preposterously truthful about his story and so refreshingly straightforward about his manner that she'd swallowed it whole. Next time she'd have to frisk him for a long-lens camera and a dictaphone, just in case.

She'd left the greenhouse door open. Slowly, she closed the distance to the heavy Victorian glazed door, with its beautiful brass handle and peeling, off-white paint. On a whim, she stepped inside before she closed the door and stood for a few moments in the warm dampness. It smelled good in here, of earth and still air, but very real. She liked real.

The assorted plants lining the shelves by the windows really were quite exquisite. She'd never seen anything like them. Venus fly-traps sat next to frilly, sticky-looking things in shades of pink and purple.

She walked over to the little plant that the gardener had saved. She felt an affinity with this little plant, recently uprooted, thin, fragile. Now in a foreign climate, reaching hungrily heavenwards with an appetite that might never be satisfied. She reached out and touched the soil at its base. It did feel good. She pulled her hand away, but didn't wipe it on the back of her jeans.

Near the door were the stubby, brown plants that had started to hibernate. Just like her. All those years with Toby now seemed like a time half-asleep. Her mind wandered to a photo of a famous actress who had graced the pages of all the gossip magazines a few years ago. She'd been snapped whooping for joy when the papers finalising her divorce had arrived. Since then she'd lost twenty pounds, received two Oscars and had been seen with a string of hot-looking younger men.

Louise frowned. Shouldn't this be the time when *she* blossomed, came into her own? She paused for a moment, tried to search deep inside herself for the first signs of germination, but she was afraid she'd be waiting a very long time. She still felt numb inside.

She turned and exited the greenhouse, closing the door behind her and marched back down the path to her new home. Once the house was sorted, she'd feel better. She'd already talked to a team of decorators who could make her vision for this old house come alive. But what she really wanted more than anything was to find some pictures of how it had been in the past, so she could take the best elements of its history and mix them with her own unique stamp.

Surely there were photos somewhere she could look at? Once she'd had a cup of tea, she'd rifle through all the forgotten cupboards and attics of the vast old house and see if she could find a photo, or some papers— something—that would help her bring this house back to life.

Louise might still be hibernating, but she had a feeling Whitehaven was ready to wake up.

It seemed odd to have so much noise and movement in the house after a couple of weeks of solitary occupation and silence. The structure of the house was sound, but it needed a little TLC. The outside was worse than the inside, having had to brave a few winters high up on a hill above a salty tidal river. Nothing a little skilled work wouldn't fix, though.

At first Louise stayed on hand to oversee the repairs and redecoration work. When she wasn't needed, she hunted through the forgotten spaces of Whitehaven, looking for any clues to the house's past. She found old newspapers and some electricity bills from a decade ago, but nothing that got to the heart of the lovely old mansion.

In the end she took refuge from the muddy boots, the endless tea-making, and took herself off down to the boathouse. That was also somewhere that could do with a bit of a spruce-up, but she'd already decided it was a project she would handle personally. If all those women on the decorating shows on telly could wield a paint-brush, then so could she. And, if she got it all wrong, then she would be the only person to see it, because this was her place, her sanctuary.

Louise wasn't scared of a bit of hard work. She'd done plenty while she'd been raising her brothers and sisters and looking after her dad. But she'd felt trapped by it, as if it were a prison sentence stretching into the future. Cleaning up the boathouse was different. It was her choice, and she found that instead of being drain-ing and weary, scrubbing down the walls and making every last inch shine was energising. She surprised her-self with how long she kept going the first day.

Even more, she surprised herself by arriving early the next morning again—flask of tea in hand, and a book to read when she took a break—ready to start again. Half-way through the morning she turned her attention to the fireplace. It was a Victorian design: cast iron hold-ing tiled inserts with a wooden surround and a firestone cut into the floorboards. She decided to take the thick layer of dust off first, then she'd be able to work out what kind of cleaning materials she could use on the tiles without damaging them. She didn't want to rub the hand-painted blue flowers off their white background with one pump of cleaning spray.

This wasn't normal dust, she realised, as she passed the duster over it. It didn't fluff and fly off like normal stuff. It seemed to be welded on. She rubbed a little harder, trying to dislodge some of the stubbornly clinging dirt, trying hard not to think about what the ingredients might be to make it stick that way.

She must have been rubbing harder than she'd realised, because suddenly the second tile down in the vertical strip of four gave way and her hand hit the wall behind. Her heart pounded. Had she broken the tile? If she had, she had no idea if she'd ever be able to match it again. But she hadn't heard a crashing noise, just a dull clang as it had fallen down behind the tiles below it. She moved closer to the fireplace and dipped most of her forearm down into the hole. Her fingers reached and flexed trying to find a hard ceramic edge. Perhaps she could just balance it back in place until she found some glue to repair it?

Louise's fingers closed around something, but it wasn't fired clay.

It was paper. And a leather binding.

It was a book.

What on earth was it doing *inside* the fireplace in an out-of-the-way spot like this? Hardly a conventional bookshelf. Could it have fallen down the back?

She stood up and checked the surround. No. It was fixed securely against the plaster wall. Frowning, she knelt down again and reached inside the square hole once more. Carefully, she pinched the book between thumb and forefinger and tried to pull it out. The hole the fallen tile had left behind was too small, but she found she could slide the next tile down out of its spot easily, and then the book was freed from its dusty prison.

She blew on it, and instantly started coughing. Regular dust, this. It flew up into her face straight away and clung to her hair the moment the air moved around it. She grabbed the duster and gave it the once over, then wandered over to the window to get a better look.

There were no markings on the outside and the tan leather cover was soft. She took a moment to stare at it before she opened the cover and looked inside. Her heart-rate tripled when she did so.

This wasn't a novel or a child's picture book. Elegant blue ink filled the pages. Hand-written sentences. Dates and times...

This was a diary.

Louise closed the cover and walked out onto the balcony.

Should she?

This was obviously someone's private thoughts. She now realised it hadn't got behind that fireplace by accident. It had been hidden. But there was one very likely candidate as to the author and Louise was burning with curiosity to find out if she was right. She sucked in a breath, looked to the sky, said a silent prayer for forgiveness, and opened the cover again.

The beginning of the diary was tame—starting in January, as new diaries often do—and detailing Laura's glamorous life: rehearsals, parties, dinners at nice restaurants with other famous people. It all seemed so wonderful, but as Louise read on, she couldn't help feeling as if there was something missing.

She sighed. Laura Hastings, with her ice-blonde hair and classic bone structure, had always seemed like the perfect woman to Louise. She'd loved her films as a child, used to watch them with her dad in the afternoons when he hadn't been feeling well. And for some reason, Louise had never even considered that Laura might have struggled with her seemingly perfect life, just as she had with hers. How odd.

Of course, it had been the same for her. Of course.

So Louise read on, reading not just the words, but interpreting the spaces between them, what was *not* said as much as what was said, and it brought a whole new sense of connection between herself and the previous owner of her home.

And then Whitehaven was mentioned…and the boat-house…

Louise sank even deeper down into the chair, forgetting completely about grime and dusters and pulled-apart fireplaces. And when Laura met Dominic, she pressed a palm against her chest and it stayed there as she read the next handful of entries.

26th June, 1952

Dominic and I have been spending a lot of time together. The nature of our job means there's a lot of time hanging around, waiting. And even when we're working we have a lot of scenes together.

He talks to me. Really talks to me. In a way Alex has never done.

I think about my marriage now and wonder why we got together. It seemed so perfect at the time—like a fairy tale ending. Industrial heir marries movie princess. But I wonder now if I just got caught up with the glamour and the whole idea of us. I know that's one of my faults, acting impulsively, getting carried away in the emotion of the moment.

I try to tell myself that's what this is with Dominic, but I don't really believe myself.

Alex doesn't see me the way Dominic does. I think, to him, I'm just another trophy he's collected. He likes the best of everything, you see. And I was flattered that he thought I was the best. But I hadn't realised that once he's got that object he's had his eye on, that he locks it away behind glass and then moves on to the next conquest. I've tried not to think about what that might mean when it comes to other women, and I've never even caught of whiff of scandal about him, but still...

No, that's horrid. I can't blame my husband for things he hasn't done, because I'm feeling guilty about having feelings for someone else. That's too low.

Alex is a good man, really. He's just rather distant and... I don't know. I don't know what's wrong with him—except that he isn't Dominic.

And Dominic trumps Alex in every way. I know he feels something for me. I can see it in his eyes, the way I find him looking at me across the set a thousand times a day. Where Alex is a good man, Dominic is an extra-ordinary one. We talk, we sit together, but he won't take it any further. I want to hate him for being so principled, but I find I can't. If I were his wife, I wouldn't want him any other way. I don't want him to lower himself to something he isn't for me. I don't want to make him less, *when I feel he makes me so much* more.

But when we have scenes together—scenes where Richard and Charity get close—I know it isn't acting. I know he's drinking every moment in, saving it up, like I am. It's taking the film to a new level. Sam hardly says a word when we have our scenes. More than once we've got an important moment down in one take.

I wrote that something magical would happen here at this house this summer, didn't I, and it has.

I met Dominic.

But I also know I'm making the film of my career. Something that will last long after I've grown old and ugly and no one will want to watch films with me in them any more.

Thank you, Whitehaven. I don't know how I am ever going to repay you.

Louise closed the diary and walked back into the relative gloom of the boathouse interior. She stared at the book in her hands, hardly able to comprehend what she'd just read, what she'd just found.

This was *Laura Hastings'* diary! And obviously written the year she'd filmed *A Summer Affair* here. This was…it was…amazing. She felt as if the house had given up one of its secrets, trusted her with it. She hugged the book to her chest until she realised it was leaving a dusty imprint on her front, and then she carefully wiped it down with a soft, clean duster.

And what a romantic story.

At least, it seemed like one from the outside. But Louise knew all about how glamorous and exciting things could seem when you read about them, when it was a whole different ball game to live through them. Part of her ached for the young Laura Hastings, too.

She'd always seemed so perfect on the screen, had

always been one of Louise's icons. Who wouldn't fall for that ice-blonde hair and those big, sparkling blue eyes? Laura Hastings had always looked so poised, so in control. She wondered if anyone had had any idea of the inner turmoil underneath the movie star surface.

She flicked back through the diary again. The entries seemed to be sporadic. Sometimes they were days apart, sometimes months. Sometimes there were gaps of a few years.

She carefully replaced the book in its hiding place and slotted the two tiles back into place. She discovered the one she'd pushed through would sit very nicely in its spot, held gently by the cast iron surround, as long as no one applied undue pressure to it. As she hid the book again, made everything look as it had before she'd made her discovery, she tried to wrack her brains about what had happened to Laura after her heyday.

She made films into her forties, but then she'd just quietly faded away. Must have lived here for some time and died an old woman. Louise was shocked to realise she didn't even know if Laura had lived here on her own or if she'd been married. And if she'd been married, who had the husband been? Alex, still? Or Dominic?

She could ask Ben, she supposed, but he seemed to be a little tight-lipped about the previous owner. And, anyway, the diary wasn't huge. It wouldn't take too long to read it and find out for herself.

Louise frowned. She didn't want to gulp it down in

one sitting—it was too beautiful for that. Maybe she'd just read a little bit each week, ration herself. Then she could make the magic last for months. She had years to uncover the rest of Whitehaven's secrets, so maybe she could be patient about finding out about Laura's too.

CHAPTER EIGHT

Almost a fortnight later, Louise was putting the finishing touches to Jack's room. She looked at her watch. It was almost one o'clock, but she couldn't even contemplate eating anything. Only five more hours and Jack would be here. Her eyes misted over as she fluffed the duvet and smoothed it out, making sure it was perfect—not bunched up in the corners or with an empty bit flapping at one end.

It looked so cosy when she had finished that she flumped down on top of the blue and white checked cover and buried her head in the pillow.

She's made the trip up to London a couple of times to see him in the month and a half she'd been here, but it had been far too long to go without seeing him every day. She sighed. It had been the longest they had ever been apart. Toby had used to moan that she didn't travel with him any more, and maybe that had been part of the reason their marriage had crumbled. Even strong relationships were put under pressure when the couple spent weeks or even months apart. But how could she leave Jack? He was everything. He always would be everything.

It wouldn't have been fair to uproot him and ask him to change schools before the half-term break. She snuggled even further into the pillow, wishing it smelled of more than just clean laundry.

Toby had agreed—thank goodness—to let Jack live with her. Her ex was away filming so often that it wouldn't have been fair to Jack to leave him at her former home in Hampstead with just a nanny for company. Even Toby had seen the sense in that.

So Jack would be with his father on school holidays, and even though Louise hadn't lived with her son for weeks, she'd still agreed to let Jack stay with Toby for the half-term week. Her ex could be a true diva, so she'd decided it was sensible to appease him, just to make sure he didn't change his mind.

But tonight Jack would be coming to Whitehaven. He'd be here.

She turned to lie on her back and stared at the ceiling. She wasn't sure whether to laugh or cry. Mostly she just ached.

Minutes, maybe even half an hour, drifted past as Louise hugged herself and watched the light on the freshly painted ceiling change as the October wind bullied the clouds across the sky. Eventually, she dragged herself off the bed and sloped towards the window.

Something shiny glinted in the bushes and instantly

her back was pressed against the wall, every muscle tense. After five seconds, she made herself breathe out. Nosing very carefully round the architrave, so only half of an eye and the side of her face would be visible from outside, she searched for another flash of light.

No-good, money-grabbing photographers!

In her effort to remain hidden, she only had a partial view of the front lawn. She remained motionless for some time, until her left leg started to cramp and twitch, and then only when she was very sure nobody was in her line of sight, did she lean out a little further.

Another glint! There!

Once again she found herself flattened against the wall. But this time she let out a groan and covered her face with her hands. It wasn't a telephoto lens but a big, shiny spade that had reflected the light. Ben the gardener-guy's spade. It was Sunday afternoon and he was here. Just as he'd been for the previous two weeks. Only she'd forgotten he'd be here in all her excitement about Jack coming.

Not that she ever really saw him arrive when he came. At some point in the afternoon, she'd become aware that he was around. She'd hear him whistling as he walked up to the top lawn, or hear the hum of a mower in the distance.

So why had she felt the need to slam herself against the wall and pretend she wasn't here? This was stupid.

She stopped leaning against the wall and drew herself upright. There. Then she walked primly across the room and out of the door. No one was hiding. She was just walking around inside her own house, as she was perfectly entitled to do. Okay, she'd chosen a path across the room that had meant she couldn't have been seen from the window, but that didn't mean anything. It had simply been the most direct route. Sort of.

She found herself in the kitchen. It was in serious need of updating, with pine cabinets that had darkened to an almost offensive orange, but it had a fantastic flagstone floor and always seemed warm—probably because, in the now defunct chimney breast, there was an Aga. It looked lovely and spoke of families gathered in the kitchen sharing overflowing Sunday lunches, but after a more than a month at Whitehaven she still had no idea how to work it.

Well, that wasn't strictly true. She knew how to boil the kettle. And, at this present moment, that seemed like a shockingly good idea. She filled the battered, thick-bottomed kettle with water, lifted the heavy lid on the Aga hotplate and left the kettle to boil.

She hoped Jack would love Whitehaven as much as she did. What was she going to do if he decided he didn't like living in the depths of the countryside, far away from the flash London townhouse she'd shared with Toby? It was the only place he'd ever known as home. Well, that and the New York apartment. And the villa in Beverley Hills. Whitehaven was charming, but it lacked the gloss of her former houses.

She'd been getting what she needed out of the cupboards while she'd been thinking, and now discovered that she'd placed two teabags in two mugs. Something she'd done regularly in the early days after her split with Toby, but hadn't done for months now.

Her first instinct was to put the teabag and mug back in the cupboard, but that urge was hijacked by another one.

She might as well make one for Ben. She gave a short, hollow laugh. It would be the nearest thing to payment she'd given him for all his hard work. The lawns were looking fabulous and, little by little, the shrubs and borders close to the house were starting to lose their wild look. Inside and out Whitehaven was regaining some of its former glory.

It wasn't that she hadn't intended to pay him. Just that she'd been heartily avoiding the issue. She'd acted like a diva herself that first week, and she didn't know how to undo that all-important first impression. As if summoned up by her thoughts, she heard the crunch of footsteps outside. A moment later Ben passed the kitchen window, probably on his way up to the greenhouses.

A cup of tea seemed like a poor effort at a truce, but it was all she had in her arsenal at the moment. Boiling water lifted and swirled the teabag in the cup. Louise hesitated. Sugar, or no sugar?

On an instinct, she put one level spoon in the cup and stirred. He looked like a man who liked a bit of sweetness.

Another laugh that was almost a snort broke the silence. Well, she'd better have a personality change on the way past the herbaceous border, then. Especially if she was truly on a peace mission. At the moment she was the dictionary definition for the absolute opposite of 'sweetness'. *Meet Louise Thornton, sour old prune.*

When Louise arrived at the greenhouse, she realised she had a problem. Two hands and two cups of tea meant that she had no spare hands to open the door, or even knock on it. But it had seemed stupid to leave her mug of tea in the kitchen. By the time she'd have delivered Ben's, discussed paying him and walked back to the house, it would have been stone cold.

She peered inside the greenhouse and tried to spot him. The structure was long and thin—almost thirty feet in length and tucked up against the north side of the walled garden to catch as much sun as possible. Down the centre was the tiled path with wrought iron grates for the under-floor heating system. The side nearest the wall of windows was lined with benches and shelves, all full of plants, but on the other side, large palms and ferns were planted in soil at floor level.

Halfway down the greenhouse a leg was sticking out

amongst the dark glossy leaves. She banged the door with her foot. The leg, which had been wavering up and down in its function as a counterbalance, went still.

She held her breath and tried to decide what kind of face she should wear. Not the suspicious glare he'd received on their first meeting, that was the sure. But grinning inanely didn't seem fitting either. In the end, she didn't have a chance to decide between 'calm indifference' and 'professional friendliness', because the leg was suddenly joined by the rest of him as he jumped back onto the path, rubbing his hands together to rid them of loose dirt, and looked in her direction.

She held up his cup of tea and then, when his face had broken into a broad grin, she breathed out. He was obviously really thirsty, because he practically ran to the door and swung it wide. She thrust the mug towards him, ignoring the plop of hot liquid that landed on her hand as she did so.

He took it from her, smiled again, and took a big gulp. 'Fantastic. Just how I like it. Thanks.'

Louise took a little sip out of her own chunky white mug. 'No problem. It's the least I can do.'

Ben lent back against one of the shelves and took another long slurp of tea. He seemed completely at ease here. She tried to copy his stance, making sure she was a good five feet away from him, but she couldn't work out what to do with her legs and stood up again.

'Um… about money…'

Ben raised his eyebrows.

'I can't let you going on doing all this for nothing.'

He shrugged. 'It started as a labour of love. I'm just sorry I haven't been able to do more.'

He wasn't making this easy. All she wanted to do was to work out what the going rate was and write him a cheque. She didn't want him to be nice. Men who were nice normally had a hidden agenda.

She put her mug down on the only spare bit of space on the shelf nearest her and drew herself taller. Only, he didn't make that easy either. Her five-foot-eight wasn't too far away from his six-foot-plus height, but however much she straightened her spine, drew her neck longer, she still felt small beside him. But this was no time for weakness. She was the boss. She was in charge.

'Well, if you could just let me know how much you'd routinely charge for this sort of job…'

He drained his mug and looked at her with a more serious light in his eyes. 'I can't say any of my "routine" work resembles this in the slightest.'

Louise crossed one booted foot in front of the other and a corner of her mouth rose. Oh, this was his game. Make it seem like he nobly didn't want anything, but sting her with an exorbitant price when it came to the crunch. And, if he played this game well, she was probably supposed to be shaking his hand and thanking him profusely for being so generous when the moment came.

She folded her arms, but only had to unfold them as he handed her back the empty mug.

'There's no rush for money. I'll send you a bill if you're really desperate for one, though.' He smiled, and it had none of the sharkish tendencies she'd expected after a conversation like that. 'Thanks for the tea.' And then he turned his back on her and went returned his attention to a large plant with floppy leaves.

If there was one thing Louise didn't like, it was being ignored. It had been Toby's favourite way of avoiding anything he didn't want to talk about. All she'd had to do was utter the words, 'You're late. Where have you been?' and the shutters had come down, the television or the game console switched on. Nobody liked to be rendered invisible. She coughed and Ben looked up.

'No rush?' She'd promised herself she wouldn't be pushed around by any man again—ever. Okay, in her mind, she'd meant *significant others*, but suddenly it felt important to stand her ground, to have this conversation on her terms. 'I'd much prefer it if we could talk figures now.'

He straightened again. 'Fine. It's just that I know you've just moved in, Mrs Thornton—'

The pause was just long enough to indicate he hadn't meant to say that, and for the first time in their conversation he broke eye contact. She realised she didn't remember telling him her name.

'I thought you might like a little more time to get settled.'

Louise felt her features harden. 'Why are you being so nice to me?'

Ben looked for all the world as if he hadn't a clue what she was talking about. Boy, he was good. She'd almost fallen for that straight-talking, man of the earth and sky nonsense. So he knew who she was, and he wanted something from her. Maybe not money, but something. People always did.

Eventually he scratched the side of his nose with a finger. 'I suppose I felt I needed to make up for being a little…awkward…the first time we met. I was angry with someone else and I took it out on you. It's not something I'm proud of.'

A man who apologised! Now she *knew* the act was too good to be true.

Still, she was prepared to play along for the moment. He'd show his cards eventually. 'Well, if you're not going to be businesslike about this, I may just have to look in the Yellow Pages and find a gardener who is.'

He didn't seem that worried about losing her business; he just went back to fussing with the floppy plant. After a few seconds he looked back at her. 'Suit yourself.'

Once again, Louise felt as if she'd been dismissed. How dared he? This was her garden, her greenhouse. Those were her plants he was messing around with. 'At least give me your card.' That was a pathetic attempt at gaining control, getting him to give up something, but it was all she could think of.

He patted his pockets. 'I don't think I have one…ah!' He pulled his wallet out of his back pocket and rummaged around inside. The card he pulled out was creased and the edges were soft. She took it from him and backed away.

Oliver Landscapes. Very grand for a one-man band outfit.

'Feel free to let me know if you don't want me to come any more, but if I don't hear any differently, I'll just assume I should pop by again next Sunday.' This time he didn't turn away and continue working; he just looked at her. Not with barely-concealed curiosity, or envy, or even out-of-proportion adoration. Those kinds of responses she was used to. No, this was something different. He looked at her as if she were transparent.

She didn't know what to do.

'Just come,' she said, and fled, leaving her mug of lukewarm tea in the shade of a wilting ficus.

CHAPTER NINE

Louise couldn't help grinning as she climbed out of the car, even though the weather was disgusting and she was about to get on a tiny little ferry and cross an angry-looking river. Just as well she could see their destination, the village of Lower Hadwell, only a few minutes away on the opposite shore.

The rear door opened and Jack climbed out, tugging at the collar of his new school uniform and looking a little uncomfortable. He was tall for his age and he had his father's good looks. Half the class at his previous school—the female half—had cried for a week when he'd told them he was moving away.

Not that Jack cared. He had no idea that his golden blond, shaggy hair was anything but a nuisance to comb in the mornings. He might have Toby's physical characteristics, but he lacked any of his father's swagger. And long may it stay that way. Louise knew from first-hand experience just how devastating a weapon all that beauty mixed with a little too much ego could be.

'All ready to go?'

Jack nodded and clutched his book bag. Louise wanted to take his hand and hug him to her. He was being so brave. Starting a new school was difficult for any kid, but Jack was going to face an extra set of challenges. She'd had a meeting with the headmistress to discuss it and they'd both decided that, quietly, the word would go round that Jack was to be treated like every other child in the school.

She laid a reassuring hand on his shoulder. Jack was a normal boy in that he wouldn't allow more overt public displays of motherly affection.

At this time in the morning there were regular ferries across the river and they walked to the edge of the high stone jetty and waited for the little wooden boat, painted white with a blue trim, to sputter up to a seaweedy flight of steps.

The ferryman paid them absolutely no attention other than to take coins off them and Louise breathed a sigh of relief. Lower Hadwell was a small community and news of her arrival in the area had to have spread. Although she'd been here for a while, she'd kept herself to herself and this was her first proper trip to the little village across the river. She just hoped they were all like this guy. Completely uninterested. And with that blissful thought in her mind, she sat on the hard wooden bench that circled the stern of the boat and turned her face into the wind.

By the time they reached the jetty on the other side of the river, she was sure her hair had picked up a bucket-load of salt that was blowing up the river from the sea. Never mind. She'd deliberately dressed down in a tracksuit and baseball cap, hoping she'd blend in a bit more with the other mums at the school gate.

Jack declared the boat ride 'sick' and jumped out the ferry in one smooth motion. Louise followed, although her clamber on to dry land was nowhere near as graceful.

The school had to be at the top of the longest and steepest hill in the whole of south Devon. It only took a minute before Louise's legs burned and her breath came in gulps. Her calves begged for mercy as they trudged past a pub, cottages in hues of cream and earthy pink and a handful of shops. Jack stopped and turned round to face the river.

She grabbed on to his coat and tried to inhale enough oxygen to talk. 'Jack!' The noise that came out of her mouth barely registered as a croak. 'Come on!'

Jack gave her his usual, I'm-eight-and-I-under-stand-the-universe-much-better-than-you look. 'Try walking backwards. It doesn't hurt so much.'

Louise couldn't work out if that was the most sensible idea she'd heard in years or the most stupid. She stared at her son as he started ascending again, this time with his backpack pointing up the hill. Stuff it. She'd do anything to stop the fire in her calf muscles. She did a one-eighty and followed suit. Her legs fairly sang with relief. This was much better!

At least it was until she came unexpectedly in contact with something tall and warm. Something that said 'oof'. Louise squeezed her eyes shut, yelled an apology and turned and ran up the hill after Jack, who had made much better progress.

Coward, she thought, as she reached the level ground just outside the school gates. But it was only a minute before the bell was due to go and she didn't need someone recognising her and delaying her by asking for an autograph or something.

Jack stopped just short of the wrought iron fence on the quaint village school. Louise bent over and tried to suck in more air. She knew from the furnace in her cheeks that her face was probably pink and blotchy and sweat was making her back feel all sticky.

She laid an arm on Jack's shoulder—more to support herself than anything else. She got down the gym every now and then. So why had this finished her off?

The jangle of an old-fashioned brass school bell rose above the screams and shouts of the playground. She stood up, put a hand on each of Jack's shoulders and stared into his eyes. 'You ready?'

Jack pressed his lips together and nodded just once. She grinned at him and, as she spoke, she turned to walk through the gate.

'Then it's showti—'

A bright flash seared her retina. At first she couldn't work out what had happened, but the guy who jumped out from behind a parked car with a whacking great camera round his neck kind of gave it away. Instinctively, she pulled Jack to her and started to run. She really, really wanted to swear, but this was neither the time nor the place.

As they reached the safety of the school building, all grey stone and arched windows, she started to chastise herself. She'd been stupid not to have been prepared for this! Of course the tabloids would want a picture of Jack starting his new school. They were desperate for any titbit about either her or Toby. And while Toby had gushed at length about the new love in his life, she'd steadily maintained her silence.

Jack was in tears. And it took a lot to make her little man cry.

Louise marched up to the school reception and fought back tears herself while she waited for the receptionist to stop fiddling with the photocopier. Maybe she should just have given an interview to *Celebrity Life* or something. Her refusal to play their game had just made incidents like this inevitable.

Jack was hugging on to her, his face buried under her arm. She stroked the top of his hair.

Now she was good and angry. She and Toby were fair game. They'd chosen this life. But Jack had no choice.

When she'd got her son settled in, she was going back outside and she would find that photographer and she would shove his camera so far down his throat that he'd be coughing up bits of his memory card for weeks. That's if they didn't make it out the other end first.

Ben was happily walking down the road, minding his own business. Well, almost. He'd just spotted a picture of the Wards' cottage in the estate agent's window and was actually paying more attention to that than the direction in which his feet were heading. He and Megan had dreamed about buying that place for years.

With his current income and the maintenance payments to Megan, could he afford it? Maybe.

But, before he could do the mental arithmetic, he was winded by some idiot charging up the hill backwards. He didn't even have the chance to say *hey!* before the track-suited figure garbled out and apology and ran off. He was so busy staring up the hill at the pink-clad bottom with the word 'Juicy' emblazoned across it that he was almost knocked over a second time by a man in a large anorak and a wild look in his eyes. He had a huge camera in his hand.

Ben shrugged. Bit late in the season for bird-watching, but what the hell did he know? Global warming was having a weird effect on the wildlife in this area. Last year some strange-looking bird only seen in the isles of Scotland had been blown down to the south coast of England by a freak storm. The local 'twitchers' had gone bananas. That man had had the same crazed look in his eye. Marauding ornithologists aside, nothing was going to stop him wandering down to the newsagent's to get his morning paper before his meeting today.

However, Mrs Green, owner of the shop for the last thirty-three years and purveyor of local gossip, was in a chatty mood. Ben valiantly attempted to tuck his paper under his arm and drop the money in her hand, but her arms stayed firmly folded across her ample chest and he was forced to hover, one hand reaching over the counter, as the inquisition began.

'I heard that another celebrity has bought Whitehaven, Mr Oliver. What do you think of that?' She narrowed her eyes and analysed his reaction. He was trying hard not to have one. Something might have given him away, because she added, 'Of course, I expect you know all about that—having been so friendly with Laura Hastings, and all.'

'I just helped out in the garden, really.' He waved the coins again, hoping the glint of something shiny might distract her.

'Yes, but you'd know if the place had been sold, wouldn't you?'

'Not necessarily.'

He didn't know why he was protecting Louise Thornton. Just that, having been the source of local gossip himself a few years ago, he knew how unpleasant, how…invaded…it could make one feel.

'Well, whoever it is…' Mrs Green leaned back and looked down her nose at him; it made him feel like a slice of something on a glass slide under a microscope. '…they'll be fine with the residents of Lower Hadwell. After all, we'd been used to living with a bona fide Hollywood legend on our doorstep for forty years, hadn't we?'

He nodded and thrust the money at her again. This time he wasn't going to be put off. Just as she started to uncurl her hand to accept it, she paused and nodded in the direction of the magazine rack that was half-hidden by a tall shelf containing pet food and assorted stationery. 'That mag that your Jasmine was waiting for has come in. I expect you'll be wanting to pick that up as well.'

Ben's mouth straightened into a thin line. He stuffed the coins back in his coat pocket and retreated to the safety of the other side of the shop, pleased he was hidden by the boxes of envelopes balanced on the top shelf.

Now was it *Pink!* or *Girl Chat* that Jasmine liked? One had a free lip gloss with it, and he wasn't sure about that, so he picked up the other one.

There was a sudden jangle of the shop door and a sudden rush of cold air. A figure slammed the door closed and darted behind the shelving unit to join him.

'Louise?'

She pulled the baseball cap she was wearing further down over her eyes and crouched a little lower. 'Shh!' she whispered loudly, without looking at him. Then she froze and slowly turned her head to look over her shoulder. 'Ben?'

He didn't say anything back. It was obvious who he was.

'You're wearing a suit,' she said, forgetting to hunker down.

Just then, the wild-looking ornithologist appeared, running down the street. Louise must have seen a hint of movement out of the corner of her eye, because she practically flattened herself against the shelves, sending a box of ballpoint pens flying. 'Did he see me?' she hissed at him, looking a little wild-eyed herself.

Ben tried to look nonchalant and peered out of the shop window, but it was difficult to get a good look with all the posters for local events and cards offering bicycles for sale and adverts for paperboys plastered over the glass.

'I think he's gone.'

Louise edged closer to where he was standing and craned her neck. 'Are you sure?'

He nodded. 'He was going at some speed when he shot past here. On a hill this steep, it's pretty difficult to stop when you've built up that kind of momentum. Why are you worried about—'

Oh. If Jas had been in his shoes she would have

slapped herself on the forehead and said *duh!* Paparazzi. Definitely not a species seen around Lower Hadwell before. It put a totally new spin on the whole 'invasion' issue.

'Couldn't you just let him have a picture and then he'd be on his way?' That seemed like a reasonable solution.

Louise looked at him like he'd just suggested she do a nude photo-shoot on the jetty in sub-zero temperatures. 'I'm so furious with him I might not be responsible for my actions. He just scared the life out of Jack as we were on our way into school.'

Her son was here? Good. Perhaps then she'd lose that slightly haunted look from her eyes. The look that unwittingly begged him to rush in and be her knight in shining armour. His armour had gone into retirement when he'd signed his divorce papers, and he'd better remember that fact.

She sighed and straightened up a little. 'A photo of us looking shocked is bad enough, but a shot of me turning pink in the face and spitting obscenities at him would only stoke the fire. By Friday there'd be a whole pack of them camped out at the local inn waiting for us.' She rubbed her face with her hand. 'Thank goodness, I'd calmed down enough to realise that when I spotted him following me again.'

She stopped talking and looked him up and down. 'You're wearing a suit. A very nice suit.'

'You already said that.'

'Won't it get dirty?'

'Nope.'

She glowered at him. 'Stop being obtuse.'

He was tempted to chuckle, but decided it wouldn't help her current mood. 'I know you only think I'm fit for weeding the flower beds, but I'm not a gardener by trade. Not exactly.'

Louise's mouth dropped open. A sensation of achievement swelled inside him. Although why he should feel so stupidly proud of the fact that *he* was bamboozling *her* for a change, he wasn't sure.

'I'm a landscape architect. I design outside spaces—town centres, open spaces, parks, private homes. This morning, I'm meeting with Lord Batterham to discuss restoring a knot garden on his estate and building an environmentally friendly play area for visitors.'

She blinked. Twice. And closed her mouth. 'Oh.'

She seemed to have forgotten all about the photographer, which had to be good news, so he decided to keep her distracted. 'You look a little different yourself.' Gone were the elegant clothes in dark, muted tones, replaced by a baby-pink tracksuit and bright, white running shoes. And what was with the cap with the ponytail sprouting through the back all about?

'I look a mess,' she muttered.

He took in her appearance again, went beyond the

surface impressions. He face was free of make-up and her cheeks rosy with fading anger. A slightly more dishevelled appearance suited her. It made her more approachable...touchable.

He took a step back.

'Every day for months I've not gone beyond my front gate without my best clothes or my make-up on. Trust some rat with a digital camera to turn up when I'm looking...well, less than perfect.' She shook her head. 'I swear they must have some kind of radar to target me on my off days.'

'You look fine.'

She tipped her head to one side and gave him a weary look. 'I think what you said was that I look "different". Believe me, it spoke volumes.'

'I just meant...not your normal self.'

That's right, Ben. Just dig yourself in deeper.

He was bad at this kind of stuff, he knew. He didn't have the ability to dress words up and make them pretty. And what was so wrong with the plain, unvarnished truth, anyway?

'Not my normal self?' she said, staring hard at him.

He sighed inwardly. Megan hadn't appreciated his 'lack of tact and incredible insensitivity' either. Some women were just too much hard work.

'Well, here's your explanation...' She pulled a magazine off the rack and thrust it in front of his face. It took him a few moments to realise the blurry picture on the cover was Louise herself—playing catch on a beach with a little boy. But that wasn't all. The caption read 'Celebrity Bulges' and large red lines circled her tummy and thighs.

He snatched the magazine from her and slapped it back in the rack, upside down and with the cover facing inward. She locked him with a steady gaze and, when she spoke, her voice was low and dry. 'Apparently, I've been letting myself go. I'm surprised you hadn't heard.'

Her ability to mock herself blindsided him for moment, but then he found himself laughing. It rocked him from the inside and burst out his mouth. And then, after a few seconds, she joined him. Her eyes widened, as if she was as surprised at her own response as he was.

It was kind of surreal to be huddling in a little country newsagent's, hiding from the press and chuckling with Louise Thornton. The laughter subsided to a level where he could get a bit of control and he wiped his hand over his face.

Louise was no longer laughing, but she was still smiling. If the topic of conversation was transformations, here was one that beat them all. The remains of his mirth died away instantly.

If she was beautiful when she was looking fierce and distant then he didn't have any adjective for how she looked now. Her eyes sparkled and her skin glowed. Why did she think she needed all that black stuff to make her look pretty? He almost wished the photographer was here right now to capture this moment.

Thinking of cameras and lenses, he walked to the shop window and looked up and down the street. 'No sign of him now. I think you're safe.'

Louise's brows changed shape as she frowned, then relaxed again. The smile vanished and the remote beauty returned. 'Of course.' She stood up properly and started picking up the pens scattered all over the floor. When she'd finished, she gave him another smile, but this time her eyes were unaffected. 'I'll see you on Sunday?'

He nodded.

'I promise I won't make you weed the flower beds, if you're really too grand for that.'

It was his cue to laugh again, but he couldn't bring himself to. 'I've been itching to sort that garden out properly for years. Just indulge me, okay?'

She nodded. And, although she was as collected and self-contained as always, he could see a hint of something in her eyes. As if she wanted to reach out but was too afraid.

'I promise I'll charge the earth and drink all your tea.'

That earned him a real smile. Small, but real.

'It's a deal, Mr Landscape Architect.' She looked at her watch. 'Speaking of which, didn't you say you were off to a meeting?'

Lord Batterham!

He hurried back to the counter to pay Mrs Green for his paper. She was standing there, holding a magazine in her hand—the same one Louise had flourished in front of his nose. She stared at it, and then at Louise, and then back at the magazine cover, as if she was playing some kind of mental tennis match.

For the first time in thirty-three years she wasn't making a sound. He plopped the change in front of her on the counter, grabbed Louise by the hand and dashed out of the shop.

Louise didn't question Ben's tug on her hand—she just followed him. He took her out of the shop, down a side street and through some alleyways, until they arrived in a narrow passage between the pub and the next door cottage on the main road that separated the village from the beach and jetty. He pressed a finger to his lips and peered out over the road.

Louise had forgotten they were running, hiding. She'd been too busy noticing the warm hand wrapped around her own. How long had it been since she'd touched someone other than Jack? And even those opportunities had been few and far between recently. How long had it been since she hadn't felt totally alone, as if it was her against the world?

Too long—if the warm feeling creeping up her left arm and into her chest had anything to do with it.

'He's there on the jetty,' Ben said as he turned round

to whisper to her, a wicked smile on his lips. 'Do you want me to just run up behind him and shove him in?'

That made her laugh softly. 'You'd do that for me?'

Was it sad that Ben's throwaway remark was the nicest thing anyone had said to her in a long time?

His smile faded and he looked down at their joined hands. Slowly, he slid his fingers from hers. 'No... Just joking. Anyway, the tide's out.' He pushed his fists into his trouser pockets.

Louise's eyes narrowed. So what if there was mostly damp, hard sand and pebbles below all but the very end of the jetty? She reckoned the guy deserved everything he got.

Ben leaned against the wall and looked out towards the river again. Louise kept herself in his shadow, blocking any view someone might have of her from the road. Whose idea had it been to wear a baby pink track-suit today? Honestly? She might as well have strapped a homing beacon onto her head.

'He's coming back this way,' he muttered over his shoulder. And then a few moments later, 'I think he's giving up.'

Not more than a minute after that they heard the noise of a car engine and a beat-up saloon sped past them on the narrow road. Louise sagged against the wall and let out a sigh of relief. 'He's gone?' she asked quietly.

Ben nodded. The look in his eyes—not pity, but understanding—made her feel a little wobbly.

'Thank you,' she said softly. 'But you didn't need to do all that. I've made you late for your meeting.'

He just shrugged. 'That's what being part of a small community like this is all about. We look out for each other.'

Louise nodded. That was what she'd wanted for her and Jack, wasn't it? To be part of village life, to fit in. Then why was disappointment making her insides plummet? She hadn't wanted to think he was doing something special for her, was she, instead of just doing a kind thing he'd do for anyone else? That would be stupid.

They waited a minute more to be sure the car didn't come back the other way, and then Ben moved out of the way and let Louise pass.

'The ferry's just arrived from Whitehaven pier,' he said, gesturing to the little wooden boat rocking on the waves. 'If you're quick you can catch it, and then there'll be no chance of getting caught waiting around with nowhere to run.'

She nodded again—words seemed to have deserted her—and then she gave him a small smile and ran across the road and towards the waiting boat. When she looked back Ben Oliver was nowhere to be seen. It was only then that she realised she'd expected to find him standing there, making sure she got on the boat safely.

Stupid, Louise. He's nothing to you. And you're

nothing to him. Why should he care if you get on the ferry?

But why should he care if she avoided the photographer, in that case? Why had he helped her escape?

Louise shook the thought away with a toss of her ponytail and she clambered over the side of the ferry and sat down in the stern. Tara was right: she was spending too much time on her own. Now a good-looking man just had to be a little bit nice to her and it was making her think all sorts of crazy things.

She deliberately focused on the little cottage that sat beyond the small pier on the other side of the ferry. Still, as the boat pulled around, Lower Hadwell came into view again. As the boat turned, Louise caught a dark shape standing on the café terrace just across the road from the pub. A man.

Adrenalin spiked through her as she thought it might be the paparazzo, back for more, but then she realised he wasn't wearing a blue coat, but a smart dark suit. And when the little ferry began to chug across the choppy water, the dark shape turned and made its way back across the road and up the hill.

CHAPTER TEN

Louise walked down to the boathouse again after she got back on dry land. When she entered she went straight to the fireplace, removed the two tiles and pulled Laura's diary out.

She'd lived here for decades. How had she managed to come and go as she pleased without being stalked?

She pulled one of the dusty cane chairs over and sat down and began to read, without even cleaning it off first. Her life was a mess and she'd dearly like to lose herself in someone else's for a bit.

17th July, 1952

I don't know how I am ever going to go home again and act as if everything is normal and that this was just another job. Today was the last day of filming. I had a lump in my throat all day. Twice I had to take a break just to compose myself. I told Sam I was just tired because it was the end of the shoot.

And Dominic and I didn't even have any big scenes to shoot—just a couple of plain conversations in a cor-

ridor. *I couldn't hold him. I couldn't touch him. And I wanted to so much.*

There weren't many of us left behind, because most of the bigger scenes had been filmed earlier in the week. Only five of us actors remained. So, Sam has planned a big wrap party back in London next week. We stragglers went across the river to the little Ferryboat Inn for a drink. I had to sit there with my gin and tonic, looking across the table at the man I loved, knowing it might be the last time I'd ever get the chance to talk to him properly, all the while listening to some dull sound man drone on about all the fishing he'd wanted to do, but hadn't had time for. Very romantic! In the end I had to get up and walk out. I felt as if I just couldn't breathe.

The beach at Lower Hadwell is small and stony, but it was a clear moonlit night and the warm air was a pleasure to walk in after the smoke and air of the Ferryboat Inn. I wrapped my arms around myself and tried to wish the clock backwards, so I could just have one more day with Dominic.

That was how he found me.

For the longest time we didn't say anything to each other. Even if I'd had the words, I'm not sure I'd have been able to get them out.

'I don't want to lose you,' I eventually told him.

He didn't need to agree. His face said it all.

'I can't see you again, not after the party next week'

was all he said, and I know it half-killed him. It certainly half-killed me.

I nodded. 'I know,' I said.

He reminded me that we'd made other promises to other people. He didn't say much about her—Jean—only that she was fragile, that he couldn't leave her.

I nodded again, wishing those promises undone from both our lips. I'd known his wife, a well-known singer, had had a troubled history. There had been rumours of instability before she'd married Dominic, but everyone thought that was in the past now she had such a devoted husband. But if anyone knows that what you read in the papers doesn't always reflect the truth at home, it's me. Why would I want to escape my 'fairy tale' otherwise?

'I promised her I wouldn't leave,' he told me. 'She needs me.'

I wanted to be selfish then, to tell him I needed him too, but I didn't. What right did I have? And I was sure that Alex would not make it easy for me to break free. There'd be a scandal that could end both our careers and I couldn't do that to Dominic. I wouldn't want to be the reason everyone hated him.

But then he surprised me by stepping in close, pulling me into his arms. I hung onto him, just hung onto him, wishing the night could last forever. And then he bent down and kissed my hair with such tenderness. I could feel him shaking beneath my hands.

'But I can promise you something, too, Laura,' he whispered. 'I will never forget you, and you will always, always be in my heart.'

And then he ripped himself away from me and strode back up the beach, not looking back, leaving me to sit down untidily on the damp shingle and cry.

Why? thought Louise. Why does love always have to die? Why does it always have to end badly? She had been hoping for something more than this, some hope, really. Unable to read any more, she tucked the diary back into its hiding place and returned to the house.

CHAPTER ELEVEN

'Mum? Can we go outside? It's stopped raining.'

Louise stopped herself from putting the kettle on the Aga for a fifth time. She didn't really want another cup of tea. It was just that, at some point this afternoon, *somebody* might want one.

'Can we? *Please*?' Jack's voice was so high-pitched on that last word she was sure dogs would be bounding towards them from all over the district.

'Can we what?

Her son ran to the back door and opened it, letting in a gust of damp November air. Louise walked over to where he stood and stuck her head out of the door. Moisture dripped from the leaves of an evergreen bush in the little courtyard directly outside the kitchen, but the clouds were now a pale, pearly grey and she even thought she saw a hint of blue before it was hurried away by the wind.

Fresh air would do her good. Fresh air would stop her waiting. Or wondering why he was late. Well, not late, because they'd never really set a time for him to come and go, but later than normal.

She shook her head and reached for the scarf and hat on a peg nearby. Ben Oliver had turned all her assumptions about him on their heads once this week already. Why shouldn't he do it again?

The grass on the sloping lawn in front of the house was still damp, but it didn't stop Jack deciding a game of football was the ideal way to burn off a bit of energy. They used a couple of the medium-sized stones lining the driveway to mark out the goals.

She'd never been good at games at school, always too tired from looking after both Dad and the younger kids. Jack was running rings around her, but then he misjudged a kick and the ball went flying past her towards the edge of the woods. She ran after it and stopped it with the side of her boot. If all went according to plan, she would have at least one goal to Jack's seven by the time they gave up and headed back inside for hot chocolate.

She swung her leg in an almighty kick. There was a jarring pain in her lower back as it met something flat and solid and, all of a sudden, she was staring at the sky. She could hear Jack laughing his head off some distance away.

'Just you wait!' she yelled, giggling slightly herself, but the mirth stopped when she attempted to move. 'Ouch!'

'Here.' The voice was as rich and low and she

recognised it instantly. She also recognised the broad, long-fingered hand that came into her field of vision—although exactly when she'd noticed the shape of Ben Oliver's hands, she wasn't sure.

Even through the wool of her gloves, his skin was warm and he gripped her hand in such a way that she knew she could give him all her weight and he wouldn't let her fall. She winced as he gently helped her to her feet. 'Ow.'

'Where does it hurt?'

She didn't want to draw even more attention to her slightly-larger-than-planned and somewhat muddy backside. 'Where d'you think?'

'Do you want me to take a look?'

'No!' Louise's cheeks went hot and she twisted out of his grip and brushed herself down, more for camouflage than for cosmetic effect. 'Don't tell me you're an almost-doctor as well as an almost-gardener.'

He laughed and she looked up at him, her irritation dissolving. It was only then she noticed the girl standing slightly behind him. She had shoulder-length, honey-coloured hair, nothing at all like Ben's dark mop, but her eyes were all her father's.

Ben grabbed his daughter's hand and pulled her forward a little. She blushed and looked at the ground. 'Louise, I'd like you to meet my daughter, Jasmine.'

'Nice to meet you, Jasmine. I'm Louise. Your dad's been helping me out with my garden.'

'I know.' The reply was barely a whisper, and Jasmine flushed an even deeper shade of red.

Her father may not have known who Louise Thornton was the first time he met her, but Jasmine certainly did. This kind of reaction wasn't unusual. Louise knew she'd acted identically when she'd started going out with Toby and he'd introduced her to the latest Oscar-winning Hollywood actress.

'Come and meet my son, Jack. He's football mad, I'm afraid.'

Jasmine shrugged and followed her across the lawn as Ben strolled along, bringing up the rear. Jack took one look at Jasmine and Louise knew he'd decided she was okay. As the child of a celebrity couple, he had an uncanny kind of radar for discerning between hangers-on and real friends. He made instinctive decisions in a second and he was rarely wrong. Now, how did she go about getting herself some of that?

Jack picked up his football and started walking in the direction of the back door. 'There's biscuits inside. Want some?'

Jasmine nodded furiously and broke into a trot to keep up with him as he raced off towards the kitchen.

Ben fell into step beside Louise as they followed their offspring. 'Sorry I had to bring Jas with me. I hope it's okay.'

'Of course it's okay. Who do you think I am? The wicked witch of the West?'

He was smirking when she looked up at him. 'You can be a tad fierce at times.'

Was she? Really? She fell into silence for a few seconds while she pondered his remark. What had happened to the shy, sweet Louise she'd once been? Where was the awkward girl with the too-long limbs that sprouted through the sleeves of her school blazer?

Eventually, she said quietly, 'If you'd been really afraid, you wouldn't have come.'

Ben laughed again. She liked that sound. She wondered if she could make him do it some more. Only, so far, it had only happened accidentally, when she hadn't actually been trying to be funny at all.

'True. I hadn't intended to bring Jas at all, it's just that…' He ran his hand through his hair. '…it's complicated.'

'Trust me. I know *complicated*. Your ex have something to do with this?'

Ben stared off into the distance for a few seconds and she stopped walking, aware that it would be better if this conversation wasn't overheard from the kitchen. Ben halted beside her.

'Megan…' He made a microscopic movement with his head, as if he wanted to shake it but was stopping himself. 'She's a good mother, really. It's just that lately her priorities have been a little skewed.'

Louise nodded.

'She seems to think that now Jas has started senior

school she can fend for herself a bit more. And, probably, she could. It's just with the divorce still in the recent past, I think Jas feels a little neglected. Megan had last-minute plans and cancelled their Sunday afternoon together. I don't think she even realises how shut out Jas feels sometimes.'

'How long?'

'Since the divorce? Two years.'

'I'm still waiting for mine to be finalised, but we split up five months ago.' Louise breathed in. 'Girls need a mother at that age.'

She had certainly ached for her mother going through those awkward years, but Mum had died just as she was on the brink of puberty, and she'd had to muddle through on her own. At least when her sisters had reached that age she'd been able to help them along.

She turned and smiled at Ben, tried to make herself seem less—what had he called her?—intimidating. 'Well, Jas is very welcome here. I understand completely.'

Ben let out a breath and smiled back, and for the first time since she'd met him, Louise felt as if she wasn't a complete mess compared to him. He might be out the other side of the divorce process, but she could still recognise the scars. But if he could pull through, maybe so could she.

Ben turned and scanned the lawn, which had sprouted magnificently since the previous Sunday, thanks to a healthy dose of West Country rain. 'Thanks,' he said, glancing back at her. 'I'd better get started. It's going to get dark soon.'

When Louise reached the back door, Jack ran across the kitchen and skidded to a halt in front of her. 'Jas says there's fireworks on tonight. Can we go?'

Fireworks? Oh, of course. Time had taken on a strange quality since she'd moved to Whitehaven. The date was… what? The second or third of November? It was only days away from Guy Fawkes' night and there would be bonfires and firework displays all over the area this weekend. She thought the bangs she'd heard last night must have been shotguns, but now it all made sense.

'I don't know, Jack. What time is it? And where?'

'I'll ask Jas!' He raced out of the kitchen before she could quietly explain that maybe it wasn't such a good idea to be out in public, that maybe the Olivers wouldn't want a couple of extras tagging along. She fiddled with her cup of tea while she waited for her son to return but, after a couple of minutes, she decided he must have found something else to get all hyper about and had lost interest.

They didn't need to go out to see fireworks. Whitehaven was perched high on a hill and there would be great views from the attic windows. They could stay here and watch at a safe distance.

***

Ben knocked softly on the back door. There was no reply. He stared at the chunky Victorian handle for a second, then gripped it, the brass chilly against his palm, and turned. The door swung open on surprisingly creak-free hinges.

'Hello?'

Louise was standing at the old butler's sink staring out the window. He could hear water sloshing and see bubbles splashing and a moment later she dumped an upturned cup on the draining rack. It fell over. She didn't even look at it, just grabbed the next bit of crockery off the pile and started washing again. He coughed.

All the sloshing and splashing stopped. She didn't alter the angle of her head, but somehow he could tell that her focus was no longer off in the distance. She was aware of him. And, somehow, that made him aware of her too.

Suddenly, she started washing the plate she was holding again. When it must have been scrubbed clean of every last speck of food, she placed it on the drying rack with exquisite care, then turned to face him wiping the bubbles off her hands with a tea towel.

'All finished?'

He nodded.

A million snatches of small talk whizzed round his head, but meaningless words weren't his forte. And Louise didn't seem to require any. She gave him a look—not quite a smile, more an expression of open-

ness, of welcome—and reached for a large brown tea-
pot.

When he'd been married to Megan, he'd got used to
having an arsenal of such phrases for the moment when
he walked through the door. She always needed him to
say something, to pay her attention, to make her feel
noticed. Not that he hadn't noticed her or hadn't loved
her. It was just that he was better at showing rather than
saying. But Megan had never been able to understand
that. When he'd tried to do nice things for her, she'd
hardly noticed, like he'd been speaking a foreign language. So, he'd adapted, because she was his wife, and
it had been what she'd needed from him.

Louise motioned for him to sit at the chunky kitchen
table and started rummaging in a cupboard. After what
he'd seen the other day, he wouldn't have been surprised if *this* woman was thoroughly fed up of being
noticed, so he did nothing to break the wonderful
stillness that surrounded her. He just drank it in and
slowly felt his muscles relax. She handed him a mug
of tea, sweetened to perfection, then pottered round the
kitchen.

Rampaging children, however, could not be counted
on to be so restful. Jas and Jack stormed into the kitchen
just as the last knot was about to ease from his shoulders.

'Mum, I'm hungry!'

Even when she smiled, wide and full, as she was

doing now, she still had a sense of elegance and poise that he'd rarely seen. At first he'd labelled it standoffishness, but he'd been wrong. She was merely reserved, shy even. But he could understand how people who didn't know her better, people who'd probably decided she was an attention hungry bimbo, could misinterpret it as snootiness. Louise Thornton was indeed an intriguing mix of contradictions.

But she didn't look very snooty now, smiling down at her son. 'You're always hungry,' she said.

'Can we have some cake? *Please?* After all, we've got guests.' Jack looked hopefully at Ben and Jasmine, and Ben chuckled. Having been a hollow-legged boy once himself, he was pretty sure Jack's request wasn't entirely altruistic. However, he wasn't about to talk himself out of a nice piece of cake, so he watched for Louise's reaction.

She rolled her eyes and pulled a large tin off the counter—the item she'd been rummaging for earlier. Clever woman. She'd been prepared.

When she opened the lid the most delicious smell hit his nostrils: treacle and walnuts and warm November evenings by the fire. He almost had to wipe the drool from his mouth with his sleeve by the time a large chunk was handed to him on a plate. He didn't waste any time doing it justice.

Now, he could make a decent casserole and a great roast dinner, but baking evaded him entirely. This must have been a prize-winning, locally-made example. As he bit into it, he was almost tempted to growl with pleasure. Light moist cake with dense spicy flavours and the earthiness of walnuts teased his taste buds. Almost half the slice was gone already. Would it be rude to ask for another one? He looked over at Jack, who had cleaned his plate, but was wearing a significant amount of crumbs over his face and down his front. Now, there was a lad who could be counted on to ask for more. All Ben had to do was hop on the bandwagon when the opportunity came.

Jack opened his mouth and Ben swallowed his last mouthful, confident that his plate would not lay desolate for long.

'So, can we go to the fireworks, Mum? Please?'

Louise frowned and put the lid on the cake tin. Ben felt taste buds whimper in protest.

'I don't know, Jack. I thought we could watch from upstairs. That way we might get to see more than one display.'

Jack pursed his lips. 'Jas says there's going to be hot dogs on the village green. Can't we go and have hot dogs?'

She looked pained as she shook her head. 'I'm sorry, darling. After the way that photographer... Well, it's just better we stay here where no one will see us.'

Jack's face fell and Louise's was a mirror image of misery. Ben wished there was something he could do. It was criminal that a mother and son couldn't do something as simple as watch a firework display without being hounded. He remembered only too well how hard he'd had to work not to stay inside every evening and mope when his divorce had been fresh and raw. With the extra pressures on Louise, he could see her turning into a hermit. And that wouldn't be good for her son, either.

Jack slumped forward on the kitchen table, his chin in his hands and his bottom lip sticking out. Ben stared at the wall straight in front of him, racking his brain for a solution. Slowly, the pegs containing hats and coats and scarves near the back door came sharply into focus. He stood up.

'I've got an idea.'

The other three stopped talking and looked at him. He grinned, walked over to the row of pegs and pulled off a fluffy, knitted hat and matching scarf. 'Come with me,' he said as he walked back towards Louise, whose eyes were wide and round, then he linked the tips of his fingers with hers and pulled her up to stand.

Her mouth moved, but no sound emerged.

He tugged her in the direction of the hallway, to the large gilt mirror he'd seen hanging there on his very first visit after Louise had moved in. He stood behind her and, while she continued to stare at him in the mirror, he pulled the dusky purple hat over her head. It was one of those tight-fitting ones with no embellishment or bobbles, and the crocheted hem came down level with her eyebrows.

Better. But she still looked like *Louise Thornton*. He scowled at her reflection and her eyebrows raised so they disappeared under the hat. It was the hair. That long, glossy dark hair was her trademark—instantly recognizable, indefinably *her*.

He brushed the hair framing her face back behind her ears and twisted the strands into a loose plait, something he'd done countless times with Jas. When his gaze flicked up to the mirror again, she was staring at their reflections, her mouth slightly open, and then she shivered and shook his hands away from her shoulders. He broke eye contact and busied himself wrapping the scarf once, twice, around her neck, letting it stand up so it covered the lower half of her face. Somehow his hands had made their own way back on to her shoulders with the flimsy pretence of keeping the scarf in place.

Only the eyes gave her away now, but there wasn't much he could do to diminish their impact. She could hardly wear sunglasses on a chilly autumn evening. That would only draw more attention to her.

'There.'

She was motionless, the only movement her eyes as they flicked between her own reflection and his. 'I'm wearing a hat and scarf. Is that your stunning plan?'

'No one will be able to pick you out of a crowd in this. It's going to be almost pitch-dark, after all. Top it off with a big, dark coat and you'll look just like the rest of us.'

'I *am* like the rest of you.'

He knew celebrities weren't a different breed of human being, so he could almost agree. But there was something about Louise Thornton that defied explanation, that made her unlike anyone he had ever met before. And he really hoped he didn't feel that way because she was famous. He didn't want to be that shallow.

They stared at each other in the mirror a good long time. Her shoulders rose and fell beneath his hands.

'Mum, look!'

The stillness was shattered and suddenly he was moving away and Jack and Jasmine were running into the hallway, bundled up in coats and hats and jumping up and down. Jack was tall for his age, and Jasmine petite, making them almost the same height. It took a few seconds for him to realise that Jack's over-excited squeaking was coming from underneath Jasmine's hat and scarf. Louise looked from one child to the other and burst out laughing. She pulled the fluffy hat with ear-flaps up by its bobble until she could see her son's eyes.

'If you'd have kept quiet, I'd have had no idea that you two had switched coats!'

Jack jumped up and down. 'Can we go? Can we?'

Louise rolled her eyes again. 'Okay, we'll go.'

Their cheers echoed round the tall hallway and up

the elegant sweep of the stairs. Pounding footsteps followed as they raced back into the kitchen. 'You can wear your own coats and hats, though,' Louise called after them.

When the silence returned, she looked at him. 'Do you really think it'll work?'

'Of course, everyone is going to be craning their necks and looking up at the sky. They won't even pay attention to who's standing next to them. And, let's face it, it has to be a better disguise than your last attempt!'

She pulled the hat off her head and spent a few seconds de-fluffing her hair. 'You don't beat around the bush much, do you?'

He shook his head. Why waste time using inefficient words when you could use a few that hit straight to the heart of the matter?

Louise unwound the scarf and held it, together with the hat. 'Was it really that bad?'

He nodded, and tried very hard not to smile. 'You looked like a celebrity trying very hard to *not* look like a celebrity. I mean, a pink tracksuit with the word "juicy" splashed all over the…um…back.'

She gave him a knowing look. 'Oh, you noticed that, did you?'

He knew he shouldn't, but he grinned back at her. 'It was hard not to.'

CHAPTER TWELVE

25th June, 1952

I know I wrote at length about how I wasn't going to attend the blasted party in London, but in the end I couldn't stop myself. It was another chance to see Dominic. How could I have stayed away?

But after the events of this evening I wish I had.

I realise now that I'd been holding on to some foolish hope that fate would intervene somehow, that all the very real obstacles to our being together would just melt away, and that I'd finally be able to have him. Perhaps Alex is right. Perhaps my job means that I do spend much of my time living in a fantasy land. Well, reality hit home this evening, and it was a stinging and unpleasant slap.

Alex came with me, and Dominic brought Jean. There was an awful moment when we met in the hotel foyer and exchanged pleasantries. I had rush of feeling at seeing him again, but it was instantly dashed away by a horrible sense of discomfort. I felt as if something was climbing around inside, clawing away at me.

It's wrong, I thought, to be standing here beside my husband, watching your wife with her arm linked through yours, and to want you so desperately I can't see straight.

I hated her. I know it's awful to admit it, she's done nothing to me—nothing!—and I am the witch in this scenario, but I really hated her at that moment. I hated her for meeting him first, for tricking him into loving her. I hated her for being able to touch him when I couldn't.

Most of all I hated myself.

Alex has been lovely since I've come home. He's seen me moping around and thought it was something to do with him, all the travelling he's been doing. And he's tried, really tried. He's even changed his mind about trying for a baby.

It's so unfair. Why couldn't he have done this before? It's too late now. I can never go back to how I was before Dominic. Even if he was the most perfect husband in the world to me now, I could never be the perfect wife to him.

I thought seeing Dominic would stop me feeling so wretched, but I was wrong. I felt much more wretched after seeing him with his wife all night, being courteous and attentive, keeping his distance from me.

Maybe it would have been better if I'd seen him look at her the way he'd looked at me down at Whitehaven, if

I'd had a sense that I had just been a momentary madness on his part, but I didn't.

Once, just once, our eyes met across the top of the crowd, and it was all still there. Everything I've been dreaming about, plucking from my memories. I hadn't exaggerated it at all in the week we'd been apart.

But she saw me. Jean saw me look at Dominic, and I saw her eyes narrow and her hand clasp his arm more firmly. I saw her steer him away to another part of the room. They left shortly after that.

I went out onto the terrace overlooking Park Lane and stood there on my own for a bit. There was a chill in the air that had been missing these last few months. Summer was finally over.

I know I'll never see him again.

I could. If I wanted to. I could track him down, arrange to bump into him somewhere... But I won't.

As I stood there, I thought about all those times I'd ached for Alex to notice me more—to really see me. How I'd wanted him to speak or show his love somewhere other than the bedroom. I know what that's like. How can I do to Jean what I know would have crushed me a few months ago? I can't. And I can't make Alex a laughing stock in front of the whole world. I might be emotional and impulsive, but I'm not heartless.

So there's only one thing left to do. I will stay with Alex. I will try to be a good wife to him, and I will have those babies I've always longed for. I've been working too hard these last few years. It's time to take a break. And maybe, just maybe, with some time away from the madness of my profession, and a child to adore, I can build something with Alex that will last, even if it never will touch me to the depths of my soul.

So, there's only one thing I can do now. Only one thing left I can say…

Goodbye, my darling Dominic.

CHAPTER THIRTEEN

'When are the fireworks going to start?'

Louise looked first to the left and then to the right and clung a little harder on to the rope strung between rusting metal poles in front of her. Lower Hadwell's village green bordered the river just upstream from the main jetty and the fireworks had been set up on the stony beach with a clear boundary marked out to stop excited children getting too close.

'Twenty minutes.' Ben's voice was calm and reassuring, but it did nothing to soothe her. 'Don't worry.' His hand rested lightly on her shoulder and she jumped.

Don't worry. That was easy enough to him to say. Every time he let his guard down, someone didn't jump out in front of him a with a digital camera in hand. So, in recent years, Louise had just stopped letting her guard down at all in public, and when things had started going downhill with Toby, she'd kept it up at home too. Pretty soon it had become a habit that had been hard to break. As a result, the tabloids labelled her 'stuck-up' and 'fake'.

She sighed and, as her warm breath flowed out of her mouth, cool night air laced with wood smoke and sulphur filled her nostrils. She smiled.

Her family had always attended the little firework display in the local park each November. The fireworks themselves hadn't been all that spectacular, but her memories were of cosiness, laughter and a feeling of belonging.

Then she'd met Toby and all that had changed.

'Mum? Can I have a hot dog?'

Louise blinked and then focused on Jack, who was tugging on one of her arms.

'Pardon, sweetheart?'

He tugged so hard she thought her shoulder would work loose from its socket. 'I'm really hungry. Can I have a hot dog?'

The smell of onions, caramelising as they cooked on the makeshift grill on the far corner of the green reached her nostrils. Hot on its tail was the aroma of herbs and meat. Her nose told her that, when Jack said 'hot dogs' he didn't mean skinny little frankfurters but bulging meaty local sausages, bursting out of their skins and warming the soft, floury bread that surrounded them. Her mouth filled with saliva.

'Jack, you're going to pull my arm off! Give me a second to think!'

She was safe here at the front of the crowd. No one could see her face, only half-lit from the bonfire on her left. But over there by the grill, a generator grumbled as it provided power for a couple of harsh floodlights, making it bright as any catwalk she'd ever walked down when she'd been modelling.

'Um…'

Ben took hold of Jack's hand, his eyebrows raised in a question as he searched her face. 'Why don't we let your mum save our spot here and we can go and get the hot dogs? If that's okay with you…' he added, a little more quietly as he leaned towards Louise.

Her face relaxed and she breathed out. She nodded and almost sighed her response. 'Thank you.'

It was only when Ben and the two kids had disappeared through the crowd that she realised she should have asked him to get one for her too. She opened her mouth to yell, but stopped herself and pulled the hem of her hat down until it was touching the bridge of her nose. Too many faces.

There were always too many faces these days. Yes, back in the beginning, she'd loved that aspect of her golden life with Toby. Dad had needed a lot of help when she'd been finishing secondary school and, after being in class so infrequently that some of the kids in her year hadn't even known who she was, it had been nice to be recognised. But she'd underestimated just how addictive being noticed could be.

Her first hit had been the adrenaline rush she'd had when that talent scout for a modelling agency had come up to her when she'd been working in the supermarket one Saturday afternoon. Within weeks she'd been flying round Europe for photo shoots, attending industry parties, meeting famous people...

Dad had been so proud of her. And she'd ignored the guilt she'd felt at letting Sarah, the next oldest, slip into her Cinderella role whilst her big sister had danced away in an imaginary world where the clock never seemed to strike midnight.

And then she'd met Prince Charming—Tobias Thornton, rising star and darling of the British film industry. After they were married she'd smothered all those nagging feelings by reasoning that now, at least, her family had decent food on the table. That they'd moved into a proper house with a bedroom for each of them...except Louise. And the school uniforms were no longer hand-me-downs or scavenged from local charity shops. Best of all, Dad had a full-time nurse to look after him.

But it had been the nurse who'd been sitting beside him when he'd died just over a year after she and Toby had said 'I do' on a private island in the Caribbean.

Tears stung Louise's eyes and the bonfire became a big orange blur. She stared at the mass of colour until it started to sharpen and move again. Slowly, she became aware of people talking and being nudged, but she didn't seem able to move. It was only when she heard Jack laugh and splutter with a mouthful of hot dog that she realised the others had returned. She carelessly rested a hand on top of Jack's head but he shook it off.

'You looked hungry, too.' There was a smile in Ben's voice and she turned to look at him, even though the world was still shimmering slightly. He was holding up a big, juicy sausage in a roll, dripping with fried onions and ketchup. 'Of course, I've heard models don't eat, so I'm prepared to make the sacrifice of eating two if you don't want it.'

'Ex-model,' she said, snatching it out of his hand and stuffing one end in her mouth before he could change his mind. Ben threw his head back and laughed. And, when she had finished chewing, she did the same.

'Mum? What's so funny?'

Louise gave a tiny shake of her head, her gaze locked with Ben's. 'I don't know, just…' Ben was still grinning, but his eyes weren't just smiling at her now. Deep underneath, there was something intense, something that drew her and terrified her at the same time. '…something.'

She breathed out and returned her attention to her hot dog, which wasn't hard to do. She hoped these had been happy pigs because, boy, they made one heck of a good sausage. Their sacrifice had been entirely worth it.

But then, sacrifices often were.

If Mum hadn't died, if Dad hadn't been ill, if she hadn't been standing at that particular supermarket till that day—looking 'haunting' as the scout had told her—then she wouldn't have met Toby. Okay, she might not have any regrets about erasing Toby from her life at this particular moment, but without Toby there would have been no Jack. And Jack was worth any sacrifice.

She looked at him, hanging off the rope and trying to edge closer to where the fireworks were being set up. Before she could reach for him, a strong male hand gently grabbed his coat and hauled him back into place.

A bonfire sprung into life inside Louise. In a place that had been cold and dead for so long, flames licked and tickled.

No. Not now. Not here. Not with this man.

Not that Ben Oliver wasn't worthy of admiration. After all, he was good-looking, thoughtful and kind. A good father. All the things a girl should put at the top of her list when searching for a prospective Prince Charming. And he had a presence, a quiet charisma that made it impossible not to search him out in a crowd or feel that he was someone you could trust your life with.

But she wasn't a princess and he was no prince. And this wasn't the time to be noticing those things about someone. This was time for her and Jack to heal, to rebuild. And she'd felt this way before, had trusted Toby with her life, and he had made it glitter and shine for a while, but ultimately he'd decided it wasn't worth his enduring attention.

So, this was her sacrifice: she wouldn't go there. She'd cut off the oxygen supply to whatever feelings were warming her core. Jack deserved all her attention and her love at the moment and he shouldn't have to share it with anyone. He wouldn't.

The fireworks started. Louise had thought herself immune to the pretty showers of colour. Last year they'd seen the New Year's fireworks in London from a balcony of an expensive riverside apartment a quarter of a mile away. It had been a dramatic display, with rockets shooting off the London Eye and barges on the Thames, but she'd felt removed from it all somehow.

There was no ignoring anything tonight. Not the way the crowd collectively held its breath waiting for a bang. Not the warmth of the bonfire on one side of her face. Especially not the breath of the man standing slightly behind her that made her right ear tingle.

In the inky blackness of a country night, the sprays of light—from pure white to red and green, and blue and gold—were reflected in a river that had stretched itself taut and flat. The effect was magical. Soon she was saying 'ooh' and 'aah' with everyone else, and clapping and watching Jack's reaction.

And finding herself catching the gaze of a warm, brown pair of eyes, then quickly looking away again.

The last firework glittered and fizzed, shooting so high up into the sky that she would have sworn that, briefly, she caught a glimpse of her big, white house on the opposite bank. And then it exploded and split into a thousand stars that gracefully fell to earth. She sighed and closed her eyes. Simple pleasures.

How odd. She'd always thought that money and fame would make it easier to find pleasure, but all it had really done was make it more complicated. Pure happiness, joy with no strings attached, was an unknown commodity in her life. When had she become so poor? And how had she become so blind she hadn't even realised what a sorry state she'd been in?

'Come on…' Ben's hand, resting once again on the shoulder of her thick wool coat, caused her to open her eyes, releasing the magic moment and letting it flutter away like the sparks from the bonfire. 'I'll give you a lift home.'

Jack, who should have been totally worn out by now, jumped up and down even harder. 'Are we going on the dingy again?'

Jas put on a very superior tone. 'It's not a dingy, Jack. You say it *ding-gee*. Dinghy.'

Jack pulled himself up to his full height. 'I knew that.'

Ben shook his head. 'No. I'll drive you.'

Louise opened her mouth to protest. It would take more than half an hour to drive down to Dartmouth, catch the 'higher ferry', as the locals called it, and double back to Whitehaven.

'I wouldn't take the kids out in the boat at this time of night,' he explained.

Louise followed him as he headed for the quiet spot where he'd parked his car and looked carefully at the scenery. It had been verging on darkness when they'd made the trip over, or at least she'd thought it had. The trees had been dark grey shapes and the sky had faded from bright cobalt at the horizon to indigo overhead but, compared to how it looked at the moment, that had merely been twilight. Everything was black if it wasn't lit up by either starlight or electricity.

'And you and Jack would have to scramble back through the woods in the pitch-dark.'

Okay, he'd convinced her. She got lost in her own back garden in daylight still. No way was she dragging her eight-year-old through those woods tonight.

As she strapped Jack into the back of Ben's car, Louise went still. Ben must have known all along that they wouldn't be able to return to Whitehaven the way they'd come. It explained why he'd disappeared when they'd first arrived to move his car—away from the main road and the village centre, where the crowds were now ambling—into a quiet side road.

She sat in the front passenger seat and fastened her seat belt without looking at him. Pretty soon they were whizzing through isolated country lanes in silence, the only hint they weren't alone inside a big, black bubble were the golden twigs and branches picked out by the headlights in front of them. The patterns the light made on the road and hedgerows shifted and twisted as they sped past. Every now and then, for a split-second, an odd tree stump or a gate was illuminated, and then it was gone.

Louise breathed in the silence. After a few minutes she turned her head slightly to look at Ben. His hands gripped the wheel lightly, but she had no doubt he was in full control. All his concentration was focused on the road in front of them. He looked at it the same way he'd looked at her in the mirror that afternoon.

The air begun to pulse around her head and a familiar craving she'd thought she'd conquered started to clamour deep inside her—the heady rush of simply being *noticed*. Immediately, she twisted her head to look straight ahead and clamped her hands together in her lap. They were shaking.

Simple pleasures.

She had an idea that Ben Oliver was full of them.

It was taking every ounce of his willpower to keep his eyes on the road ahead. Having Louise Thornton in the front seat of his car was proving a distraction. And not an oh-my-goodness-there's-a-celebrity-in-my-car kind of distraction. Unfortunately. He could have talked himself out of that one quite easily.

And it wasn't even because she was the most stunning woman he'd ever laid eyes on. She was way out of his league, he knew that. The logic of this situation would catch up with him eventually.

At the start of the evening, she'd stood tall and still, and a casual onlooker would have thought her relaxed and confident. But, unfortunately, he'd discovered he could no longer regard Louise casually.

He'd noticed the way her gloved hands had hung on to the boundary rope as if it were a lifeline. He'd seen the panic in her eyes when she thought she'd have to face the crowd and might be recognised. He had the oddest feeling that the real Louise had shrunk small inside herself, hiding beneath the thick outer shell. How long had she been that way?

Then, as the evening had worn on, he'd seen her hands unclench from the rope and noticed the unconscious, affectionate gestures that flowed between mother and son. He'd heard her laugh when ketchup dripped onto her chin from the hot dog, and had heard the soft intakes of breath with every bang and crackling shower of the fireworks.

He didn't want to notice these things about her. He didn't want to know how warm and rich her laugh was, or how tender and gentle she was below the surface. He just wanted to see the surface alone—much in the same way he only saw the rippling surface of the river and never the rocks and currents beneath.

He would rather remember the bare facts: that she was still in the middle of a divorce, that the last thing he and Jas needed in their lives at the moment was another woman with too much baggage for him to shoulder.

He'd known that Megan had had 'issues' when he first met her, but they seemed inconsequential compared to the situations facing Louise. Yet she faced them with such dignity and poise…

There he went again, admiring her when he should be concentrating on other things.

A flash of movement across the road caused his foot to stamp instantly on the brake. All of the joke-telling and giggling from the back seat stopped.

'It's okay,' he said, his heart pounding. 'Only a rabbit—and he's away up the hill now.'

Jas and Jack returned to their knock-knock jokes and he put the car into gear. He pulled away gently, aware of the slim fingers that had flown to the dashboard and were now curling back into her lap.

Getting freaked out by a rabbit? What was happening to him? They darted in front of the car all the time and he never usually reacted this way. He pressed his foot on the accelerator, the car picked up speed and soon they were flying down the country lane as if nothing had happened. Ben concentrated on the road and pretended he didn't know how to answer his own question.

The other occupants of the car fell into silence and it wasn't long before he was pulling into the long drive that led to Whitehaven. Louise shifted in her seat, as if she was preparing to dart out of the door as soon as the wheels had stopped turning. Good. If she didn't feel the need to linger in his presence, that was fine by him.

'Can I have cake when I get in, Mum?'

Ben stifled a smile as he slowed the car and brought it to a halt outside the front porch. And then his tummy rumbled. It had fond memories of that cake.

'Jack, it's past your bedtime! Of course you're not going to have—'

'Cakes!'

They all turned and looked as Jas, whose eyes were wide and a hand was clamped over her mouth. Then she started to cry. He scrambled out of the car and opened the rear passenger door. 'Jas? What is it?'

Jas's lip trembled. 'C—cakes. My class are doing a tea party for the old people in the village. Mum was going to help me make cakes this afternoon, but she went away…'

Ben tried to not let the irritation show on his face. Megan could waltz off to Timbuktu for all he cared, but when her flaky ways affected Jas it was a different matter entirely.

'I'm supposed to take them in on Tuesday morning or I won't get any house points!' Jas wailed. 'Can you help me, Dad?'

'Um…' There was nothing he'd like more, but he wasn't sure Jas would be getting any house points for anything he tried to bake.

'I can help.'

As one, he and Jas swivelled round to look at Louise and stared. Her face was expressionless. Had he really heard that right?

Ben turned back to Jas. 'Can't you do it on your own? I'll supervise.'

There was a loud snort from the passenger seat. He ignored it.

Jas was wearing the end-of-the-world face common to all eleven-year-old girls in a crisis. 'I don't know. I can never get the beginning bit right when you have to mix the eggs and flour together.'

'Eggs and sugar.' Louise spoke quietly. In his experience, that tone was deceptive. He just might be in big trouble.

'Yeah, eggs and sugar. That's what I meant,' Jas said absently.

Ben sighed. 'Can't we just buy some?'

Jas shook her head and started to cry again.

'I can help.' This time Louise's tone was more insistent.

'Home-made cakes?'

'What do you think you were eating earlier? Scotch mist?'

Reality dropped away and Ben felt as if he was standing on nothing. '*You* made that cake?' He could tell by the look on her face that he was probably sabotaging Jas's only chance—which was a pity. He hadn't meant his words to come out quite like that, but they'd escaped before his brain had had a chance to give them the once-over.

Louise glared at him. 'No, the cake fairies left it on the doorstep.'

Okay. He'd deserved that.

Jas, who was wiping her eyes with her coat sleeve, piped up. 'I thought that if Jack needed cakes for school you'd just buy them at Harrods.'

It seemed his daughter had inherited his capacity for opening his mouth for the sole purpose of changing feet.

Louise clamped a hand across her mouth and, just as he was expecting her to flounce out of the car, slamming the door, her eyes sparkled and she let out a raucous laugh.

Ben was floored. This wasn't the shy giggle he'd seen earlier; it was a full-bellied chuckle. And it was pretty infectious. When the surprise had worn off, his mouth turned up at the corners and it wasn't long before all four of them were crying with laughter. Louise was clutching onto the door for support and Jack's titter was so high-pitched it was starting to hurt his ears.

Still giggling, Louise managed a few words, even though she was a little short of breath. 'Sometimes…sometimes…when I was really busy…I *did* get them at Harrods!' That just set them all off again.

When they all managed to get back on the right

side of sanity he felt as exhausted as if he'd done a cross-country run. Man, it hurt to breathe.

Louise let out a long, happy sigh. Her face was soft and relaxed and her cheeks were flushed. It was just as well there were two children in the back of the car, because he had the stupidest urge to kiss her.

That sobered him up pretty fast.

'Are you sure? I'm sure you're really busy. We don't want to put you out, do we, Jas?'

Jas didn't say anything, but pleaded with her eyes.

'Busy doing what? The contractors keep shooing me away when I try to help with the redecoration.' Louise raised an eyebrow, and then she winked at him—actually winked at him. 'I'd be happy to help. You gave us a great night out tonight.'

Ben stuttered. That was the problem. In his mind, tonight had been about making a nice final gesture to make sure Louise was settled into the neighbourhood before he backed off. Now, how was he supposed to do that if she was going to be installed in his kitchen tomorrow?

CHAPTER FOURTEEN

After she'd put Jack to bed that night, Louise couldn't sleep. Didn't even want to try. It must have been the fresh air or something.

She found herself flopped on the big velvet-covered sofa in the drawing room, the remote control in her hand, flicking through endless cable stations searching for something to watch. A fire glowed in the hearth and the lights were low. The rich, deep colours and luxurious textures of the fabrics in here truly had made a large, draughty room incredibly cosy.

After ten minutes she let the remote drop on the sofa and gave up. Then she remembered that she'd sneaked Laura's diary up from the boathouse yesterday and it was still in her bag. Although she'd already read a couple of entries this morning, and she was trying to ration herself so she could mull it all over, getting to know Laura through it slowly, surely a few more pages wouldn't hurt?

Laura was so brave where she was so cowardly. She leapt in and gave her heart freely and completely. Comparing herself to Laura, Louise realised she'd locked her heart away—which was good, because that meant it was safe—but she also knew it was the cowardly thing to do.

She fetched the soft leather notebook from her bag, snuggled back down on the sofa and began to read. The next entry was some months after the one made on the night of the party…

2nd December, 1952

Even after all these months I miss him so much it hurts. I scan the papers every morning just to see if there's a mention of his name. It's the one weakness I allow myself now that I'm trying to patch things up with Alex.

I've taken a break from filming. The doctor thinks the rest will help me fall pregnant.

'No stress, Mrs Wallis,' he says. He's the only person I know who uses my married name. Everyone else just sees me as Laura Hastings. Apart from Dominic—who sees me as just Laura. And she's a very different creature from her movie star namesake. Very different indeed.

I thought it would get better, the ache inside, but if anything it's got worse. I didn't count on the way it would gnaw away at me, or the guilt that would magnify it.

I know nothing happened between us, not really. I'd

have had to kiss Dominic anyway—it was my job. Alex knows that and he doesn't care. But I do feel horribly guilty. For loving a man who is not my husband. Especially as I now realise I never loved Alex properly, not the way I do Dominic. I mistook flattery, affirmation, a sense of security, for love. I needed Alex. To give me things I should have found inside myself.

I hope he's happy with me. He seems to be. Because now I realise I could have short-changed him badly by agreeing to be his wife. I should have waited. And maybe, if I had, fate would have found a way to give me Dominic.

Louise stopped reading and wiped a tear from her eye. She'd never thought about it before, but that was exactly the same reason she'd married Toby. Not for who he was, but for all the things he could bring her. That was selfish, wasn't it? She'd never loved him the way Laura loved Dominic, not even right at the start. She'd been too worried about not being good enough for him, of letting him down. Which made her seem humble, self-effacing, but those things had just been a smokescreen for being self-absorbed. It had all been about *her*.

She gently closed the diary. No more tonight. It was too sad. And it was stirring up things she didn't want to think about. Things that made her start to wonder if her divorce was a black and white matter, that maybe she'd contributed to the downhill spiral of her marriage…

Perhaps she'd watch a DVD instead. She got up and walked over to the pile of cases near the television. Under one of Jack's kids' films, she found one that arrived in the post a couple of weeks ago that she'd forgotten about. A film that had been an impulse buy while she'd been browsing for books on Whitehaven and Georgian architecture.

A Summer Affair.

Feeling almost guilty, she slid it into the DVD player and returned to the sofa and zipped past the trailers to where the film started. Laura had been so beautiful when she'd been younger. Her ice-blonde hair, pale skin and blue eyes looked fabulous in gaudy nineteen-fifties Technicolor ®.

The on-screen chemistry between Laura and Dominic was sizzling hot. She'd always thought that, but now she knew the story behind the story, every touch, every kiss had a bittersweet quality to it. She sighed and settled down to watch, a chenille cushion hugged to her chest.

There was a scene halfway through the film, just after lovers had started to act on their feelings for each other that had been filmed on the balcony of the boathouse. A picnic was set out on a little table with a red and white checked cloth. The sun was shining, and shy, heated glances were flying between hero and heroine.

Louise sighed. That was what love should be like, she mused as she covered her mouth with a hand to stifle a yawn—overly bright and colourful, the sun always shining. The zing of electricity in the air. And the way he looked at her—as if he could see right through her and into her soul. As if he wanted to drown in her. That was what love *should* be like.

But it hadn't worked for Laura, and it wouldn't work for Louise.

What a pity love was only like that in corny old movies, she thought, as the Richard pulled Charity into the shadowy interior of the boathouse and wrapped her in his arms.

Louise's eyes were closed. A gentle summer breeze warmed her skin and she could hear the waves half-heartedly lapping against the jetty below the balcony. She let out a long, therapeutic sigh, stretched her legs and opened her eyelids.

The sky was the colour of cornflowers and the sun a glaring dot of white gold high above.

'Perfect timing.' The male voice was warm and lazy, and accompanied by the dull pop of a cork exiting a wine bottle. 'I thought you were going to sleep all afternoon.'

She shook her head and stood up. The chequered red and white cloth on the small table fluttered, lifted by the warm air curling in and out of the boathouse balcony. Self-consciously, she reached for the wine glass he offered her and dipped her head to hide behind the curtain of her hair.

'Don't do that. Not with me.'

She froze, anticipation and vulnerability sending both hot and cold bolts through her simultaneously. He stepped forward and brushed the hair away from her face. His thumb was warm and slightly rough on the skin of her cheek. The tips of his fingers threaded through her hair until he held her head in his hand. She couldn't help leaning into it, letting him support her.

Slowly, he tipped her head until she was looking him in the eyes.

'You don't have to hide from me.'

Oh, she would have given anything to believe that was true. Tears sprung to her eyes and clung to her lashes. Even in the bright sunshine, she could see his pupils growing, become darker and darker. But it wasn't just desire she could see there. Deep in the blackness were the answers to all the questions she'd ever wanted to ask.

Yes, the eyes said. Yes, you are good enough. Yes, you deserve to be loved like this.

One tear escaped, pulled by gravity, and raced away down her cheek. She couldn't move, not even to swipe it away. It carried on running as he continued to stare at her, his expression full of texture and depth, until it trailed down her neck.

A question flickered across her face—she felt it as surely as the salty river air.

Do *you?*

He didn't move a muscle, except to stroke the skin of her temple with the edge of his thumb. The eyes held the answer once again. *Yes.*

Something inside her, something that had been clenched tight and hard for years, unfurled. And Ben Oliver stepped back into the cool darkness of the boat-house, pulling her with him and repeated his answer over and over again with his lips on hers.

Louise woke up with a gasp, her eyes wide. The fire was little more than burnished embers and the film had ended. A blank blue screen bathed the room in an eerie light.

She pressed a hand to her pounding chest. Just a dream. It had only been a dream. Calm down, you daft woman. Is this how pathetic you've become? A man shows you just a little bit of concern and neighbourly decency and your subconscious decides he's the love of your life? Just how starved of affection have you been?

Well, her subconscious could just think again. Starving or not, this was one meal she was going to refuse. All her brain had done was jumble up the events and people of her day with the events and characters of the late-night film. A simple crossing of wires, that was all. In the morning, when she was coherent again, she'd make sure everything was rerouted back the right way.

She straightened the stiff arm she'd been lying on and was rewarded with a click. Serves you right for falling asleep in front of the telly, she told herself. Although love *should* be like falling in love in a cheesy old movie, it wasn't. And it never would be. The sooner the logical side of her brain caught up with that fact, the better.

CHAPTER FIFTEEN

At three-thirty the following afternoon, Louise still wasn't sure of she'd won the battle with her subconscious. She pressed the doorbell on the Olivers' cottage door and tried to work out where all the butterflies in her stomach had migrated from. Wherever it was, it seemed they were making themselves at home.

There was a click and the door started to open. Louise stopped breathing.

The blonde-haired woman who answered frowned slightly. 'Yes?'

Louise swallowed. 'I'm… er… here to help Jasmine. Mr Oliver is expecting me.'

The woman nodded, opened the door wide and Louise stepped inside and followed her into a funky, modern kitchen with glossy red cabinets and a black granite work surfaces. Not exactly what she'd pictured Ben Oliver would have chosen but, then again, maybe he hadn't chosen it. Maybe the now ex-Mrs Oliver had had something to do with it.

Right there was a good reason to stamp on all the

butterflies waltzing inside her. Both she and Ben had too much history, too much baggage.

'Hey!' Jasmine was sitting on a cushioned stool next to a breakfast bar with a glass counter. She jumped off and walked towards Louise, her hands in her pockets. A blush stained her cheeks and she looked at the floor as she came closer.

Louise smiled. It didn't seem that long ago that she'd been all awkward gestures and blushes herself. 'Hey, yourself. Ready to bake?'

Jas nodded. 'Is Jack with you?'

Louise shook her head. 'He's gone to football and then to a friend's for tea.'

'More cake for me, then!' Jas said and giggled.

'Is… um…' Louise glanced at the anonymous woman, who was standing in the doorway, staring at her with undisguised curiosity. 'Is *everyone* joining in?'

'Oh, no.' Jas shook her head. 'Just you and me.' She scowled at the woman, who took the hint and sloped away. 'Don't mind Julie. First of all, her nose is out of joint that she can't stay and snoop on a famous person, but most of all she's probably worried she won't get as much child-minding money if you're looking after me.'

'Your dad's not here?'

'Nah. He doesn't finish work until five o'clock and probably won't be home until six. She looks after me until then most days.'

Louise wasn't sure whether to be relieved or disappointed. Relieved, she told herself quickly. It was much better to be relieved. Still, that didn't explain the black hole that had opened up inside her tummy that the butterflies were now being sucked into.

Even before Ben's key had turned in the lock, the most amazing smells hit his nostrils: warm butter and cinnamon, sugar and vanilla. He'd been on a site visit most of the day and lunch had merely been a fleeting fantasy as he'd tried to explain to his client, in the most polite way possible, that his ideas for a visionary garden were actually going to be a blot on the landscape. His stomach rumbled, and he ordered it to get a grip.

He didn't want any cake. He didn't want to be hungry for anything at all.

He found Julie sulking in the sitting room reading a magazine. She really wasn't the greatest substitute for the regular child-minder, but at least she'd been amenable to relocating to the cottage today so Jas could cook. With Louise.

His stomach gave up growling and did something more akin to a backflip.

Get a grip, Ben.

It meant nothing. It would always mean nothing. He'd just not been on a date for a while, that was all. He nodded to himself as he made his way to the kitchen. That was it, he was sure. Lack of female company had left him a little hypersensitive to having a woman around. Especially a woman as beautiful as Louise Thornton. It was just his testosterone talking.

But did it have to yell quite so loudly?

His hand was almost on the kitchen door, but he snatched it back and veered off in the direction of his study. He closed the door firmly behind him and let out a long breath. Work would distract him. And he needed to update his files on today's project and come up with something that fulfilled his client's brief to be 'ground-breaking' and 'organic' without being hideously ugly.

Instead of turning his computer on he reached for a large sketch-pad and a soft pencil. All his best ideas came when he did the designing the old-fashioned way. Somehow, just holding a pencil and having a creamy sheet of cartridge paper beneath it made him want to fill it with shapes and shading and curves, to change the blankness of the bare paper into something that came alive.

He threw the pencil and pad down on his desk, took off his jacket and hung it over the back of his chair, then sat down and set to work, his empty stomach momentarily forgotten.

Half an hour later, he stood back and surveyed his handiwork.

Great, just great. Best ideas? What a laugh.

He squinted at the drawing and then turned the pad ninety degrees. A long, low groan escaped from his mouth and he ran his hands over his face. He had a wedge-shaped paved area, a semi-circular lawn finished off with a small round water feature at the far side. In other words, the aerial view of the garden loosely resembled a giant cupcake with a cherry on top. Why, when he'd been thinking of lawns and borders, had he come up with this?

Best thing to do was admit defeat. He should just go into the kitchen, say hello and then leave again, proving to himself he was just working himself up about nothing. And maybe this evening he would call his pal Luke and get him to set him up with one of his wife's friends. Gaby had been trying to matchmake for more than a year now. Perhaps he should just put her out of her misery?

Ben grinned, but it turned into a grimace. The truth was he didn't really want to go out on a date with anyone. Nobody he'd met in the last couple of years had been anything more than pleasant company for an evening. No one had been the sort of woman he could envisage fitting into his and Jas's lives. Even Camilla.

Camilla had been stylish and intelligent and funny, but there'd just been no spark—even though he'd done his utmost to get something to ignite. For a while now, he'd just thought it would be better to wait until Jas was older. She deserved love and stability after all she been subjected to because of his and Megan's mistakes, not a string of unsuitable girlfriends being tramped through the house. Not that he'd actually brought any of them home, anyway.

Unsuitable. That was a good word.

Louise Thornton was totally unsuitable, no matter how mouth-watering her cakes might be. Okay, she wasn't the airhead the tabloids made her out to be, but her life was full of turmoil, and that was the last thing he and Jas needed at the moment. He'd do well to remember that.

He pushed open the kitchen door and found exactly what he'd feared—turmoil. He blinked at the two females giggling on the other side of the room as a puff of icing sugar billowed up from a glass bowl and settled on them like microscopic snow. 'Not that way...' Louise was saying. 'Gently!'

Jas was laughing so hard she inhaled some of the icing sugar and started to cough and sneeze at the same time. Louise, who was starting to cough herself, started to pat Jas on the back. Neither of them had any idea he was there.

He looked around the room. On every available space there were cake tins and wire racks, assorted cake ingredients and almost-clean mixing bowls with finger marks in them. Megan would have had a fit if she'd have seen her precious kitchen like this. It looked wonderful.

'Dad!' Jas spotted him, pulled away from Louise and ran over to him.

'Jasmine.' He tried very hard to keep a straight face. Someone had to bring some sanity into the proceedings.

'Come and see what we've made!'

Before he could argue, she slipped a sticky hand into his and pulled him across the kitchen to where a row of cooling racks stood, with various cakes, all in different stages of decoration. Louise was there, standing straight and tall. She'd been laughing a moment ago, but now her eyes were watchful and her mouth was clamped shut. He saw her gaze sweep around the kitchen.

'Sorry,' she mumbled. 'We kind of got carried away.'

He wanted to say something grown-up, sensible, but not one word that fit the bill entered his head. He was too distracted by the smudge of icing sugar on Louise's nose.

She blinked at him. 'What?'

'You've got—'

Ben leaned forward, meaning to brush it away, but she stepped back and went cross-eyed trying to see what he was looking at. Then she rubbed at her nose with the heel of her hand, which only served to add a drop of jam to the proceedings.

He stayed where he was. She could sort out herself out. It was better that way.

Louise was staring at him. Slowly, she walked over to the double oven and checked her reflection in the glass door. He handed her a piece of kitchen towel and she took it, without looking at him, and dabbed at her face. When she stood up again, she was blushing.

It was so unlike her normal, armour-plated façade that he couldn't help but smile. 'Much better.'

She blushed harder and smiled back. 'Good,' she said quietly.

Only, he wasn't sure if it was better. There was something rather appealing about an icing-sugar covered, vanilla-smelling Louise Thornton in his kitchen. She seemed…real. Not unapproachably beautiful or spikily vulnerable. Just real.

'It's time we started clearing up, Jas.' Louise reached for a tin and headed for the dishwasher.

Ben waited for the whining to start, but Jas just nodded and started closing up bags of flour and putting egg cartons back into the fridge. He shook his head, then decided to put the kettle on—mainly to distract him from the rows of cupcakes, sitting silently on the counter, just *waiting* for someone to notice them. Saliva started to collect in his mouth and he found himself swallowing three times in a row.

He turned round to offer Louise a cup of tea and found her standing right behind him, a plate full of cakes in her hand. He swallowed once again.

'Would you like one?'

Now, if it had been Jas doing the offering, he would have immediately responded with, *what do you want?*

However, Jas was earning her halo washing up the wooden spoons. He looked at Louise and just nodded.

'Raspberry and lemon muffins, jam doughnut muffins or iced fairy cakes?'

His eye fell on something golden-yellow and covered in sugar.

She smiled. 'Jam doughnut muffin it is, then.' She looked down at the cakes for a few seconds then up into his face. 'Actually, I'm trying to butter you up.'

She was? 'You are?'

Louise nodded. 'I watched that film that was made at Whitehaven last night…' her eyes glazed over and she seemed adrift for a few seconds before she caught herself and carried on. 'The garden…well, it looked lovely and I wondered if you'd consider, um, taking on the job of landscaping it properly for me.'

He was speechless. For years he'd wanted to have free reign at Whitehaven. Now was his chance. He should be whooping with joy and dancing round the kitchen hugging someone—hugging *Jas*, of course.

'You do that kind of thing, don't you?' She was looking at him strangely.

Twice his head dipped in a nod. He'd started off in landscape gardening and when that had been going well, he'd trained as a landscape architect. The resulting design practice, with specialist teams to do the ground work when required, was one of the things that made his firm so successful. However, he didn't seem to be able to articulate any of this to Louise.

'Good. Perhaps we can chat another day—during work hours. I don't expect you to give up your time to…' A tiny frown creased her forehead and she stared at him for a couple of seconds, then her gaze dropped the plate in her hands. 'Still want one?'

The muffin was still warm when he picked it up and, when he bit into it, liquid raspberry jam burst out and added its acidity to the dense but moist texture of the muffin. Pure heaven. Louise just smiled. Oh, she knew she was good! She knew exactly how much her baking had reduced him to a salivating wreck. And she was enjoying it.

Ben stood up very straight and resisted the urge to lick the sugar off his fingertips. Suddenly, this wasn't just about cakes any more. But perhaps it had never been about cakes.

Yup, he was pretty sure he was in big trouble. Because, despite all his efforts at logic, he was starting to think that, far from being the wrong kind of woman, Louise Thornton might suit him just fine.

CHAPTER SIXTEEN

Louise looked up as rain started to lash against the boat-house windows. She put the paintbrush that she'd been holding down and stood up to stretch her back. There was no electric light in the boathouse and the gathering clouds meant it was far too gloomy for decorating. The paint was off-white and it was difficult enough to do a second coat when the light was good.

She pressed the lid back on the pot of paint and did what Gerry, one of the contractors, had shown her to do and wrapped the wet paintbrush in cling film. She stood back and surveyed her handiwork. The light reflected off the wet paint in patches, revealing that she hadn't been as even as she'd thought with her strokes, but she still felt the warm glow of accomplishment.

She walked over to one of the windows and peered out. Further off, the clouds were pale and bright, and moving quickly in the stiff breeze. This was only a shower. Give it ten minutes and she might be able to continue.

Time for a tea break.

She reached for the large metal flask she'd filled with scalding tea before she'd walked down here and poured herself a cup, then she remembered the solar-powered lantern she'd rescued from the boot of her car and pulled it from a box near the door. Its dull blue glow was no help in the painting and decorating stakes, but it added a little light to the corner of the small room.

Louise took it over to the small desk that sat against the far wall, looking out over the river, and put the lantern on one side. She pulled a small, tarnished key from her jeans pocket and unlocked the small, central drawer, then eased it open and removed Laura's diary.

She'd brought it back here. However, she had plans to use the fireplace once she'd finished redecorating, and she was worried she'd scorch the precious book if she put it back behind the tiles. The desk had seemed like a good compromise.

After retrieving her flask lid full of tea, she sat down and carefully parted the pages where she'd last left off.

28th May, 1953

I was doing so well, and then I dreamed of Dominic one night. Since then I haven't been able to get him out of my thoughts, either sleeping or waking. I dreamed we were at Whitehaven, that somehow all the things keeping us apart had melted away.

I was standing on the front lawn in the sunshine, looking out over the river, and he came up behind me

*and folded his arms around me, kissed me in the hollow
of my neck. I closed my eyes and just drank it in, even
though it was just a dream.*

*We've never had that. The easy familiarity of that
kind of affection. Even the stolen moments we had were
played out in front of a film crew, and as much as we
tried to disguise it, there was a tinge of desperation to
every time we touched or kiss, knowing that time was
short that we had to grab what we could while we had
the chance.*

*It was both beautiful and terrible that my subcon-
scious conjured up what I could never have. Beautiful
to experience it so vividly, but terrible that I have not
been able to tuck the thought away in the past where it
should stay.*

*I keep going back to it, pulling it out from its hiding
place, reliving it, embellishing it. Now it's not just a
moment, but a whole scene—a whole life—has begun
to grow in that shadowy place. I imagine what our bedroom would look like, what meals we would eat in the
kitchen, that our children are running down the lawn
and building Indian forts in the woods.*

If I can't have Dominic, at least I can have this.

*Maybe it's because my stomach stays worryingly flat,
that any nausea I have is just from forgetting to eat
some days. Alex says he doesn't mind, that I am enough
for him. I wish I could respond in kind. I really want
that baby, and I fear if it doesn't come along that I will*

*fall apart completely. It's the only hope that keeps me
going, keeps me giving the performance of my career in
my own life.*

Louise closed the diary and loving fingered the
leather cover. She'd hug it to herself, somehow trying
to comfort the sad, lonely woman in its pages, but she
was scared she'd mar it with paint if she did.

She knew what that was like. That sense of encroach-
ing loneliness that could not be completely kept at bay.
Carefully, she placed the diary back in the drawer and
locked it again.

Had Laura found the happiness she'd craved? Had
she been able to find peace? Suddenly, Louise really
needed to know.

Of course, she could go back up to the house and
get on the Internet and find out within five minutes,
but somehow that seemed like cheating. Reading it in
Laura's own words, making the journey with her, was
somehow important.

She drained the last of her tea and put the lid back on
her flask. While she'd been reading the wind had done
its job and cleared the skies. She would just have to be
patient. Laura would reveal her secrets in due time, and
until then Louise had a boathouse to decorate.

She tipped her head on one side and surveyed the
drying paint on the other wall.

Yep. That was a shocking attempt at a second coat.

***

The next couple of weeks disappeared in a frenzy of activity. The builders and decorators stepped up their schedules, determined to be finished well before Christmas, and the landscaping began in the garden. Louise just took herself off down to the boathouse, slowly continuing her restoration job. It wasn't as slick and professional as the work in the main house, but she liked its slightly rustic, haphazard style. It was all hers.

When it was finished, she was going to get a sofa or a daybed to put in here, along with a couple of comfy chairs and a rug. In the summer, it might even be nice to sleep down here, close to the river, where she could hear the gentle waves licking against the jetty when high tide was up.

But as her project neared completion, she began to feel restless. Even more so, when, up at the main house, the flurry of vans and men in work boots diminished to just a few painters and a sole carpenter.

For a couple of months, making Whitehaven a welcoming home for her and Jack had been her priority. What was she going to do when it was finished? She couldn't just sit around all day and stare at the wallpaper, no matter how nice it was.

Around her, everyone else moved with purpose. Aside from the contractors, Jack was busy studying and fitting in at school. Ben was overseeing the landscaping of the more formal gardens near to the house. From the plans he'd shown her, she knew he was very good at what he did. Even, Laura, whose presence Louise felt through the diary, had excelled at something. She'd been one of the leading British actresses of her day.

But what was Louise good at? What was she *for*?

She'd been a successful model once, but her body had expanded and her looks no longer held the glow of youth many clients preferred. She liked baking, but it was hardly a life's calling.

It was odd, she thought, as she passed the main lawn and headed up round the side of the house—just to walk, to take in the transformation just a lick of paint and some deftly applied plaster had made to Whitehaven's exterior—she wasn't used to having nothing to do.

For most of her life she'd been running at full speed. First keeping her family together, and then being the wife of a Hollywood actor and all the extra drama and patience such a role involved. And then she'd been a mother. Unlike many of her contemporaries, she hadn't hired a nanny, preferring to be hands-on with Jack herself as much as she could. Even though she'd wished it otherwise sometimes, after sleepless nights and harried shopping trips, she just hadn't been able to leave Jack with a stranger and waltz off on her own. That was what she'd done to her father, and she'd always, *always* regretted it.

She reached the top lawn, where the greenhouse was,

and walked past it. There was a bench leaning against the wall of the garden and she paused and sat down on it, breathing in the chilly air and soaking up the meagre warmth of the frosted winter sun.

As she sat there she thought about her life with Toby.

She'd thought he'd needed her, but that hadn't been true, had it? She'd just been convenient to have around, to put up with, while he found his fun elsewhere.

But she'd made it easy for him, she realised. She'd walked into that relationship and taken on the only role she knew how to play: carer, giver. Just as she'd had to be a grown-up well before her time at home, she'd had to be the grown-up in her relationship with Toby too, and she'd fallen into looking after him the way she had her father and her brothers and sisters.

However, where her family had needed her love and indulgence to get them through tough times, by the time she'd met him Toby really hadn't needed another person indulging him. She'd done it anyway, hadn't she? Because she hadn't known how to be any other way. It was all so clear to her now. Why hadn't she been able to see this before?

She'd *helped* Toby take her for granted.

Of course, that didn't mean she deserved what he did to her, but maybe, if she'd been a little stronger, asked more of him, things might have been different. That should make her sad, but it didn't. It just made her puzzled.

She got up and wandered in the direction of the old stable block, not too far from the kitchen door. Now there was a real project, something she could really get her teeth into. Horses obviously hadn't been at Whitehaven for decades, because this building would need more than just a lick of paint and a little remedial plastering to see it right. Louise got quite excited at the thought, until she realised she already had a house with more rooms than she could use, and that, really, this would just be a great way of stalling, of filling in the time so she didn't have to think about the one question that had been hounding her since she'd walked out the door of Toby's house and had never looked back.

What on earth was she going to do with the rest of her life?

CHAPTER SEVENTEEN

December, so far, had been incredibly mild, but a cold snap was coming. He could feel it in the slicing wind that raced every now and then up and down the river. Ben hunched his shoulders up to try and escape the draught snaking down the back of his neck as he steered the little dinghy through the sharp, steely waves.

Jas moved into the stern with him and he held up an arm for her to snuggle under. He smiled down at her and she buried her head further into his side. His lips were still curved when he returned his attention to the river. It didn't matter if the weather was cold enough to freeze the Dart solid, the fact that he'd managed to create a living thing so wonderful would always melt his heart.

This was one of those perfect snapshot moments that would live in his memory forever. Everything on the river seemed to be in shades of grey and silver—the waves, the reflection of the pearly sky. And, directly in front of him on the hill, perched on the hill like a queen on her throne, was the bright white house he was heading towards. In their waterproof coats—his dark green and Jas's vibrant purple—they were the only blobs of colour on the river spoiling the effect.

'Do you think it's going to snow, Dad?'

He pursed his lips, thinking. 'I don't know. It would be nice, though, wouldn't it? The last time we had a white Christmas I was younger than you.' He hugged Jas to him, then released her as they neared the jetty below Louise's boathouse. 'We'll have to wait and see.'

After tying up the dinghy, he stood for a moment and stared up the hill. The house was hidden by the curve of the land and by the trees, but he knew which direction it was.

There were ugly gashes in the earth near the house which his team had created in the midst of doing the hard landscaping. It would look a mess when he approached the front lawn. But, in his experience, things often had to get a lot messier before they were transformed into something beautiful. In the spring, the digging and paving would be finished and they'd be able to plant. Come summer Whitehaven's garden would be transformed. And, over the years, it would mature into something unique and stunning.

Unique and stunning…

How easy it was for his thoughts to turn to Louise.

Recently Jas had taken to showing him any photographs of her she found in the Sunday papers or magazines. Most of them weren't current, as she hadn't really been anywhere to be photographed recently.

'Ready, Jas?'

Jas, who had been throwing stones into the water, nodded and ran off up the hill. Ben tucked his hands into his pockets and strolled after her. As he walked, the image from the article in one of the Sunday magazines filled his head. Tobias Thornton had given an extensive interview about his new life with a blonde actress whose name Ben was struggling to remember. Of course, there had been photos of Louise and Toby in their glory days.

He punched his hands deeper into his pockets. What did it mean if he admitted to himself that the photos had made him feel sick? He couldn't figure out why; they were fairly innocuous shots of the then Mr and Mrs Thornton on the red carpet somewhere. The body language had been convincing—he'd had an arm around her waist and she'd hooked a hand around his neck. They'd been smiling.

Ben kicked a stone on the path and watched it hit a tree trunk then roll down the hill out of sight. And then he thought about her eyes. There had been a deadness there, just a hint. Most people, if they'd noticed it at all, would have just assumed it was because it had been the five-hundredth photo they'd posed for that evening. Not him.

That same soul-deep weariness had been in her eyes

the day he'd first met her, and no one had been watching her then. He had a good mind to track her ex down and give him a piece of his mind for putting it there.

Ben stopped in his tracks. What he really wanted to do was teach Tobias Thornton a lesson. When had he suddenly got so primitive? He never wanted to hit people. It just wasn't him. Not even Megan's new man.

Probably because he kind of felt sorry for the guy…

Slowly, he started walking again, then picked up speed because he realised he couldn't see Jas any more. He called out, and a few moments later saw a flash of purple in between the trees up ahead.

His heart rate doubled. Would she be up there on the lawn, strolling as Jack played? Or would she be waiting from him in the kitchen, the kettle blowing steam? He could easily have sent a guy to care for the carnivorous plants in the greenhouses, but he'd kept on coming on Sundays anyway, hoping she wouldn't ask why.

Sunday was now officially his favourite day of the week. And he had a feeling that Louise knew the plants were just an excuse. Each week they spent more and more of his visit talking, walking round the grounds. He'd never drunk so much tea in his life. But if those giant mugs kept him leaning against the rustic kitchen counters while she hummed and pottered round the kitchen, stopping every now and then to smile at him, how could he complain?

At that moment the trees parted and he saw her. It

felt as if every molecule of blood had drained from his body. She was chasing both Jack and Jasmine, who were running round in circles, and when she saw him, she stopped, brushed the hair from her face and waved.

Normally, he didn't have any problem speaking his mind. He was never rude or insensitive, but he just called things as he saw them. So why, when all he could think about was asking her out to dinner, or seeing if they could spend some time alone—just the two of them—did the syllables never leave his lips?

He was now within shouting distance. Hands that had been cold and stiff were now clammy in his pockets and he took them out and did a half-wave with one hand. Louise smiled and his insides jumped up and down for joy. The warm laughter in her eyes erased any form of sensible greeting.

Just admit it, Ben. You've got it bad.

He was here.

She waved, just to seem friendly. And, of course, if she didn't smile too it would look funny, so she did. Only she didn't seem to be able to control how wide, how sparkling it was.

He took long strides across the lawn, minding the gouges of red earth at the edges. Something to do with re-establishing the rose garden, she'd been told. The details were a little fuzzy at present. He gave a little wave, but his face remained serious.

She didn't care. She liked it when he looked serious. His jaw would tense sometimes when he was in this kind of mood and his eyes became dark. She allowed herself a little sigh before he got close enough to see the exaggerated rise and fall of her chest.

She was playing with fire, she knew. But there was nothing wrong with fire if you kept your distance, let it warm you but not scorch you. And that was what she intended to do. To keep her distance from Ben Oliver— romantically, at least. But it had been so long since she'd felt this alive.

What was the harm in a little crush? To feel her blood pumping and all those endorphins speeding round her system. It was good for her. And no harm ever came from a little bit of daydreaming.

Laura had done it. It had kept her sane to think of Dominic when everything else had seemed grey and lonely. She gave silent thanks to the woman who had stopped her going mad fighting with herself. This way, she could indulge her crush but she'd be safe.

Daydreaming was all it would ever be. It was all she'd allow herself.

It would have to be enough, because she'd felt this way before—worse even—and it hadn't ended well. She'd fallen so totally in love that she'd lost herself completely, had allowed herself to become completely overshadowed. It would happen again if she let it. When she fell, she fell hard, completely.

She took a sideways look at Ben as he joined her and they silently started walking towards the kitchen. Jas and Jack had already disappeared inside and were probably trying to work out how they could raid the biscuit barrel without being rumbled.

He was walking with his head bowed, looking at the ground in front of his feet, but he must have sensed her looking at him, because he mirrored her and the smallest of smiles crossed his lips. Without warning, another sigh snuck up and overtook her.

Ben Oliver was all the good things she'd once believed a man could be: strong and kind, thoughtful and funny—although sometimes without meaning to be, but that just made it all the more charming. Honest. That was a big tick on the list, honesty.

He was all wrong for her, of course.

Or, maybe, more to the point, she was all wrong for him. She could picture a new wife for Ben quite clearly in her mind: someone who was capable and strong. A woman who had a quiet confidence, a gentle heart. And when evening came, and it was time to turn out the light, he would reach across and stoke her face with the palm of his hand, look deep into her eyes…

Tiny pinpricks behind her eyes took her by surprise and she was glad they'd reached the back door and she could busy herself removing her coat and hat and putting the kettle on before she had to face him again.

He hadn't said it out loud, but she knew he would do

anything to keep his and Jas's life on an even keel. And so it should be. It was just such a pity that the only thing she could bring him were the ups and downs of a roller coaster life—a life that was way out of control and she was powerless to stop. She didn't wish it on herself, so how could she wish it on him when he'd worked so hard to build a solid foundation for himself and his daughter?

Louise watched Ben as he sat down with the kids at the kitchen table and refereed as they argued about who had had the most cookies. Another sigh. And this one hurt right down to her toes. If only this could be real...

No. Dreaming was fine, but wishing was dangerous.

She shook herself and made the tea. There was no point wishing for things that couldn't be, but something about Ben made her feel like a proper person again. So she was going to hang on to that feeling as long as she could and use this crush, this infatuation—whatever it was—to help her heal.

And, one day, when she was good as new, she wouldn't need to dream about him any more. Then she'd let the fantasies go and watch them swirl up into the air and blow away like the autumn leaves.

Louise looked round the boathouse. It was finally finished. The wooden floor was painted, the walls smooth and even in the off-white colour she'd chosen, and now the day bed had arrived and two armchairs faced the fireplace. The desk still sat in its corner near the window, and she'd also added a bookcase on the wall opposite and a small sideboard which housed a camping stove and tea and coffee-making supplies.

And she'd done it all herself. From choosing the soft furnishings to painting to walls and varnishing the floor. Okay, she'd had help getting the furniture down here, but she wasn't superwoman.

In the grand scheme of things, it was a tiny triumph. It shouldn't have made her feel so good, but it did. Maybe because for the first time in a really long time she'd done something for herself. Not because anyone else wanted her to. Not because anyone else needed her to. But for her. To make herself happy. It was quite a giddy feeling.

As a reward, she unlocked the desk drawer and pulled Laura's diary out. It had sat unread in there for quite a few weeks. She hadn't quite been able to bear finding out how Laura's story ended for a while. At the moment, they were two lonely women battling against the world. If Laura found her happy ever after, Louise would have been all on her own again.

But now she thought she was ready to take a peek.

She hugged it to her chest and took it over to the day bed, piled high with cushions so it could be used as a sofa, and sank back into them.

New Year's Eve, 1953
I can hardly believe the blissful state in which I began

this new year—with Dominic's lips on mine. I feel that everything has turned around, that finally I can shake this sense of heaviness that has plagued me since last summer…

Slow down, Laura. Start at the beginning. You'll want to remember this later, because this was the moment when everything changed.

Sam Harman, director of A Summer Affair, *invited me to one of his legendary parties at the Ritz. Alex was travelling again—off to Greece to do some deal—and I thought 'why not?'. I had nothing else to do.*

I didn't expect to see Dominic there, so that wasn't why I went. After the last party, I knew I couldn't bear seeing him and Jean there together, so I checked—very subtly—with Sam. He told me that Jean had written to tell him they'd been invited by the Duke of Argyll to stay in his castle for Hogmanay. I thought it would be safe.

I was doing such a good job of pretending to be the sparkling film star—circulating the party with a champagne glass, laughing at people's jokes, flirting with the young men—and then it felt as if I'd run into an invisible glass wall.

There standing on the other side of the room, stealing all my breath and commanding my gaze, was Dominic. He looked more handsome, more wonderful, than I'd ever seen him. I hadn't realised how much I'd been yearning for him until that moment. I'd thought I was doing better. But don't they say that the starving man loses all sense of hunger eventually? And then I saw Dominic and my appetite for him was back, twice as powerful, twice as desperate. It was all I could do not to run across the room and fling my arms around his neck.

The only thing that stopped me was that I could see matching famine in his eyes too. If we'd touched, right there, right then, no one would ever have been able to pull us apart, and this party of Sam's would have become legendary, not for the bucket loads of champagne or famous performers, but for the scandal he and I would have created in the centre of the dance floor. I wouldn't have stopped, not until I'd had everything I'd ever dreamed about having from him and more.

That's shocking, isn't it? To know that a well brought up girl like me could think such wicked things. I surprised myself.

It was agony, continuing to mingle with the other guests, when every molecule in my body was focused on him. I knew who he talked to, how many drinks he had. I was the compass needle and Dominic was my North. So I knew when he stopped keeping away and started to make his way, group by group, person by person, towards me, and—God help me—I didn't move. I waited for him.

But I've spent every moment of my life since last summer waiting for Dominic. How could I do otherwise?

He held out his arms as he reached me and I walked into them, placing one hand on his shoulder, one hand in his. The dancing had begun maybe an hour before, and this was one way we could be seen together and not start tongues wagging. Even so, even with only my palm and fingers touching his, I felt I could melt into a puddle at his feet.

'I didn't think you'd come,' I said. Very sophisticated, wasn't I?

Dominic shrugged. 'Sam invited me and my other plans fell through.'

My heart stuttered. Jean. I'd forgotten all about Jean. Was she here too? I'd been so consumed by seeing Dominic again, I hadn't even remembered she existed! He must have read my mind—or my panicked expression—because he told me they'd cancelled their trip because Jean had been feeling under the weather. They'd been staying with her mother over Christmas, so they'd just stopped there instead of going home. She'd insisted he get out and enjoy himself instead of being cooped up with such a bore, he said.

'I hope it's nothing serious,' I said. Being polite, but not being honest...as much as it pains me to admit it.

He shook his head. 'She's just been very tired recently. And she thinks the rich Christmas food disagrees with her. Her mother does tend to go a bit overboard.'

I nodded. I really didn't have anything else to say. I didn't want to talk about Jean. I didn't even want to remind myself she was real. I wanted this night to be our little bubble of time—mine and Dominic's—and I resented her for nudging her way in, even in conversation.

So we didn't talk. Just moved. Looked. Breathed each other in.

But it couldn't last. We had to break apart, talk to other people, dance with other people, otherwise it would have looked bad. However, every now and then we found our way back to each other, stole another few moments, another few touches.

When midnight came close, I realised I couldn't see Dominic anywhere. I wasn't foolish enough to think I could kiss him, but I wanted to be able to see him, share at least that with him. I turned round and round, scanning the room, started walking this way and that as Big Ben's musical peals boomed from a wireless somewhere, but he'd gone. It was so unfair.

The chimes started and I just froze to the spot, tears welling in my eyes.

That's when a warm hand touched my arm. I knew before I turned that it was him. Maybe it was his smell, or the unique feel of his skin on mine. Maybe it's just because something inside of me recognises him.

I turned and pressed my face against his cheek, hardly daring to move my arms so I could hold him. All around us the party was heaving. No one was paying any attention to us. For a few snatched seconds we could be ourselves.

And then everyone was cheering and shouting and

clinking glasses. Dominic just leaned in and pressed his lips softly to mine. Just for a second. A peck that could have been as innocent as it looked.

'I need to go,' he whispered.

I placed a hand on his chest, searched his face as one tear escaped and dripped down my face. 'I can't say goodbye again,' I sobbed, and I bunched his lapel in my fist.

Slowly, he stroked my fingers until they unclenched and flattened. He waited until I looked at him, until I focused on him properly. 'Neither can I,' he said. And my world flipped upside down. 'Have lunch with me next week. I have to come into town to see my agent.'

I nodded, barely able to breathe, let alone speak. Inside, I felt feverish and shaky. I knew what this meant. That lunch may well not just be lunch. I also knew it was wrong, but I just didn't care any more.

Who says love is pure and lovely and wonderful? Not me. It has turned me into something I despise—a grasping, weak, greedy creature, who is willing to selfishly take what she wants and everyone else be damned. Yes, even him. I try to care that this might end his marriage, spoil his perfect family, but I can't.

Louise closed the diary, her eyes wide.

This was not easy to read. She felt slightly nauseous. Was this how Toby had felt about Miranda? Had he thought so little of Louise, been so consumed by his need to have the other woman that he'd turned into something awful and greedy?

She looked at the closed leather book on her lap. She'd wanted Laura to find happiness, she had, but did it have to come at such high a price? While the portrait Laura painted of Dominic's wife wasn't very flattering, Louise knew all about skewed perceptions. Half the people she'd ever met, and thousands more who'd never had the pleasure, thought she was a miserable old cow. If Jean's husband was obviously in love with someone else, why *wouldn't* she have been sour and whiny?

But Louise had to admire Laura's guts. She drank life in, lived every emotion to the full. Whereas what did she do? She hid away in her big house, scared of meeting anyone new, lavishing her attention on soft furnishings and floor plans. At least Laura had lived.

She placed a palm on the diary, as if by doing so she could absorb some of Laura's boldness and courage. In comparison, she seemed pathetic. Laura dreamed of her man, but she was about to make those dreams come true. All Louise did—all she was prepared to contemplate—was the first part of the equation.

She replaced the diary back in its drawer, turning the key and then pocketing it. She wasn't ready to read more yet. Not while she was only ready to *wish* instead of *do*.

CHAPTER EIGHTEEN

Louise had convinced Jack to help her make ginger-bread decorations for the Christmas tree. However, she'd overestimated the attention span of an eight-year-old less than a week before Christmas. Once Jack had consumed vast amounts of biscuit dough—mainly while she'd been demonstrating how to use the different-shaped cookie cutters—he'd run off. She'd had to tell him off for sliding down the banisters twice already.

Carefully, she removed another tray of golden-brown angels from the oven, replaced them with uncooked stars, and shut the oven door, smiling. She really should stop, but she was having too much fun. As it was, they'd have enough biscuits for ten Christmas trees!

Later this afternoon, once Jack calmed down a little, they'd decorate the tree in the drawing room. She couldn't wait to see his little face when they dimmed the house lights and hit the switch for the twinkle lights. Yes, late afternoon would be best, when the sun was behind the hills and everything was getting gloomy.

In the meantime, she had twelve minutes to kill until the next batch of biscuits was ready. As she scooped the slightly cooled angels off the baking sheet and onto a cooling rack she drifted into one of her top-ten day-dreams…

It was a balmy summer day. A large picnic blanket was stretched out in the walled garden. Somewhere in the distance children squealed. Her eyes were closed and her head lay on Ben's lap as he twisted lengths of her hair around his finger, then released them again. Time had slowed, the seconds now hummed out by the bees in the lavender rather than the hands of a clock.

Louise sunk into a chair and rested her elbows on the kitchen table. Supporting her chin in her hands, she shut out reality by lowering her lids.

In the daydream, she opened her eyes. He was look-ing down at her, pure admiration on his face, and she knew he saw into every part of her. It took her breath away. For so long, all she'd seen in men's eyes was a certain predatory hunger. They admired the packag-ing, but very few were prepared to take the trouble to unwrap it. And those who did, like Toby, considered the gift inside disposable.

She shook her head. This was supposed to be the bit where Ben leaned in to kiss her, and she was not having it invaded by the likes of Toby. He had no place here in her summer garden.

Just as the imaginary Ben blocked out the sun by leaning forward, leaving her in a cool shadow, better able to see his darkening pupils… just as she could feel his breath on her skin…

The phone rang. The real phone.

Damn!

Louise snapped her eyes open and she jumped up from the chair. She could let the answering machine get it, but whoever it was would only ring back and interrupt her later. Reluctantly, she grabbed the handset from its cradle on the kitchen counter.

'Hello?'

'Hello, Lulu.'

The rich deep voice was as familiar to her as her own. All thoughts of bees, lavender and sunshine vanished.

'Toby.'

She wasn't going to ask him how he was; she was past caring, actually. And she certainly didn't need to hear about his cosy new life with twenty-year-old Miranda, thank you very much.

Toby said nothing, and she was tempted to put the phone down on him. He'd always done this—made her do the talking, ask the questions, prise information out of him. Well, she wasn't playing his games any more. He obviously had something to tell her or he wouldn't be phoning. He could just spit it out all on his own.

He coughed. Nope, she still wasn't biting. Not even to say, *What do you want?* This time *he* could do all the work, do all the giving instead of the taking.

'Louise?… I wanted to talk to you about Christmas.'

'Talk away.' She leaned against the counter and waited.

'Well, you see… I've been given a freebie, a holiday in Lapland. And I wondered if you'd mind if Jack came with me.'

Louise's stomach went cold. She'd been trying very hard not to think about the fact that Jack was spending Christmas Day and the following week with his father. It would be her first Christmas without him. But Lapland… Jack would be enthralled!

'That's fine with me, Toby. I'll pack warm clothes for him. Are you still coming down on the twenty-fourth to pick him up?'

There was an uncomfortable silence for a few seconds.

'Toby?'

'The flights are booked for the twenty-first.'

Monday? That was a whole three days early! Just like that, the bottom fell out of Louise's Christmas.

'Can't you change it?' she asked, forgetting to hide the panic in her voice.

'Sorry. It's now or never.'

'I… I…'

Toby let out an irritated breath. 'Come on, Louise.

Lapland. Jack will love it—and I've missed seeing him since half-term because I've been on location. It will be just Jack and me. Father and son time. He needs it.'

Unfortunately, Toby was right. Jack did need it. He'd missed his dad terribly since he'd left London.

'Just you and Jack? What about…' she wanted to say *her*, but she managed to force her mouth into the right shape '… Miranda.'

There was a short silence on the other end of the line. 'Miranda decided she'd rather see her family.'

Louise's eyebrows rose. Toby didn't seem very happy about that. Much as she didn't want to admire the tramp who'd stolen her husband, Louise couldn't help it. At that age, all she'd been able to say to the man on the other end of the line was *Yes, Toby…No, Toby…* She wasn't sure if she was irritated or impressed that the pre-schooler had more backbone than she'd given her credit for.

Louise had already said a giant *No* to Toby when she'd asked for a divorce, and now she found she didn't want to say anything but no to him. Silly, but true. However, this was Jack's Christmas too, and she knew he'd dearly love the trip. Saying yes to this didn't mean she was a pushover; it just meant she was a good mother, thinking of her son, keeping relationships with his father amicable.

She sighed. 'Okay. You can take Jack to Lapland, but I want extra time at Easter.'

Toby blew out a breath. 'Sure.'

Louise almost dropped the phone. She'd been all geared up for a fight, hadn't expected it to be that easy.

'Thanks, Lulu,' he said, sounding less like the movie star and more like the decent man she'd once married. 'I appreciate that. I'll need to pick him up tomorrow afternoon, though. We have to leave early Monday morning from Gatwick.'

Disappointment speared through her, harder and deeper than before. 'Fine.' She brightly, even though no one could see her. 'See you then.'

And then she hung up without waiting for any pleasantries and drew in a long steadying breath. Now all she had to do was tell Jack the good news without bursting into tears.

There was a strange car parked slap-bang in front of Whitehaven. Ben noticed it the moment he stepped out of the woods and onto the front lawn. Strange, because it was unknown to him but also strange because no one in their right mind would drive such a low-slung sports car in countryside like this. If it rained hard, he'd give the owner five minutes before it stalled in a ford or got stuck in some mud.

He was just wondering if he should check whether Louise was okay when she emerged from the house with Jack in her arms. She was hugging him tight, oblivious to anyone else. A man followed her out of the house, dressed all in black and wearing sunglasses. Ben snorted to himself. They were only days away from the solstice and there was no crisp afternoon sun, just relentless grey clouds.

The guy removed his glasses and shoved them in a pocket and Ben suddenly realised who he was. Weren't most people in films supposed to be shorter and uglier than they looked on screen? Unfortunately Tobias Thornton was neither. He looked every inch the action hero. He smiled at his soon-to-be ex-wife and kissed her on the cheek. Ben thought he lingered a little too long, but Louise smiled up at him.

Right. There was no use standing here like a lemon. This was family stuff. Private stuff. He might as well go and check on the greenhouses, as he did first every Sunday afternoon.

On reflection, he thought he might have over-pruned the first plant that received his attention in the greenhouse. Seeing Louise and Toby standing there in front of the house had reminded him of all those photos Jas kept shoving under his nose.

It was as if, until that moment, he'd *known* that Louise was Louise Thornton, but the woman in the magazines and the single mother who liked baking and walking in the countryside had seemed like two very different people. But now, without warning, those two completely separate universes had collided. It had left him reeling.

He spent as long as he could watering and feeding the plants. Then he tidied up the greenhouses and swept the floors. All the while, a snapshot of Louise smiling stayed in his head, her lips stretched wide, her teeth showing. He stopped sweeping and rested the broom against the wall.

Realisation hit him. That was as far as the smile had gone. Her eyes had had the same hollow look he'd seen in those magazine pictures. She'd been faking it. For Jack.

Ben smiled to himself. The sun was starting to dip low in the sky and he was now definitely ready to head towards the kitchen for one of Louise's bottomless cups of tea.

But when he reached the back door it was locked. There was no warm cloud of baking smells wafting through the cracks. No light, no noise—nothing. He tried the front of the house but it was the same story. There was no movement in the study or the library. The curved French windows round the side of the house revealed nothing but a darkened drawing room with a bare Christmas tree standing in the corner.

Where was Louise? Had she gone off somewhere with *him*?

Well, if she had, it was none of his business. And, since his work was done here, he might as well go home.

He hardly took in the scenery as he tramped through

the woods on the way down to the boathouse. He did, however, spot the loose brick in the boathouse wall as he passed it. Someone might guess the key's hiding place if it was left like that. Slowly, he slid it back into position until everything on the surface looked normal again.

It was only when he had jumped into the dinghy and was about to untie it that he noticed a glow in the arched windows of the boathouse. Someone was in there. And he had a pretty good idea who. What puzzled him was *why*. Why was she hiding out in a dusty old boathouse when she had a twenty-roomed Georgian house standing on the top of the hill?

There was only one way to find out.

He clambered out of the boat again and ran round the back of the structure, up the stone staircase and rapped lightly on the door. 'Louise?'

The silence that followed was so long and so perfect he started to think he must have got it wrong. Maybe a light had been left on a few days ago…but, he hadn't noticed it when he'd arrived. His fingers made contact with the handle.

A weary voice came from beyond the door. 'Go away.'

A grim smile pressed his lips together. No, his first instincts had been right. She was hiding.

He pressed down on the handle and pushed the old door open. Everything was still inside. She didn't move, not even to look at him, and at first he was too distracted by the transformation of the once dingy little room to work out where she was sitting. The inside of the boathouse now looked like the inside of a New England cabin. When had all this happened?

The cracking varnish on the tongue and groove walls was gone, sanded back and covered in off-white paint. The fireplace was still there, along with the desk and cane furniture, but something had happened to them too—everything was clean and cosy-looking. Checked fabric in blue and white covered the chair cushions and a paraffin lantern stood on the desk, adding to the glow from the fire.

A movement caught his eye and he twisted his head to find Louise, sitting with her knees up on something that looked like a cross between an old iron bedstead and a sofa, the firelight picking out her cheekbones. She was looking at him, her face pale and heavy. She didn't need to speak. Every molecule of her body was repeating her earlier request.

Go away.

He wasn't normally the kind of guy to barge in where he wasn't invited, but instead of turning around and walking out the door, he walked over to the opposite end of the sofa thing and sat down, hoping his trousers weren't going to leave mud on the patchwork quilt that covered it.

'What's up?'

Louise returned to staring into the orange flames writhing in the grate. 'Christmas is cancelled,' she said flatly.

He shifted so he was a little more comfortable, avoiding the multitude of different-sized cushions that were scattered everywhere. 'That explains the tree, then.'

Louise made a noise that could roughly be interpreted as a question, so he pressed on.

'The one in your drawing room—standing there naked as the day it was born.'

Another noise, one that sounded suspiciously as if she didn't want to find that funny. 'There didn't seem to be much point in decorating it now. Jack's gone to Lapland.'

'Lapland?'

She turned those burning eyes on him. 'Father Christmas? Reindeer? Who can compete with that?'

He shrugged. 'Think yourself lucky. At least Lapland is worth being deserted for. All I'm competing with is a few days in the Cotswolds with mum and the suave new boyfriend and I still came in second best.'

Okay, that got a proper snuffling sound that could almost be interpreted as a chuckle.

'You win, Ben. Your Christmas stinks more than mine. Pull up a chair and join the pity party.' She gave him a long look, taking in his relaxed position on the opposite end of the sofa-bed thingy. 'Not one to stand on ceremony, are you?'

He grinned at her. 'Nope. So…how does one throw a pity party at Christmas? Is it the same as an ordinary pity party or is there extra tinsel?'

A loud and unexpected laugh burst from Louise. Very soon there were tears in her eyes. She wiped them away with the side of one hand. 'You rat, Ben Oliver! You've just ruined the only social event on my calendar for the next two weeks. I'm going to have to reschedule my party now…Will the twenty-fifth suit you?'

It was good to see her smile. He knew from experience just how lonely a childless Christmas could be—and the first one was always the killer.

'This place looks nice,' he said, standing up and walking around to room to inspect it further.

Louise nodded, pulling her knees into her chest and tucked the cream, red and blue quilt over her legs. 'It's not bad, is it? I've even had the windows draught-proofed.' She glanced around the room and then her eyes became glassy. 'I'm tempted just to camp out here for the rest of the festive season. The house is just so…it's too…you know.'

He nodded. The bare Christmas tree had said it all.

He took a deep breath and walked over to her, holding out a hand. She frowned at him and pulled the quilt tighter around her.

'Come on.' He wiggled his fingers. 'I've got a lamb casserole that will feed about twenty ready to heat up at home. Come for dinner.'

She didn't move. 'Won't Jas mind?'

'Mind? She'll have so many invitations to go to tea after a visit from you that I'll hardly see her until she's twelve. I'll even let you be miserable at my house, if you really want.'

Louise smiled and shook her head. 'No, you wouldn't.'

He stuffed the hand he'd been holding out in his jacket pocket. 'Don't you believe me?'

'To quote a man I know: "Nope". In my experience, people say they want to you to be *real*, but only as long as it involves living up to their expectations of you at the same time.' She wrinkled her nose. 'I learned a long time ago that disappointing them costs.'

He held out his hand again. 'Well, I already know how grumpy you can be, so I wouldn't mind at all if you disappointed me on that front.'

Despite herself, she smiled at him, the firelight reflected in her eyes. 'You're not going to give up, are you?' She lifted her arm, placed her long, slim fingers in his and pushed the quilt aside.

They both smiled as they anticipated his response.

'Nope.'

His hand closed around hers, slender and warm, and he pulled her up to stand. Without her shoes she seemed smaller and he stared down into her face. The fire crackled and the light of the paraffin lamp flickered and danced. He realised that neither of them had taken a breath since he'd taken hold of her hand.

Louise dropped her head, letting her hair fall over her face and disentangled her fingers from his. 'I think you might be my guardian angel, Ben Oliver.'

He liked it when she said his whole name like that. Somehow it made it seem more intimate rather than more formal. She walked over to a hat stand by the door and pulled her coat off of it. While she did up her buttons, she risked another look at him. 'You always seem to be there when I need someone to make me think straight.'

He pretended not to be touched as he turned off the lamp and ushered her out of the door. And he tried very hard not be stupidly pleased at being what Louise Thornton needed.

Louise locked the door and hid the key in its usual hole and they walked the short distance down to the jetty in silence. He was still mulling it over, standing in the boat with the rope in his hand, ready to cast off, when Louise stepped into the boat beside him and, as she brushed past him to sit down in the stern, she stopped. He felt her breath warm on his face as she leaned close, just for a second or so, and the soft skin of her lips met his cheek.

He whipped his head round to look at her, but she was already sitting on the low wooden bench looking up at him. 'Thank you, Ben.'

A realisation hit him with as much force as the cold waves buffeting the little boat. He *wanted* to be what she needed. And he wanted to *keep* being what she needed. But she didn't need a man in her life right now. It was too soon. The divorce wasn't even final.

What she really needed was a friend. He fired up the motor and untied the boat before heading off across the choppy water and as he crossed the river he knew just how he could cheer Louise up.

And cheering Louise up would be a good idea. Because then she wouldn't look so lost and lonely, and he wouldn't have to fight the knight-in-shining-armour part of himself that wanted to charge in and be *everything* she needed.

CHAPTER NINETEEN

The house seemed empty without Jack in it. Maybe moving to the country had been a mistake. If she'd been staying in London, she could have lost herself in the last-minute Christmas Eve panic in Oxford Street. It might have even been fun to try and spot the most harried male shopper with a look of desperation in his eyes.

Louise stopped by a shallow pool surrounded by bamboo. A copper statue of a Chinese Buddha, covered in verdigris, stared back at her. He was the closest thing to human being she'd seen since having dinner with Ben on Sunday evening. The statue stared past her, looking serenely through the trees to the river below, and she decided he probably wasn't the life and soul of the party, anyway, and moved on.

She only entered the house to collect a few things and make a flask of tea. In the last few days she'd spent a lot of time at the boathouse, preferring the cosy little space to the multitude of echoes that seemed to have appeared around Whitehaven.

Tonight, she was going to sleep in the boathouse, tucked up under both the duvet and the quilt, with the fire going and a good book for company. Hopefully, Santa wouldn't discover her hiding place, set between the beach and the woods, and he'd fly straight past. There wasn't anything she wanted this year.

She pottered around the house, wandering from the kitchen to her bedroom and back again, picking up the few things she'd need. All the while, she distracted herself with her favourite Christmas daydream. At least in her imagination she could keep the loneliness at bay.

The fire was glowing and coloured fairy lights twinkled on a huge blue spruce in the bay window of a cosy cottage sitting room. It was early in the morning, the sky a deep indigo, and Jas and Jack were squabbling half-heartedly about who was going to hand out the presents. She and Ben were laughing and eventually they let the kids get on with it, just to keep them quiet.

Then, amidst the sounds of giggling children and wrapping paper being ripped, Ben drew her to one side and presented her with a silver box with a delicate ribbon of white velvet tied round it. She stopped and smiled at him, a look that said 'you shouldn't have' glowing in her eyes.

Then she gave in and tugged the wrappings free with as much abandon as the children had. Before she

opened the box, she bit her lip and looked at him again.
Then she prised open the lid to reveal...

This was the bit where she always got stuck. What could be in the box? She didn't want fancy jewellery and body lotion and stuff for the bath was just a bit too *blah.*

Louise stood from where she was, putting a change of warm clothes into a holdall, and stared in her bedroom mirror. You're losing it, girl. Seriously. Hasn't this fantasising about the gardener gone just a little bit too far?

It had. She knew it had. But it was warm and comforting—like hot chocolate for the soul—and heaven knew she needed a bit of comfort these days. And it was the one Christmas comfort that was one hundred percent calorie-free. She'd end up the size of a house if she resorted to the other kind.

She zipped up the holdall and slung it over her shoulder. The clock on the mantelpiece said three. She needed to go soon. No way was she trudging along the rough paths coated with soggy leaves in the dark.

Louise took her time wandering back to the boathouse. There was something hauntingly beautiful about her wild garden in winter. However, when she was only minutes away from her destination, the sky grew darker. Rain came in hard, stinging drops and she picked up her pace.

She ran up the stairs to the upper level of the boathouse, only pausing to retrieve the key from its hiding place, and burst into her cosy upper room only to stop in her tracks, leaving the door wide open and a malicious draft rushing in behind her.

What…?

She couldn't quite believe her eyes. What had happened to her sanctuary while she'd been gone?

On almost every available surface there were candles—big, thick, tall ones, the sort you'd find in churches—some balanced on saucers from the old china picnic set she'd rescued from the damp. The fire was burning bright, crackling with delight at the fresh logs it was hungrily devouring. There was holly and ivy on the mantle and, in the corner, near one of the windows…

Louise laughed out loud. How could this be?

A Christmas tree? Not a huge one, but at least five feet high, bare except for a silver star on top. She walked over to it and spotted a box of decorations sitting on the floor, waiting to be hung. Red, purple and silver shiny baubles would look amazing in the candlelight. She picked one out of the box and fingered it gently.

How…? Who…?

An outboard motor sputtered to life outside and suddenly all her questions were answered. She ran out onto the balcony and leaned over. 'Ben!'

The little wooden dinghy was already moving away

from the jetty and he looked up at her, a sheepish smile on his face. He waved and yelled something back, but his words were snatched away by the billowing wind.

Her natural response would have been to stand there and shake her head in disbelief, but the rain—which was rapidly solidifying into sleet—was bombarding her top to toe. She pushed her wet hair out of her face, ran back inside and closed all the doors.

Not knowing what else to do, she sat cross-legged in front of the fire, staring at the patterns on the blue and white tile inserts until they danced in front of her eyes.

Toby had been good with show-stopping gifts—diamonds, cars, even a holiday villa in Majorca once—but none of those things measured up to this. None of those gifts had this depth of thoughtfulness, this knowledge of who she was and what she needed.

Louise stood up and placed a hand over her mouth.

Oh, this was dangerous. All at once, she saw the folly of her whole 'daydreaming is safe' plan. It was backfiring spectacularly. Her mind now revolved around Ben Oliver, her thoughts constantly drifting towards him at odd moments throughout the day. And now her brain was stuck in the habit, it was starting to clamour for more—more than just fantasies. Especially when he did things like this. She was aching for all the *moments* she'd rehearsed in her head to become real.

Heaven help her.

So much for standing on her own two feet and never letting a man overshadow her again. Ben Oliver was an addictive substance and she was hooked. She should have known from Laura's diary that letting her imagination run free might be the path to destruction. The last thing she wanted was to lose herself again, not when she'd come so far. In the last few months she'd started to feel less like Toby's wife and more like someone else, even if she wasn't sure who that woman was yet. But it would be so easy to fall into the role of the woman who adored Ben, and nothing else.

Dangerous.

She looked around the room. As a declaration of independence, she ought to just pack it all up and leave it outside the door, but she couldn't bring herself to do that. If she did, the boathouse would seem as stripped and hollow as the mansion sitting on the hill, and she'd come here to escape that.

The decorations piled in the cardboard box twinkled, begging her to let them fulfil their purpose, and she obliged them, hanging each one with care from the soft pine needles, hoping that the repetitive action would lull her into a trance.

When she'd finished, she pulled the patchwork quilt off the day-bed, draped it around her shoulders and sat on the floor in front of the fire, her back supported by one of the wicker chairs. In the silence, all she could hear was the sound of her own breathing and the happy licking of the flames.

After sitting that way for a few minutes, she decided she needed something to do, something to distract herself from the thoughts bombarding her brain, so she retrieved Laura's diary from its home and sat back down on the floor with it. Perhaps Laura had the answer.

Had her dreams turned into reality without dragging her down, or had she and Dominic just destroyed everything and everyone around them? Suddenly she really needed to know. Maybe it would help her decide what to do about her own fantasy man.

6th January, 1954

I waited nervously for Dominic at a little restaurant in Pimlico. No point in going somewhere in the West End—we'd have been spotted in a second. Instead of dressing up for lunch, as I'd so wanted to do, I had to dress down. Nicely cut dress, but it was grey, not the green one I'd wanted to wear, and I put a raincoat over the top. I also covered my hair up with a scarf.

I was early. A mix of reasons: partly because I was so desperate to actually see him and partly because I was so terrified of being late that I left more than half an hour extra for the taxi ride from Victoria.

Dominic had asked for something away from the window and the waiter showed me to a little cramped space near the kitchen where a table for two only just fitted. I stared at it in dismay before I sat down. Love is supposed to be grand and glorious. One is supposed to want to shout it from the rooftops. But Dominic and I can't even sit in the window with the winter sunshine falling on our faces; we have to hide away in a dingy corner, disguising our love from the world.

Not for the first time a shiver rippled through me. Was this what I really wanted? And was I prepared to strip my feelings for Dominic of all their sparkle and grandeur just so we could be together? Something about this little table felt seedy. Tarnished.

I took off my gloves, folded them and placed them in my handbag, and then I sat down, staring out towards the chink of window I could see. I waited for twenty minutes, and then another thirty.

Just as I was pulling my gloves back out of my handbag, a shadow fell over me. I looked up to find him standing there.

At first I jumped up, ready to throw my arms around him, because I was so thrilled at seeing him that I didn't really register the look on his face. I stopped halfway to flinging myself into his embrace and my arms dropped back down to my sides.

His mouth was straight and his lips were thin, a horrible shape for them to be, but it was his eyes that were the worst. At first I thought there was a hardness there, a coldness, but then I realised it was because the emotions swirling underneath were so strong, so dark, that he had to be that way to hold it all together.

I said his name, and my voice wavered.

He shook his head. He didn't sit down.

'I can't...' he said. 'We can't...'

Then the coldness was inside me too, swirling down inside, freezing everything it touched. My question must have been written on my face, because he answered it without me even opening my mouth.

Why?

'Because Jean is expecting my child,' he said. 'I can't go through with this, Laura. I can't be that kind of man. I will *not*.'

I nodded.

I understood, even as my heart was breaking.

'I can't see you again,' he said, and I cried at the pain in his eyes. I cried like a fool. And for the first time, I didn't cry for myself, because I couldn't have the man I loved; I cried for him, for his pain.

He reached inside his pocket and pulled out his handkerchief. He didn't even touch me, just laid it on the table where I could reach it. And then, while I was still sobbing and mopping up my tears with a square of cotton that smelled like him, he took a step back.

'Goodbye, Laura,' he said, and then he was gone.

That was when I cried for myself, for the foolish longings I'd let grow out of control, for the wasteland that my marriage would always be after this, no matter how *hard we both tried. But mostly I cried because Jean had won. She'd trumped me, and I could do nothing about it.*

Louise was still staring at the pages, her mouth slightly open, when there was a knock at the door. Unable to move, she just transferred her gaze and stared at it instead.

Whoever it was—and let's face it, she'd win no prizes for guessing who—knocked again. She rose to her feet slowly, keeping the quilt wrapped tightly around her and walked over to open it. Her heart jumped as if it were on a trampoline when she saw him standing there, his wet hair plastered to his face, a large brown paper bag in one hand and a rucksack in the other.

'Ben.'

Nice, she thought. Eloquent.

'Louise.'

At least they both seemed to be afflicted by the same disease.

He brandished the paper bag. 'Can I come in?'

She stepped back and let him pass and he handed her the paper bag, which was warm and smelled of exotic spices. He moved past her and placed the rucksack on the floor.

'I ought not—seeing as you've already indulged in a spot of breaking and entering today.' She kept her voice deliberately flat and emotionless.

He stopped halfway through struggling off his green waxed coat. 'You don't like it? Oh, Louise! I'm so sorry. I was just trying to…'

The look of remorse on his face was like a punch in the gut. She'd tried to be cross, but she couldn't. How could she? She grabbed the back of his coat with one hand and tugged at it, signalling for him to stay, take it off. 'You succeeded.'

The relief on his face was palpable. 'Thank goodness for that. I have food in here and I didn't want to have to sail it back across the river and eat it cold.'

She peered in the top of the brown bag. 'Curry? That's not very traditional.'

Ben took the bag from her and began unpacking its contents on to the low coffee table in the centre of the room. 'Nonsense. I'm sure I read somewhere that Chicken Tikka Masala has now overtaken traditional Sunday roast as the nation's favourite dish.'

Louise reached for the old picnic set she'd found in a box when she'd cleared out the boathouse and pulled out a couple of plates and some cutlery. Pretty soon they were sitting in the wicker chairs, feasting on a selection of different curries and side dishes. She broke a crunchy onion bhaji apart with her fingers and dipped it in some mango chutney. While she chewed, she looked at Ben, who was absorbed in his meal. Finally, when he glanced in her direction, he froze.

'What?'

How could she say how much this all meant to her? There just weren't enough words. And maybe that was okay. Maybe the true depth of her feelings should go unexpressed. She settled for simple and elegant. 'Thank you, Ben.'

The hesitation in his eyes turned to warmth.

'Why did you… I mean, why… all this?'

He put his plate down and looked at her long and hard. 'I remember how awful it was my first Christmas without Jas.' He gave a half-grin. 'Put it down to me being a single dad with too much time on his hands. Jas is away, my parents live in Spain now and my sister has gone to visit her in-laws. I can't even rely on work to be my saviour—no one wants any gardening done at this time of year.'

Oh, that just sounded too good to be true. Too nice.

'Yes, but you didn't have to do all *this*.' A horrible nagging thought whispered in the back of her mind: nobody does anything entirely altruistic reasons. He must want *something*. People always wanted something.

The little scratchy voice whispered louder. *Perhaps you've got him all wrong. Perhaps you've been fooled by him, just like you were with Toby.* She tried to drown it out, but it just kept spiralling round, growing louder, until she had to do something to stop it.

'I'm not sleeping with you,' she blurted out.

Oh, Lord! Had she really just said that? Her cheeks flamed and burned.

Ben's grin turned to stone and he stood up, and practically threw his naan bread down on the table. 'If that's what you think, I'd better leave.'

Instantly, she was on her feet. 'No! I'm so sorry! I don't know what made me say that. After you've been so kind…' At that moment, she hated herself more than she'd ever done for wearing fake smiles in front of the paparazzi and pretending her life with Toby had been a glorious dream.

Ben was pulling his coat on, his back to her. She laid a hand on the still-wet sleeve, tears blurring her vision. 'Please, Ben! It's just…' Oh, hell. Her throat closed up and she couldn't hide the emotion in her voice. '…nobody ever does something for me without wanting something—without wanting *too much*—back. I'm just not used to this.'

He turned to face her, his expression softening slightly. 'Really? No one?'

She shook her head, too ashamed to speak any more. How did you tell a man like him nobody had ever thought enough of you to make that kind of effort? She always had to earn people's love—by being the one who gave and gave and gave. Even Toby had only kept around as long as he had because it was good for his image, nothing more. And she'd let her younger brothers and sisters grow up thinking she was strong, that she never needed anything. She hadn't wanted to burden them the way she'd been burdened. And they'd believed it. They *still* believed it. And why should she tell them otherwise? They had their own lives now. It was their turn to shine. She'd had hers.

'I'm so sorry, so sorry...' she said, sinking into the nearest chair and covering her face with her hands. 'I'm no kind of company at the moment, so maybe you'd better just go.'

CHAPTER TWENTY

Louise mumbled something through her hands. It sounded very much like: 'Oh, God. I'm such a mess.'

He wasn't sure what to do. Louise had the ability to make his head swim, to prompt him into doing outrageous things that the sensible side of his brain knew he shouldn't be doing. He looked round at the holly, the candles, the stupid tree. It was all too much, wasn't it? He'd tried to fend her off by being nice, and the knight-in-shining-armour had swooped in and turned it into a grand gesture.

A grand *romantic* gesture.

One that he wasn't sure Louise had appreciated. Not if her outburst was anything to go by.

But then he looked at the tree again. It was dripping with baubles. He'd abandoned the box when he'd seen Louise emerge from the woods, deciding it was best not to be standing there like a prize banana when she walked in. But while he'd been away getting the curry she'd decorated the 'stupid' tree. Something warm, something that felt suspiciously like hope, flared within him.

She was sitting all curled in on herself, staring at the floor.

'Louise…? What's going on? I don't get it.'

She shook her head, still staring ahead blankly. 'Neither do I.'

He shrugged off his coat and threw it on the sofa then came round to sit in the wicker chair opposite her. 'You're used to having so much…such luxury… Why are a few bits of holly and some borrowed Christmas decorations such a big deal?'

She blinked very slowly, as if moving those tiny muscles was a huge effort. 'It wasn't always that way. The money…the *stuff*…that all came after I married Toby. Before that I was…we were…poor.'

He leaned forward, hoping she'd turn and look at him sometime soon. 'I didn't know that.'

She raised one shoulder and let it drop again. 'It's no secret. Tabloid fodder in the early days. But they don't know it all. Hardly anyone knows the truth…' She moistened her lips and met his gaze. 'My mum died when I was twelve and my dad got ill the following year. His work were great at first, but then he was on sick pay and then on benefits… With five kids to look after, it didn't stretch very far.'

She stopped talking and just gazed into the fire. He wanted to say something, but he had the feeling she hadn't talked about this in years and that if he made a sound she might clam up completely. Instinct told him that wouldn't be a good thing.

'I did my best to fill mum's place, but it was just like when I used to dress up in her shoes and clump around in them when I was little.' She paused to smile at the memory. 'I did my best, but I wasn't her. I cooked, cleaned, was nurse to my father and sergeant major to the other kids, but I was out of my depth and no one came to help me.'

She rolled her eyes and gave him a wry smile. 'In my dramatic teenage way, I imagined myself a modern-day Cinderella—overworked, unpaid, at everybody's beck and call... But what we lacked in money and glamour we made up for in other ways.'

Ben had a feeling *nobody* knew any of this about Louise. They wouldn't judge her if they did, but he knew her well enough to know she wouldn't broadcast this. She wasn't full of herself, but she was proud.

'And then Cinderella's fairy godmother turned up?'

She let out a dry laugh. 'If I ever see that woman again I'm going to have her prosecuted under the Trade Descriptions act. I thought fairy godmothers were supposed to bring *happy ever afters*, not *divorce and disaster*.'

And then her expression grew more serious, lines creasing her forehead. 'She brought me Toby. He was handsome, rich, famous… and he looked at me as if I was something more than the no-hope skinny girl who was failing all her exams, like I was destined for more than trudging through the crappy jobs that no one else wanted to do day after day.'

Well, at least the big-headed lump of an ex-husband had got something right. 'You are worth more,' he said softly.

Louise paused for a moment, but then she carried on talking, as if she wasn't quite sure how to react to his words. She rested her elbows on her knees, put her chin in her hands and looked at him. 'Was it first love with Megan?'

He nodded. That seemed such a long time ago now, as if it had happened to two other people in another life. 'I had the biggest crush on her at school, but she was so shy it took me months before I could manage to tell her about it. But when she finally let me know she was interested too… That was it. I knew right then she was the one for me.'

And she could have been the one for him, if she'd only just believed it. Instead she'd pulled the plug and had given up, leaving their marriage to flatline.

Louise sat up again and nodded. 'First love…it's a bitch,' she said. 'I fell as hard and fast as first loves come.' She let out a gentle self-mocking laugh that was more of a loud breath. 'I thought Toby was my salvation, my knight in shining armour, charging in to save me from my life of drudgery. I just didn't realise the price tag would be quite so high…'

He reached over and touched her hand. 'What seventeen-year-old girl would have been able to resist that? It must have seemed like the answer to everything.'

'I should have known.' She shook her head. 'Mum would have realised. She would have told me I was just dazzled, that I needed to slow down and think instead of rushing into marriage… But I was too selfish and too impatient.' She shrugged. 'I suppose I got what I deserved.'

Ben stared at her. How could she believe that? How could she believe that what her husband had done to her was in any way her fault?

'It doesn't work like that, Louise.'

She raised her eyebrows. 'Well, could you please tell karma that, because I think, in that case, I've got someone else's just desserts.'

That's when the realisation of why she'd freaked out at his kind gesture finished creeping up on him.

Louise Thornton, the woman the press believed had everything, didn't know how accept a simple gift, even one of time and effort rather than money and things. How odd, when she gave of herself constantly—any fool could see that if they looked hard enough. But he had a feeling she'd forgotten that giving was only half of the equation.

Or perhaps she'd never known.

What she'd said earlier had been true. Nobody did nice things for her with no strings attached. She just didn't know how to handle it. He decided it was time to diffuse the impact this small bit of thoughtfulness on his part had made.

'I don't know about you,' he said, 'but I could do with something to drink.'

Louise's mouth formed a circle of surprise. 'Drink?'

He smiled to himself and reached down into the rucksack he'd dropped by the chair earlier and pulled out a bottle of red wine. Nothing extravagant. Just a bottle of supermarket Cabernet.

In one smooth second, Louise unclenched. She smiled at him, started to speak and then just shook her head. She rose, extracted a couple of teacups from Laura's picnic set and plonked them on the coffee table. After pouring a generous amount of wine into each cup, he handed one to her.

'A toast—to Christmas,' he said as they cheerfully clinked teacups.

'Something weird is happening here...' She shook her head, as if she was trying to shake away confusing thoughts, but then she raised her teacup and smiled at him. 'What the hell? To Christmas!'

Ben took a sip of the warm, rich wine and kept his thoughts to himself. He knew exactly why he'd phrased the toast that way. Christmas was about giving—and receiving. That weird feeling Louise didn't recognise? That was the warmth that came from letting someone show you they cared. If there was one thing he could give her this Christmas, it would be to show her that not all gifts had hidden traps, and that receiving them could be a simple and uncomplicated pleasure.

She needed a friend. A true friend. And that was the sort of gift a *friend* could give safely.

As they worked their way through the bottle of wine, a tiny teacup at a time, they retreated to the sofa thing that was piled high with cushions. Even though it was on the opposite wall to the fire, the boathouse's upper room was small enough for them to get all the benefits of its warmth. They talked about anything and everything before falling into a comfortable silence. The candles flickered, the sun set and the temperature outside began to drop.

He was just starting to think that it was about time to get going when Louise suddenly said, 'I don't think I know who I am any more.'

Uh-oh. Good deeds, practical gestures, he was good at. Touchy-feely, girl-type conversations were not his forte. Thankfully, Louise seemed happy for him just to listen.

'The curse of being an ex-WAG,' she said, turning to smile at him weakly.

'You're not a WAG,' he said. 'Don't be daft.'

She gave him a wry look. 'Well, not for much longer—the divorce should be final after Christmas.'

Ben shook his head, frowning. He couldn't see how that definition could ever have applied to Louise. He was about to say so, but she pre-empted him again.

'Oh, I was at the start,' she said. 'I embraced it wholeheartedly—the parties, the magazine covers, the *bling.*' She chuckled to herself.

Didn't she realise what a rare quality that was—to be able to laugh at oneself?

'But eventually, it grew old. I was famous because of him, because I was Tobias Thornton's wife, not because of anything I had done.'

He shifted to face her a little more. 'I thought you were a model when you met him.'

She nodded and looked into her teacup of red wine. 'I was. And we made it work at first. But it was hard to keep a marriage going when we spent weeks at a time on different continents. And then Jack came along and it seemed only right to give him a home and some structure…'

Why was she punishing herself for that? That was Louise all over—she'd thought of her family first instead of selfishly pursuing what she wanted.

She was lost in a daydream, staring at the rain lashing against the windows. There was a wistful expression on her face, as if she was remembering something or wishing for something she couldn't have.

Maybe it was time Louise did something for herself, got something for herself. Not out of selfishness, but because she deserved it. He rubbed his chin with his thumb. Problem was that he didn't know what she wanted, let alone how to go about getting it for her.

Pulled out of her daydream by some unknown thought, she turned her head, and the look she gave him sent a shiver up his spine.

Surely not.

Her pupils were large and dark, and there was such a heat in her eyes. He'd received that kind of look before from women, but he'd never expected to receive it from her. Surely, she didn't want… him?

His heart rate tripled.

That put Being What Louise Needed on a whole new level.

What she really needed, Louise thought, was to stop looking at Ben as if he were a Christmas present she wanted to unwrap.

It was easier said than done.

The different-sized baubles on the Christmas tree twinkled, reflecting the light from the candles placed all around the room. This wasn't her festive daydream, starring Ben, but it was close. There was the tree, the fire, the sense that someone had thought about her for a change…

Actually, reality was better. The meal, the wine, the

companionship had been a much sweeter present than the anonymous gift in the silver box in her fantasies. But, whatever was missing, whatever had changed from her daydreams, one thing remained the same. Ben. It all revolved around him.

The other thing she needed to do was to stop babbling on about losing herself. But the babbling was helping keep a whole other set of urges at bay, so it would do nicely for now. She folded her hands in her lap and smiled at him. 'So… that's what I am. A WAG. A woman who defined herself by her husband and is now adrift with no direction in her life, no purpose.'

Ben began to disagree, but she was on a roll, so she just kept going. 'I've got plenty of money, so I don't need to work, but I do need to do more than just look after Jack and—' she waved a hand to indicate the freshly refurbished room '—decorate. But apart from knowing how to pout for the camera, I have no qualifications. I didn't even finish school.'

There. That would scare him off. He'd have to believe she was a bimbo now. Only, when she dared to look at him, he didn't seem convinced. She would just have to try harder.

'Oh, I tried all sorts of jobs while I was married to Toby. He was always encouraging me to do some of the things his friends' wives were up to. I did the whole charity circuit, then I tried a bit of television presenting on a fashion show—and was supremely bad at it.'

She let out an empty little laugh and Ben fidgeted on the other end of the day bed. 'They never asked me back. I even designed my own range of sunglasses. They ended up in the bargain bucket at a supermarket.'

She looked at Ben and waited for reaction. He shrugged, as if to say *so what*?

Yeah, so what? That's what the buying public had thought too. It had been an utter flop.

She took a breath, searching for another stupid exploit to fill the silence with. Nothing came. What a waste. She was thirty years old and this was the sum total of what she'd achieved in her life. It was pathetic.

'Why didn't you finish school?'

She looked at Ben, expecting to see that same superior look that many people gave her when they found out that little bit of information. Everyone knew that models were thick, and wasn't she a glowing representative of the stereotype?

'Louise? What happened?'

He genuinely wanted to know. She frowned and looked away. He might just be the first person to ask why and mean it.

'Dad's illness got worse when I was about fifteen. Some days he needed me at home. Of course, there were home helps and health visitors, but the area where we lived was rough and the local services were overstretched.' She looked away. 'On his bad days, it wouldn't have done any good to go to school, because I wouldn't have been able to concentrate anyway.'

Ben reached over and simply took her hand. That one gesture was enough to roughen her voice and moisten her eyes again. She ought to stop, but she couldn't. She'd needed to say all of this for such a long time. She stared at the fire while she talked, unable to meet his eyes.

'In my last year of school, when I should have been taking my GCSEs, he deteriorated even further. I'd missed so much by then that I didn't even want to go in. And some of the girls were horrible… you know how girls can be. But dad was in so much pain, he became angry and difficult sometimes and took his frustrations out on me—not physically—just verbally. But I understood, really I did.'

Ben's thumb gently stroked the back of her hand and she felt something hard inside herself crumple. More tears flowed and she pulled her hand away to mop them up with a tissue. Things were getting far too maudlin. It was time to brighten the story up.

'Anyway, Cinderella got her happy ending,' she said brightly, tuning her head back to look at him. 'the rest, as they say, is history.'

He held a box of tissues out to her and she took another one. 'What happened to the rest of your family?'

The noise she made using the tissue was truly disgusting. 'Well, my wages helped buy a new house, pay for university fees and things like that. Sarah, the next eldest after me, is a lawyer now and she emigrated to Australia five years ago. The rest have all gone out to visit her this year, but I didn't want to be away from Jack for that long. Billy and Charlotte still live in London—he manages a restaurant, she's a hairdresser. And Charlie, the youngest, is just finishing university. He wants to be an actor.' She rolled her eyes. 'There's no telling some people.'

Somehow, her hand was back in Ben's and he was stroking it again.

'What about your dad?'

Drat! Why did this man have to be so good at reading between the lines?

'He died a few years after I started modelling.' She looked into Ben's eyes, desperate in this moment for someone else to understand what she'd done. 'I let him down,' she whispered. 'I should have been there.'

And then she started crying, really crying. None of that sissy sniffing nonsense she'd been doing up until now. Big, fat tears rolled down her cheeks. She tried to talk, but her vocal cords had gone on strike.

Gently, slowly, so she wasn't even sure how they'd got there, a pair of strong arms wrapped around her. Time seemed to slow as she sobbed against his chest, but it could only have been a few minutes.

'I've kind of blown your plan for a merry Christmas right out of the water, haven't I?' she whispered, thinking she should pull away, but doing nothing about it. 'But thank you for trying. I'm not sure there was ever much hope for a woman who doesn't know who to be any more.'

Ben shifted beneath her. His hands came up to cradle her face and he made her look at him.

No one had ever looked at her that way before, as if she were delicate, precious. Her heart, which had been shrivelled like one of the dates her Auntie June used to serve up on Boxing Day, swelled.

His voice was low and scratchy. 'Louise, you are… I…'

For a man who always had a direct answer, he was a little short on words at the moment. That couldn't be a good thing. Ben's features clouded and she could tell he was struggling.

Say something, she shouted in her head. *Tell me! Tell me who you think I am! I need to know!*

He was no longer looking at her, but was staring at a piece of blank wall behind her, his mind whirring and, when he looked back at her, her heart stood still for a beat. In his eyes was a renewed sense of purpose and she knew he had something to say. She waited. And Ben just looked at her as if there weren't adequate words to communicate what he was thinking. Oh, how she wished he would try.

His gaze dropped her lips and her breath caught as she felt them part.

He was going to kiss her. The world started to somersault.

Slowly, he bent his head to meet hers, giving her ample time to move away if she wanted to. But, despite all her ground rules about keeping things 'safe', about keeping things locked away in her daydreams, Louise found she didn't want to move. She wanted him to come towards her. She wanted an experience her daydreams had never been able to provide—she wanted to taste him.

The touch of his mouth on hers was tender, soft as a whisper. She closed her eyes and gave up all hope of keeping fantasy and reality separate.

Oh, this was better than she'd ever imagined. As Ben kissed her again, still with the same soul-wrenching gentleness, the nerve endings in her lips burst into life. He moved his hands from her face, ran through her hair, and pulled her closer to him as he fell back against the pile of cushions.

Louise followed him gladly, relishing the fact that she was in total control. Now, instead of *being* kissed, *she* kissed. And Ben liked it—she could tell from the low sound he made on the back of his throat.

They kissed each other sweetly, slowly, as if time had stopped for them and all that existed was this moment. After a while, the intensity of their kisses deepened. His lips sought her neck, her jawline, her earlobe, and Louise began to tingle all over.

She wanted to lose herself in this feeling. Of being desired. Of being feminine. And of being powerful. Rolling over, she pulled him on top of her, giving her hands access to the strong, broad muscles of his back. Ben responded by running a hand down the side of her torso, skimming the curve of her waist. The air between them crackled and popped like the logs on the fire.

Hadn't she said something tonight along the lines of not knowing what she wanted? Well, she had no problems pinpointing that now—it was all blazingly clear. She wanted Ben. All of him. Right here. Right now.

Taking a deep breath, she wiggled her hands between their bodies and fiddled with the top button of his shirt. A shiver of nerves ran through her.

There had been nobody else but Toby—and he'd grazed in other pastures. What if she wasn't any good? What if she disappointed him? What if this all didn't live up to the fairy tale in her head? For years, Toby had looked at her with a familiar apathy, and she couldn't bear the thought of seeing the same deadness in Ben's eyes in the morning. She was just going to have to pull out all the stops.

Ben, who had been trailing kisses from her collarbone to just below her ear, went still. Her heart began to pound. He looked as if he wanted to stop and say something but just couldn't control himself. He kissed her again—hot and sweet and deep enough to make her toes burn.

She trembled as she tried to find a second button on his shirt, her fingers clumsy in the haze of her desire. Ben dragged his lips from hers and his hand closed over her fingers, which were still fiddling fruitlessly with the button.

'We don't need to rush into this,' he whispered.

She knew what he was trying to do. He was trying to be the gentleman, to give her an out. Her gaze locked with his. 'Perhaps we do.'

Once again, he held her face in his hands and, this time, he delivered the sweetest kiss yet. She wiggled her fingers under his and succeeded in popping the button out of its hole. He gripped her hands more tightly.

'Really, Louise. It's not that I don't want to...' the look of frustration that passed over his features confirmed that nicely for her '...but we should do this for the right reason, because we both want to, because we're both ready. Not just because we're feeling lonely on Christmas Eve. Maybe this isn't the right time to make this kind of decision. I don't want to wake up in the morning and feel as if I've taken advantage of you.'

He traced the line of her jaw with his thumb and, although his eyes dropped to look at her mouth once again, he didn't kiss her.

She looked at him. Even though she'd never met Dominic Blake—Laura's Dominic—at this moment,

Ben reminded her of him. So full of honesty, even to his own hurt. A man like that was worth keeping, and she didn't want to scare him away.

But, like Laura, she found herself wanting to be selfish. She didn't want to give this up yet. Moments like this were like Christmas itself—fleeting, magical. Tomorrow the glitter and the wonder would be gone and life would return to being grey and cold and ever so slightly emptier than before.

A slow, gentle smile crept across Ben's face, and she couldn't help but smile back as his eyes glittered with fierce intensity.

'Trust me,' he said. 'We don't need to rush. I'm not going anywhere.'

Louise let out a shaky breath. It was very hard to believe that any of this could survive the night and live beyond the dawn. Her eyes must have betrayed her, because he lowered his head and kissed her again.

Carefully, he shifted until he was lying behind her and she was spooned up against him, her head resting on his arm. He pulled the quilt over the pair of them and they lay in the silence, staring into the fire and drawing strength and warmth from where their bodies made contact.

CHAPTER TWENTY-ONE

Louise's eyelids flickered. Her head was filled with crackling fires, spiced wine and silver boxes wrapped with ribbons. She yawned and stretched one arm. That was the best night's sleep she'd had since...

She wasn't alone.

Foggily, she tried to decipher what her senses were telling her. There was a warm body wrapped around her, breathing rhythmically... a strange bed... and a *Christmas tree* in her bedroom?

The Christmas tree!

Her eyelids pinged the rest of the way open and, suddenly, she was very much awake. That warm body tangled with hers belonged to Ben Oliver. She didn't dare move, just in case it was all just another delicious dream.

Slowly, she made herself relax back against him. He mumbled something in his sleep—nonsense—and pulled her closer. She smiled.

This is what contentment felt like. She'd forgotten its taste, its flavour.

Her eyes scanned the room once again, this time taking in the details. The fire was out, as were quite a few of the candles, but even with the flickering yellow glow from the few that were left, there was an odd silvery-blue light bathing the room.

Mind you, she'd never been in the boathouse this early in the morning before and she had no idea what time it was. Perhaps this was the colour of dawn down here so close to the river.

No, that wasn't it. Gut instinct told to go and look out of the window. She dropped one leg over the edge of the day bed and started to move, but Ben grumbled again and pulled her back, nuzzling into the side of her neck.

Half-asleep, he was adorable, but whether he'd feel the same way when he was fully conscious was another matter. She'd humiliated herself last night, trying to seduce him and being knocked back, and the atmosphere between them was bound to be awkward. Things often looked different in the cold light of day.

But thinking about cold light fired her curiosity up again and she wriggled out of his arms, wrapping the patchwork quilt around her and leaving him covered with the goose down duvet. As she stood, and could see out of the window, she grasped. Even a tug at the trailing quilt couldn't stop her running to the door, flinging it wide and walking out onto the balcony.

Snow.

Fresh and white and everywhere. It weighed down

the bare branches of the young trees and topped the large stones on the beach so they looked like giant cupcakes. It seemed as if the whole world was buried under a blanket of purity, the past forgotten, everything new.

She twirled around in amazement, taking it all in, then reached for the layer of snow, only an inch deep, that topped the balcony railing. The icy crystals crunched under the weight of her fingertips.

A floorboard creaked behind her and once again she was wrapped up in Ben Oliver. He'd brought the duvet with him and he folded it over them both. She held her breath. She'd thought that maybe he'd been giving her the brush-off last night, but the way he was holding her now, as if he wanted to seal their bodies together, laid those fears to rest. He rested his chin on her shoulder so his head was right next to hers and kissed her cheek near her ear.

'Merry Christmas, Louise.'

She twisted her head to look at him, her eyebrows raised. She'd been so caught up in the magic of last night, the beauty of this morning, that she'd completely forgotten that it was Christmas Day.

'Merry Christmas,' she whispered back, suddenly feeling very shy. But, as she went to shake her fringe in front of her eyes, he stopped with a gentle hand.

'Don't do that,' he said, moving so they were now facing each other.

She wasn't foolish enough to say, *Do what*? After

glancing away for a second, she tilted her chin up and met his gaze.

'That's better.'

He smiled and, just like that, any residual awkwardness she'd been feeling evaporated. There was such warmth and light in his eyes, so many possibilities, that she felt an answering smile spread over her own face. So they stood there like that for goodness knew how long, grinning stupidly at each other, saying nothing and everything.

Then his eyes sobered and began to communicate all sorts of other things. Louise didn't wait for him this time. There wasn't much of a height difference so she reached up behind his neck and pulled him closer, lifting her heels off the floor just slightly.

Kissing Ben Oliver on a snow-dusted balcony on Christmas morning had to be one of the most romantic things she'd ever done. Not only were the kisses perfect, but the crisp cold air on her cheeks and the chill in her toes only seemed to increase the heat spreading from her core. She felt as if she was glowing from the inside out, so much that shivers rippled through her.

Ben pulled away, just enough to focus on each other without going cross-eyed, and tucked the quilt tighter around her.

'How do you feel about cold curry for breakfast?'

She grinned. 'My absolute favourite.'

And, as he playfully pulled her back inside the boat-

house, she took one last look at the picture-perfect
scene outside. The river reflected the colour of the iron
sky perfectly and smoke puffed from the chimneys in
the village across the river. As far as the eye could see,
the rolling hills were bleached and frosted like the icing
on a giant Christmas cake.

It didn't matter to Louise if winter had stolen all the
shades and tones and left everything monochrome. To
her, this morning, life was very much in Technicolor ®.

Ben ran up to his bedroom, slammed the door open
and stripped all his clothes off in under a minute. The
last sock still hadn't hit the floor when he ran into his
bathroom and jumped in the shower.

He felt like a man possessed. Like a man with too
much adrenaline coursing through his system, who
was about to spontaneously combust. When he realised he'd just started to wash himself with conditioner,
he forced himself to stand still and take a few deep
breaths.

No good. He still felt like whooping aloud, or like
running down the street and knocking on every door
just to tell them he'd kissed the most astounding, marvellous, complicated woman in the world and, once he
was clean and changed, he was going to go back and do
it again.

Unfortunately, the only yelling he did was when the
shampoo got in his eye.

Slow down!

This time, he was more successful. He managed to rest one hand against the tiled shower wall and watch the rise and fall of his chest slow a little. *Relax. You can do it.*

He finished his shower in a speed that could be classified more as 'brisk efficiency' than 'mania', cleaned his teeth and wandered back into the bedroom, whistling, a towel slung round his hips.

What time was it? He checked the digital alarm clock on his bedside table. Ten.

That meant he'd been gone about forty-five minutes. And it would probably be another hour until he saw her again.

Without really paying attention to what he was rummaging for in his chest of drawers, he pulled out clean clothes and got dressed. One last look in the mirror. He ran his hand through his wet hair, then stilled. Is this what Louise saw? A thirty-six-year old man, with dark hair and brown eyes? That description could probably fit hundreds of thousands of men up and down the country. Apart from the insane grin he couldn't wipe away completely, he was just an ordinary guy.

Okay, he wasn't desperately bad-looking, but he'd be kidding himself if he thought he could compete with the men in Louise's world. A world in which he clearly didn't belong.

But Louise isn't with one of them, a little voice

whispered gleefully in his ear. *She's with you. She kissed you. She even wanted to make love with you.*

At that point he told his male pride to get a grip.

Even so, the unquenchable grin widened.

He grabbed his watch, fastened it on his wrist and jumped down the stairs only two at a time. But when he got downstairs he couldn't find his keys. He never lost his keys. He searched the pockets of his jacket, which he found on the floor rather than on its usual hook. Nothing. Rather than dropping it again, he pulled it on.

Okay, now he was scaring himself. He sat down on one of the chairs in the kitchen and thought about where he could have possibly left his keys since he'd run through the front door. Best thing was to retrace his steps. He went to the cottage door, opened it and found his bunch of keys dangling in the lock.

What was happening to him? The sky was under his feet and the earth above his head. When exactly had the universe turned itself inside out so everything was back to front? An image popped into his mind: Louise, wrapped in a quilt, standing on the boathouse balcony, tipping her head up to meet his eyes and daring him to love her.

He realised it was a challenge he hadn't refused.

Now he wasn't so sure he wanted to wake all his neighbours up and share the news. Was he crazy? Quite possibly. How could whatever was happening between them have a future? Yet, while his head told him to back out while he had the chance; his heart told him to not lose faith.

He pulled his keys out of the lock and returned them to his pocket, then closed the door. He'd loved Megan, he was sure of that, but she'd never shaken his foundations like Louise did. What did that mean? Was this romance doomed or did that promise great things?

He ought to stay away, he decided. He'd tried to be what Louise needed. It had never been part of the plan to develop a craving for her in return. He ought to make an excuse to back out and stay away. That was the sensible thing to do. He nodded to himself, took off his jacket off and carefully placed it on its hook.

But five minutes later he was in his dinghy, motoring across the river in the direction of the boathouse jetty.

Christmas was its own little universe for Louise and Ben. They shared a festive dinner of lasagne, which Louise found in her freezer, then retreated to the boathouse for the evening, where they talked and laughed and kissed and wished—not out loud, of course. Some things were far too delicate to be spoken aloud.

But this little universe was finite and, as night fell on Boxing Day, ugly reality started to shred the perfect picture they'd created.

Louise was sitting in one of the wicker chairs close to the fire with a book in her lap and Ben was stretched out on the day bed, trying not to doze. Suddenly, he raised his head and looked at her.

'Louise?'

Her heart did a silly leap. Shouldn't she be able to control that by now? It had started on Christmas morning when he'd reappeared, slightly damp and smiling, at her back door with a Christmas pudding big enough for ten and a bottle of port. Now, *that* was the way to spend Christmas. Especially if it involved being spoonfed the pudding in front of the fire.

She couldn't remember a Christmas as perfect. Not even Jack's first Christmas. Toby had spoiled it by getting drunk and disappearing off to a nightclub with one of his useless so-called friends.

'What's up?' she said carefully.

Ben shifted himself onto one elbow. 'What are we doing?'

'Well, I'm supposed to be reading the book on the history of the River Dart I borrowed from you and you're trying to pretend you didn't finish off the last quarter of that plum pudding.'

Ben didn't laugh as she expected him to. He gave a half-smile, then jumped off the day bed and drew the other chair over so he could sit opposite her, leaning forward. 'No, I mean you and me. What is this?'

She placed the book open on the coffee table. She'd been staring at an old photo of the river's most famous resident. Laura's vibrant smile and laughing eyes looked back at her, mocking her. The photo was of her and a handsome young man she'd had a relationship with before her marriage. She bet Laura wouldn't have got all tied up in knots about something like this. Laura would have thrown caution to the wind. She was confident and sophisticated. In an awkward moment, she'd have probably said something droll to make her lover laugh or swoon at her feet.

But Ben wasn't her lover, and it seemed that Louise was the one closest to swooning at present. This was all so new—this thing with Ben—that sometimes it felt raw, even though it was wonderful at the same time.

'Are you asking me if I want to be your girlfriend?'

There. That was as droll as she could manage. But she didn't manage to pull off the knowing sophistication that was supposed to go with it when he leaned in close, gave her a lopsided grin and said, 'Yeah, I suppose I am.'

She grabbed him by the shirt collar and pulled him in close for a long, slow kiss.

He rested his forehead against hers. 'It's just that...'

What? Her heart began to thump. It was too perfect. *Something* had to go wrong, didn't it?

'Jas is home tomorrow and...'

She nodded. This had been a time out of time. Tomorrow they had to go back to their real lives, which seemed to be on parallel tracks, running close, but maybe never destined to cross and merge again.

'I understand, Ben.'

He pulled away and looked intently at her face. 'No… No, Louise. I meant what—if anything—are we going to say to the kids? Are we going to keep this a secret or are we going to shout it from the rooftops? We need to decide how we're going to handle it.'

Relief flooded through her. Followed hastily by confusion. What *were* they going to tell the children? Jack was the worst blabbermouth known to man. She frowned. 'Do we need to tell *anyone*?'

And what would they say if they did? How should they define it?

And there would be other consequences too if they let the cat out of the bag. 'You do realise we might get media attention if we go public?' she said.

Ben's face was a picture of surprise, as if he totally forgotten about that side of her life. That only made her want to kiss him again. Everybody else always saw the glitter first and nothing second. With Ben she was a woman, a person in her own right.

For the first time in days, she felt as if she were on familiar territory. 'Believe me, you don't want photographers camped on your doorstep. Why do you think I chose to live in such a remote place as Whitehaven? In the village, you and Jas would be easy pickings.'

'Jas?' There was more than a hint of panic in his voice. 'You think they'd take pictures of Jas?'

Just great. This relationship was dead in the water before it had even begun, wasn't it? She knew Ben well enough to know that creating a steady life for his daughter was paramount.

She stroked his arm. 'Who knows? The paparazzi are a law unto themselves. But I think we have to consider the possibility.'

They both stared at one another.

There were no easy answers to this one. The only way to really protect Ben and Jasmine was to call the whole thing off right now. She broke eye contact and stared at her feet. Just the thought of saying goodbye to Ben now made her hurt—physically hurt. Cold fear shot through her.

He gently brushed his fingers under her chin and tipped her face up to look at him. 'Hey.' The word was filled with such tender softness, she felt her eyes moisten. He smiled at her. 'I told you before—I'm not going anywhere, okay?'

She nodded and the cold, sharp feeling gradually withdrew.

'Here's my idea,' he said. 'We tell Jas and Jack shortly—because they going to work it out anyway—but we don't tell anyone else yet. It will buy us some time, give us and the kids a chance to get used to things first.'

Sensible. He wanted to wait before letting the world know, just in case it didn't work out.

'I've got to wait at home for Megan to bring Jas back tomorrow, but I still want to see you.'

Good. She wanted to see him too.

'Jas is due back at noon and it's going to be quiet tomorrow—everyone recovering after Christmas. If you come for one o'clock and drive round, using the lanes, rather than coming through the village, nobody will see you. Once you're here, we'll put your car in the garage.'

'Okay,' she said. 'I can do that.'

She was greedily going to grab every chance to be with him. That much at least she could learn from Laura.

CHAPTER TWENTY-TWO

Once Ben had gone home, Louise returned to the diary. She'd almost forgotten it while he'd been here over Christmas, too caught up in the present to think about the past, but now her eyes kept falling on the desk in the corner, as if something in her subconscious was pecking at her. Maybe Laura's story would give her hope that she could find her own happy ever after. After all, she'd lived at Whitehaven for more than forty years, and by all accounts she'd been happy there.

She went to the desk and fetched it, noticing as she began to read that the next entry was almost a whole year since previous one.

23rd August, 1954

Alex has sent me away for a holiday. He says the sea air will do me good, that I've been working too hard. He's right. I have been working too hard. Mainly because being someone else is better than being myself. I don't want to be this wretched creature who mopes around and can't shake herself out of the doldrums.

I was doing quite well at holding it all together until I opened the paper one morning and saw the news that Jean Blake had given birth to a perfect baby daughter. There was even a quote from Dominic about how smitten he was with his new bundle of joy.

I hate that expression: bundle of joy. I'm certain it's something Dominic would never say. He'd say something clever, like 'She'll be my leading lady forever…'. At least, that's what I've imagined he'd say in my idle dreams, when I block the bleakness of reality out and pretend that everything—opinions, gossip, situations and people—that stop us being together have magically vanished.

In my dreams we live in a beautiful old house on a hill, high above a river. The sun always shines, as it did that wonderful summer. We don't do exciting things; we just live. And how we live. With laughter and smiles and colour, with intimacy and affection. And with a handful of flaxen-haired children racing round the house and squealing in the garden. Whitehaven is the sort of house that should have children running across its lawns…

Enough.

I can't think this way any more. These dreams, these vapid wishes, they're like poison. They seem so warming, so comforting—and they are at the time—but when they're over they leave me feeling bleak and dissatisfied. They suck the life out of me. No wonder I can't climb my way out of this pit.

Finally, Alex noticed it was more than just tiredness, that I was low. So here I am on Burgh Island off the Devon coast near Kingsbridge. It really is a marvellous hotel, the only building on the small and rocky island, and at low tide you can practically wade to shore. But it's the sort of place one should share with someone and I'm here on my own. Alex has gone to Belgium—something to do with expanding his empire—and the only other person I'd want to share it with is rocking his new baby daughter and looking at his wife with new admiration and gratitude.

I've been here a couple of days now, and it truly is relaxing. But all the discreet butler service and gourmet cooking in the world can't soothe my thoughts. They rage so, like the surf against the rocks beneath my window.

Now I hear Alex's voice in my head, telling me I'm being melodramatic again. Perhaps I am, but what does he expect? He married an actress, for heaven's sake!

Anyway, I've decided I need to get off the island and take a day trip tomorrow. The plan is to do something that will clear my muddled head of its clutter. Whether it's the plan of a genius or a fool will only be known tomorrow evening, when I'm back here, sorting through my thoughts with ink and paper.

Until then...

As much as Louise tried to ration reading these diary

entries, she found she had no self-control any more to put the book away and mull on the possibilities until next time. The diary did not go back in the drawer. The key did not turn in the lock. Instead, it stayed open in Louise's hands, giving up its truth as her eyes lingered on every sentence.

24th August, 1954

It took some time to get to my destination, mostly because of the winding rivers that insist on dividing up the land in this part of the world. But I hired a car and asked the driver to take me all the way to the ferry at Lower Hadwell. It would have taken much longer by road and I wanted to catch glimpses of Whitehaven through the gaps in the trees as I crossed the river.

The first glint of white stone in the sunshine set my heart fluttering. I knew he wasn't there, but I feel as if he's etched into that land now somehow, forever connected. As I am. But it wasn't just that. It was also excitement at seeing that beautiful place again. It soothed me last time I was there and I was hoping it would do it again. Somehow, although things have gone horribly, horribly wrong, I feel this house has the ability to put things right, bring things to peace, and peace is certainly something I could do with presently.

I took my time walking up the hill then crossed through the gardens until I reached the house. Thankfully, the owners had been very receptive to a visit when

I'd telephoned yesterday, but they insisted on dragging me inside and giving tea and scones—all the while grinning at me inanely—before letting me loose to wander the grounds. They wanted to show me the way down to the boathouse, but I insisted I knew the way and hinted I'd appreciate a little solitude. Thankfully, they were far too well-mannered to argue.

It was cool in the woods, with the sun filtering through the leaves. Every now and then there'd be a hole where a tree had come down and tall grass and wild flowers abounded in the sunny patch left behind.

A strange mixture of feelings hit me as I saw the boathouse again after all this time. Longing, for Dominic, but a sense of warmth and nostalgia too. I had to brave the dust and go inside, make my way out onto the balcony and just stand and breathe.

It was here I whispered my words to the river breeze—words of sorrow and regret, words of love and promises, but mostly they were words of farewell.

Once again I said my goodbyes to Dominic. Once again I cried like a child.

But as I sit in my suite this evening, although I feel raw and ragged and puffy-eyed, I also feel as if something inside has come to rest. Whitehaven has given me a gift. It has let me take some of its peace away with me. It is a gift that I will treasure fiercely.

Louise flicked through the remaining pages of the

diary. She was almost three quarters of the way through now. Could the final entries provide the answers to Laura's history? She frowned as she tried to remember snatches from a documentary she'd tuned into late one evening—oh, at least a decade ago—on Laura and her career.

She remembered her buying this grand old house, and then something about a husband. Could that have been Dominic instead of Alex? And, if it had been, how could he have stood to leave his wife and daughter?

She shook her head. It would be dark soon, and it would be a good idea to get back up the hill to the house before night fell. The mystery would have to wait for another day.

CHAPTER TWENTY-THREE

The roar of a distant car engine got louder. Ben knew not to hope this would be Megan bringing Jas back. She'd rung twenty minutes ago saying she was 'running a little late'. And when Megan usually said 'late', she didn't mean ten minutes late. He'd be lucky if he saw Jas before teatime. Megan had probably only just left the country house hotel near Stow-on-the-Wold where they'd been staying—not that her breezy message had communicated anything of the sort. He just knew.

Abruptly, the engine cut out and he dashed outside to open the garage doors. This must be Louise. He checked his watch. Yup, five minutes early. From one extreme to the other.

Louise grinned at him from inside her car as he guided her inside and closed the garage door behind her. He walked round to the driver's window and waited as she pressed a button to wind it down. Acting on impulse, he leaned in through the open window and surprised her with a swift kiss.

The rush of endorphins he got every time he just

laid eyes on her was amazing, but a long-lasting relationship took more than just feel-good chemicals whizzing round his system. While Louise wasn't the high-maintenance woman he'd mistaken her for, she was still smarting from a recent break-up. Only a fool would rush in too quickly.

A crick in his neck forced him to draw back and let her out of the car.

'Good morning, yourself,' she said, smiling sweetly at him. Then she looked around. 'Where's Jas? I would have thought you'd have wanted to talk to her first rather than have her catching us like that.'

He grimaced. 'Megan is running late. Very late. We have some time to ourselves.' He tangled his fingers with hers and pulled her out of the side door of the garage and across the garden, where small patches of snow still lingered. Most of the village now was back to normal, a warm wind from the west having melted the snow in all but the shadiest of spots.

Once through the back door, he kissed her again, taking his time this time, not rushing *anything*. The endorphins started partying.

Louise was different this morning, calmer, more peaceful. Since Christmas Eve she'd been like a skittish horse, jumping at every little thing, sensing danger where there was none. But something had changed. He could tell it from the way she kissed and held him, from the sound of her voice, even the way she moved.

Still kissing her, he pulled her hat and scarf off and threw them in random directions. She laughed against his lips. 'Not fair,' she murmured. 'You've only got your indoor clothes on.'

She undid the top button of her coat, but left the others fastened as she kissed him again. Everything went blurry for a bit and all he was aware of was the sweet spiciness of her perfume, the shallowness of their breathing, the pull of her fingers as they hooked into the belt loops at the back of his jeans and contracted into fists.

Then, after hesitating for a second, she ran her hands under his sweater. He flinched as her cold fingers met his warm flesh, but the sensation was anything but unpleasant. He pulled her closer and deepened the kiss. Louise responded eagerly, surprising him by sliding her hands up his back, taking the sweater with them. Cold air rushed around his torso, but his blood felt hot and slick as it pumped through his veins.

Finding it impossible to go any further without breaking lip-contact, she pulled back from him and continued to tug his top upwards. Just before she pulled it over his head, she looked him in the eyes. They stayed there like that while the kitchen clock announced the seconds.

Wordlessly, he lifted his arms over his head and she disappeared as his sweater blocked his vision. The jumper went the same way as her scarf and hat.

'Not fair,' he said, trying very hard not to let on he was shaking. And he didn't think it was because he was cold. 'You've still got your outdoor clothes on.'

He reached for her, first dealing with the remaining large buttons on the front of her coat and pushing it off her shoulders before stroking her face with his fingertips. That perfect bone structure might make her seem untouchable and proud, but he knew that the woman inside was soft and tender, carrying the scars of the years. He wouldn't add to them. He promised himself that.

The teasing humour evaporated and suddenly everything felt very serious, momentous. Should he stop her now? Was she really ready for this? 'Louise…is that what you really want, what you really need?'

Because what Louise *wanted* and what Louise *needed* might be two very different things. And they might not be the same as his wants and needs—although the *needing* part of the equation was making it very hard to think.

She silenced him with a kiss. 'I don't want to just wish and dream any more. I want it to be real.'

He kissed her fiercely, then drew back to look at her, hoping his eyes conveyed the storm surge of feeling that was crashing over him. She had to have guessed how he felt about her. It was stamped in every look he gave her, in every touch.

Her answering kiss was rich and soulful. Her fingers

traced the muscles of his chest and he felt them quiver in response. '*You* are what I want, Ben. *You* are what I need…'

Then how could he say no? He wanted to give her everything, and he'd do anything to fill that empty hole inside of her. It was about time somebody tried. It was about time someone made her feel loved. He would. Even though it was too soon to say the words yet, he'd show her how much. He would make sure that she never doubted for a second, ever again, how rare and precious she was.

He kicked her fallen coat out of the way, picked her up and carried her straight out of the kitchen and into the hallway. His foot was on the bottom step when the doorbell rang.

'Cooo-eee!'

Both of them froze.

He would have known that irritating little sound anywhere. Megan.

The word he wanted to say, he couldn't, just in case Jas was standing outside and she heard it through the door.

Louise slithered out of his arms and ran back into the kitchen. Megan's blonde head was detectable as she tried to peek through the little window in the centre of the door. Thank goodness the old glass was not only obscured with a pattern, but rippled and bowed. The bell sounded again and he jumped.

'Ben? Is that you?'

Realising he couldn't very well answer the door in his present state, he charged back into the kitchen and started to fight with his sweater. Why, in situations like this, did the neck hole and the armholes seem to switch places? When he'd finally popped his head out of the right opening, he ran back to the front door, yelling, 'Just coming!'

Megan did not look impressed when he swung the door open. Jas jumped into his arms. 'Daddy!'

'About time too,' Megan said, pushing past him into the hall. Never mind that she didn't live here any more and, technically, she was supposed to wait to be asked. 'Come along, Jasmine.'

Jas gave him one last kiss and turned to grab the handle on her roll-along case and followed her mother inside. Ben, in a fit of adrenaline, managed to slam the door, charge past his ex-wife and daughter and make it to the kitchen door first.

Megan eyed him suspiciously. 'What are you up to, Ben?'

He ran a hand through his hair and leaned against the door jamb, blocking her way. 'Nothing.' The problem with priding himself of being a straight-talker was that he didn't get much practice at lying. Megan was looking at him strangely.

'Coffee?' he asked, although the words felt as if they came out sideways. In the effort to maintain harmony and stability, he always offered Megan a drink when she dropped Jas home. Most times his ex was far too busy being fabulous to stop and chew the fat, but today she was showing no inclination to rush off.

'Thanks,' she said dryly and pushed the kitchen door open.

Louise, hat and scarf on and coat in hand, was heading for the back door when she heard the kitchen door creak open. Quickly, she turned and hung her coat on one of the overcrowded pegs. If she couldn't disappear altogether, she was going to have to make it look as if she'd just arrived. Her skin felt hot and her cheeks were probably flushed but, hopefully, she could blame it on coming in out of the cold weather.

'Louise!' Jas shot into the room like a bullet and threw her arms around her middle.

'Hey, Jas!' she said softly.

Jasmine looked over her shoulder and shouted at the woman who had just entered with Ben. 'Mum! Look! Louise is here!'

'So she is.'

Ben's ex-wife was nothing like Louise had pictured her. She'd imagined a housewifey sort, but Megan was only what could be described as a 'yummy mummy'. Her long blonde hair fell past her shoulders and ended in a blunt, straight line, and she was wearing a designer coat, military style, pulled in tight at the waist. Her high-heeled boots made a fingernails-on-a-blackboard sort of noise as she crossed the tiled floor and offered her hand.

Louise's jeans, jumper and clumpy fur-lined suede boots suddenly seemed rather casual. She pulled the hem of her jumper down, rumpled as it had been from being whisked into Ben's arms. The memory was still doing odd things to her insides.

'Hello.' Not exactly original, but it was polite and it didn't give too much away.

Jas, still hyperactive after a longish car journey, abruptly let go of her and dashed towards the door. 'Dad! Wait till you see the really cool presents I got from Granny and Grandpa! Can I get them from the boot, Mum?'

Megan nodded, pulled a bunch of keys out of her pocket and threw them for Jasmine to catch. The girl's exit left the adults in an uncomfortable silence.

'Nice to meet you.' Louise stepped forward and offered her hand. Megan took it, but the contact only lasted the barest of seconds.

'Megan.'

Something about this woman reminded Louise of a cat arching with all its fur frizzed up. Somehow that made the whole situation easier. Being Toby's wife had made her used to this kind of response from other women. She was always a threat, the enemy, never someone that they wanted to gossip over cappuccinos with.

'I'm doing Louise's garden for her.'

Both she and Megan turned to look sharply at Ben, who seemed to be pulling every mug he could find out of one of the kitchen cupboards.

Garden? Good one. She'd forgotten all about the garden.

'Yes,' she said, nodding a little too hard. 'Ben is sorting out my rebellious garden for me…We were going to have a look at the plans.'

Don't wince, she told herself. You *were* going to look at the plans today—just later. Much later.

'Today? It's still Christmas, the holidays.' Megan's voice was flat and she looked at Ben, then at Louise, then back at Ben again. Nobody moved.

Okay, the only way to get round this was to milk the rich-and-famous angle and play the I'm-a-diva-and-people-jump-when-I-snap-my-fingers card—much as she hated it. 'Yes. I'm sure you understand, Megan. My life can be so hectic, you know, travelling all over the place…' The silly little laugh she gave turned her own stomach. She hadn't meant to do it; it must be the nerves. 'Sometimes we just have to squeeze the project meetings in whenever we can.'

'I'm sure it'll be marvellous,' Megan said, and Ben did a double-take and looked in astonishment at his ex-wife. 'Ben really is very talented.'

Louise stifled a smile as, from behind Megan, Ben gave her a dry look, pointed at his ex-wife and held up a pint-sized mug up, then shook his head. Megan's back was to him, thank goodness, so she didn't see him reach for the smallest mug of the collection and, after giving Louise a wicked smile, spoon instant coffee into it.

Megan sat down at the kitchen table, her mouth pursed a little too tightly for Louise's liking. 'I must say, you're all Jasmine has talked about while we were away.'

Louise shot a nervous look at Ben, who was now making a cup of coffee with record-breaking speed. 'Well…Ben has brought Jasmine up to Whitehaven a couple of times. My son, Jack, is only a few years younger than her and it made sense for the children to play together while Ben was looking after the garden.'

Megan nodded and twisted to look at Ben as he plonked the mug of coffee in front of her then dropped into the seat opposite Louise, his expression guarded.

'Well, Louise. I'm sure you'll appreciate that you're not the only one who leads a busy life. Ben and I have some *family* stuff to discuss—' as she said 'family' she laid a hand on Ben's arm '—so if you wouldn't mind…'

'Dad!' Jasmine burst back through the kitchen door, her arms full of presents. 'Look what I got!'

Much as Louise would have liked to walk over to Ben, slide her arm around his waist and stake her claim, this was neither the time nor the place.

Ben turned to look at Megan, an exasperated expression on his face. 'Louise and I have an appointment. She shouldn't have to leave.' The words *especially as you were supposed to be here at one* hung in the air.

Louise stood up and did an extra knot in her scarf. 'No, it's okay Ben. Family stuff comes first. I'll call you when I have an opening in my schedule. Goodbye, Jasmine…Megan.'

She collected her coat from near the back door and Ben rose and escorted her out of the kitchen and into the hall. She looked a little puzzled, but followed his lead. As she reached for the door latch, he grabbed hold of her hand. 'Don't go.'

She bit her lip and shook her head.

He turned her hand over, pulled it to his lips and planted a kiss into her palm. 'Actually, you can't go yet—not without giving away that your car is parked in my garage, which will only make Megan more suspicious.'

Okay, that was true, but she could always use the ferry and come back for her car later.

'If you could just…I don't know…take a walk on the beach for half an hour, I'll see what she wants to get off her chest and I'll call you when the coast's clear. You do have your phone with you, don't you?'

She nodded. This was getting sticky, complicated, just as she'd feared when Ben had only been a day-dream. That was the problem with reality. It was so…messy. She ought to take the ferry and leave them alone. But she found herself nodding and heading for the beach anyway.

Ben closed the door behind Louise and then pressed his face against the little window to watch her disjointed shape walk down the garden path. There were some days when he regretted not being able to make his marriage work, but today certainly was not one of them.

Whatever he did for Megan was never enough. It never had been.

When she'd left him, he'd felt empty. Not really because he missed her—by then he'd been too exhausted to feel anything but regret on Jas's behalf. No, the emptiness had been more a sense of being bled dry. He was a pretty decent bloke, he thought, and he'd put his heart and soul into his marriage but, in the end, he'd had to accept that his best had not been enough.

Megan had wanted more. She'd been so needy—he could see that now. Blindly, he'd thought he could help her grow, be the foundation that she could build on. But she was the sort of woman who needed constant attention, constant flattering, and he just hadn't been skilled at that. It had been like feeding a gaping hole that had never been satisfied.

He scrubbed his face with his hands and headed back to the kitchen. It was going to take all his energy for the next half hour to make nice and hear what her latest gripe was without telling her to get over herself.

The young woman he'd married, who'd been fragile but full of promise, had not blossomed into the strong and confident mother he'd thought she would. She was still full of all the same insecurities. And what little confidence she possessed hadn't grown into self-esteem, but had hardened into self-involvement. She was the world's axis, and heaven help anyone who didn't agree with her.

When he re-entered the kitchen, he was disappointed to discover that her coffee mug was still mostly full. He sat down beside her.

'What's so urgent?'

She gave him a withering look. 'Thank you, Ben. I had a lovely Christmas. How about you?'

'Dad? Look at this journal…It's got an electronic lock and a password. I can keep all my private stuff in here. Mum says it'll help me grow emotionally to keep a diary.'

Ben resisted the urge to growl. 'It's lovely, Jas.'

Placated, his daughter started to flick through the book, full of *all about me* pages. He'd really like to 'lose' that diary after Christmas. The last thing he wanted was for his ex to pass on the message to their daughter that life was *all about her.*

Turning back to Megan, he raised his eyebrows. She glanced at Jasmine, then motioned for him to join her on the other side of the kitchen. Too cloak-and-dagger for him, but it was easier to play along than have a row in front of Jasmine. He hauled himself back out of the chair and followed her, hoping that filling in the diary would command one hundred percent of Jas's attention.

Megan's idea of 'subtle' was talking in a stage whisper.

'I want Jasmine to come and live with me.'

He shook his head. No way. They'd decided all of this when Megan had moved out. Jas needed to stay in Lower Hadwell for school, for continuity. It had been Megan's idea to up and move to Totnes, South Devon's new age hotspot, to 'discover' herself. He didn't like the idea of Jas being influenced by all of that mumbo-jumbo at such a young age. And some of Megan's friends...

Megan's voice rose. 'She's going to be a teenager soon. I think a girl that age needs her mother close by.'

The rustling noises reaching from the kitchen table stopped.

He grabbed his ex-wife by the arm and propelled her out of the kitchen. Megan forgot her stage whisper and protested loudly.

'Pity you didn't think she needed a mother when you upped and left us.'

She ran a hand through her long hair. 'I realise what a mistake that was now, and it's time to put it right.'

'Right for whom?'

Not for him, not even for Jasmine. This was all about what Megan wanted, about what was good for Megan.

'Dad?' A nervous shout came from inside the kitchen.

Still fixing Megan with his fiercest stare, he yelled back, 'I'll be right there, Jellybean.'

'Yes, that's right, Ben. Take the easy way out, run away from the main issue.'

Lord, he really wanted to grab this woman by the shoulders and shake her.

'Megan,' he said from between clenched teeth. 'Wouldn't it have been more appropriate to discuss this on our own, somewhere Jasmine couldn't hear us?'

She made a gesture he could only describe as a flounce. 'It should be her decision, you know.'

Give him strength! 'We are not doing this now! Okay? You are going to collect your handbag, say goodbye to your daughter and leave. And I will phone you during the week so we can discuss this properly.'

Megan glared at him. 'Fine.' She stalked into the kitchen, followed his suggestions to the letter—which had to be a first—slamming the front door behind her. She was going to stew on this for days, he just knew it. Which was only going to make the coming negotiations worse, but how could he let Jas overhear? She'd witnessed enough rows already.

As he headed back into the kitchen he heard the screech of tyres in the lane.

Well, that ought to put any of her ridiculous ideas that he was still carrying a torch for her to rest. And about time too.

Louise put her phone away. The coast was clear. Although, from the sound of it, it would be better to leave father and daughter to some quality time this evening. Despite Ben's protests, she'd insisted she was merely returning to collect her car then she'd be on her way.

She stepped over the low wooden fence that separated the lane from the stony beach and headed back towards Ben's cottage. Only a moment later, she had to flatten herself against the hedge as a flashy four-wheel drive hurtled towards her.

Megan was in the driving seat, and she looked like she'd just sucked a whole pound of lemons. The car slowed briefly as she spotted Louise. At first, Megan's face registered surprise, but when she got closer her face contorted and she gunned the engine, leaving Louise coughing on exhaust fumes.

CHAPTER TWENTY-FOUR

Louise still daydreamed about Ben, even that night, after she'd returned home after eating supper with him and Jas. Even the following morning, when she wandered down to the boathouse just as it got light.

Unlike Laura, who'd been wishing for someone she couldn't have, Louise was seeing a man who was free to be with her. That made it different. Safer.

But now her dreams didn't just involve significant looks and first kisses; they'd moved on, matured. These were no seedling fantasies. Now they were putting down roots, burrowing deep inside of her and they stretched far into the future.

She and Ben living at Whitehaven, talking easily in the kitchen, eating round the large oak table with Jas and Jack...

Waking up with Ben in her bed, a circle of gold on his finger...

Sitting outside on the lawn on a bright summer's day, the squeals of the children ringing out as they chased each other in and out of the woods...

Okay, she'd borrowed that last one from Laura a little bit. But Whitehaven *was* the sort of house that should have children running on its lawns.

She reached the boathouse and went instantly to her destination: the desk.

7th November, 1954

I know I shouldn't be surprised. In fact, I'd steeled myself for the news already, eerily sure of what the doctor wanted to tell me. I thought I was ready.

And yet, when he said the words—so kindly—when he told me I probably wouldn't ever have children, I fell apart and made a terrible scene. It was the one thing I'd been hanging onto, you see. The one thing that could keep me cemented to Alex.

I don't know what to do now. There is nothing left to hope for.

19th February, 1955

My marriage is dying a slow and painful death. The sad thing is that it wasn't until I said to Alex that I wanted to leave him that I realised how much he truly cared about me. He's always so quiet, always so restrained.

And yet my big, stocky businessman of a husband wept when I told him I couldn't go on any more.

'What?' he begged me, 'What more can I do for you to make you stay? I love you, Laura. I have always loved you.'

I didn't say anything. What could he do to make me stay?

Be Dominic. That's all I could give him, and even I am not cruel enough to say that.

He told me he knew he wasn't good with words, but that he did his best, that he tried to tell me how much he cared in all the ways he knew how. That's true, I suppose, when I think back. Alex likes to give gifts. He's bought me more diamonds than I could ever wear, but I always thought they were just window-dressing for his trophy. I learned to despise them.

But I can't say that about the other things, the things I'd hardly noticed and taken for granted—the way he always opens the door for me, or that he'll fetch my coat if I so much as shiver. But you can't build a marriage on little civilities. There has to be adoration. There has to be passion.

For me, there has to be Dominic.

And if I can't be with him, I don't want anyone else. It's not fair to Alex to keep him tied to a woman who doesn't love him. As much as he says he doesn't want me to go now, he'd just end up hating me in the future. I'm doing this to save both of us from that.

Louise put the diary down and frowned. It all sounded so romantic, this desperate love for Dominic, but she couldn't help feeling sorry for poor Alex. She had a feeling he'd been a good man, that he'd loved Laura far more than she'd realised.

Louise knew she'd never have divorced Toby if he'd been half as attentive and kind as Alex had been to Laura. Good men like that were hard to find.

She looked at the closed diary and shook her head.

Poor Laura. No chance of being with the man she adored, and no desire to stay with the one who just might have adored her. But that still left a question hanging.

If there had been a husband with Laura at Whitehaven, who had it been?

CHAPTER TWENTY-FIVE

As Ben motored across the river in the dinghy, he couldn't quite wipe the smile from his face. Life had a funny way of throwing surprises at you. If someone had told him six months ago that he'd fall in love with one of those glitzy women from the magazine covers, he'd probably have hurt himself laughing. But, in his eyes, Louise wasn't one of *them,* anyway.

Through a series of text messages that morning, they'd decided that since it was a Sunday he should come to Whitehaven as usual. The hike up the hill towards the house seemed to last forever. It didn't stop Jas complaining that he was going too fast and pulling on his jacket to slow him down. Finally, he caught a glimpse of white masonry between the trees. Jas started running—probably because she had cakes on the brain.

Two seconds later, he sprinted after her.

When he laid eyes on Louise, who had obviously been hovering in the empty kitchen waiting for him, he hadn't counted on how hard it would be to be only feet away, but not able to pull her into his arms and kiss her senseless. Not yet, anyway.

It was torture, having to go out to the greenhouse and look at the plants while Louise and Jas made banana muffins together—bonding time. When he returned, he drank his cup of tea so fast he scalded his throat. Did he care?

'Come on, Jas. You and I are going for a bit of a walk.'

Jas rolled her eyes. 'Aw. Can't I have another muffin?'

'When we get back.' He walked over to the back door and handed her coat to her, then, over the top of Jas's head, he winked at Louise. She rewarded him with a smile.

As soon as the door closed behind them and they started making their way along the path towards the old stable complex, his heart began to thump. 'Jas? You like Louise, don't you?'

Jas bent down to pick up a stick. 'Yeah. She's cool—and really pretty.'

No arguments from him there.

Suddenly his mouth went dry. 'How would you feel if she…if we…' heck, this was more nerve-wracking than when he'd proposed to Megan '…if she was my girlfriend?' he finished in a rush.

Jas twiddled the stick in her fingers. 'Cool!' she said, suddenly, smiling up at him. 'Can I have another muffin now?' And, without waiting for him, she ran off back to the house.

He shook his head as a grin spread on his face. How easy had that been? He'd been expecting tears, arguments about why couldn't he and Mummy live together again, but Jas had taken it totally in her stride. Maybe he wasn't doing such a bad job of bringing her up after all.

Then, realising he could now go back to the house and, at the very least, hug Louise in front of Jas, he started to jog. If only telling the rest of the world could be that simple and uneventful, but he didn't have to worry about that yet. For now, this was their little secret.

Ben should have suspected something was up as soon as he walked into the newsagent's to collect his morning paper. Instead of the buzz of gossip, the rustle of paper and the ding of the old-fashioned till, there was silence, only broken by the echo of the brass bell that had announced his arrival.

There were around six people in the shop and they all stopped what they were doing and looked at him.

He felt decidedly uncomfortable as he headed for the rack full of newspapers. Had he turned green overnight or grown an extra head? What was up with these people?

As he bent to pick up his usual broadsheet there was a collective gasp.

Okay, that was enough. He stood up, and turned around to face them, his arms wide. 'What?'

Still, no one uttered a word but, one by one, they all looked at something behind him on the magazine and newspaper rack. He had the feeling that if he turned round a trap door would open underneath him and he'd be standing on thin air.

Slowly, he twisted round and scanned the display. The other villagers burst into motion and chatter. More than one darted out of the shop without buying anything.

What the…?

He shut his eyes and opened them again, just to make sure he wasn't hallucinating. There was a woman he knew very well on the front of one of the tabloids, looking grim and angry with her arms crossed and her eyes blazing. Only, it wasn't Louise.

It was Megan.

'LOUISE GOT HER CLAWS INTO MY MAN,' the headline screamed in tall white letters on a black background. Below were two smaller pictures, one a heart-shaped photo of him and Megan from the last summer holiday they'd shared together—graphically altered by putting a jagged rip between the two of them—and a headshot of Louise, taken from below, so it seemed as if she was looking down her nose at something.

He snatched the paper off the shelf. *What the hell?*

Megan had to have something to do with this. How else had the paper got that photo of them? What on earth was she playing at? Didn't she think *any-thing* through? What if Jasmine saw this? Or even her friends?

At first he was relieved that there only seemed to be three copies on display but, eventually, his brain kicked in and he realised that must be because the rest had been sold. He grabbed all three of them, marched up to the counter and threw a few coins down. He wasn't about to wait for change.

'You should be ashamed of yourself for selling such trash,' he told Mrs Green.

She gave him a stony look. 'Well, Mister Oliver, we all know Megan's been gone a while, and that Thornton woman has only just arrived, but you know what they say…'

Suddenly, he *really* didn't want to know what the mysterious 'they' had to say about anything. He turned and walked towards the door. Mrs Green raised her voice, just so he wouldn't miss her pearl of wisdom as he opened the door and exited the shop.

'There's no smoke without fire.'

What a pity the old stable block had deteriorated so badly. Louise pushed gingerly at one of the doors. The building was huge—a double-height room with gigantic arched doors at one end, big enough to take a carriage or two. The low-ceilinged central section had enough stalls for one, two, three…eight horses.

There was a hatch in the ceiling above one of the abandoned stalls. What was upstairs? Those skylights in the steep slate-tiled roof had to be there for a reason. She was dying to find out. Or, at least, she was dying to think of something other than the email that had blithely pinged into her inbox earlier that morning, and pulling buildings apart and putting them back together again was a familiar displacement activity for her at present. Safe. Comforting. All-consuming.

In a corner she found a stepladder, obviously not authentic Georgian as it was made of aluminium. Still, it would do. She dragged it underneath the hatch and unfolded it, making sure the safety catches were in place.

She was up the steps in a shot and, when she pushed the hatch door, she was showered with dust and dirt and probably a hundred creepy-crawlies. Holding onto the ladder for support, she brushed her hair down with her free hand.

When she'd stopped coughing and blinking, she poked her head through the hole. Enough light was filtering through the streaky grey skylights for her too see a long loft, with fabulous supporting beams in the roof. She turned round to look in the other direction. Goodness, this must run the whole length of the stables. It was easily sixty feet long. Just think what an amazing guest house this would make! There was room for at least four good-sized bedrooms.

Louise turned round and sat on the large, flat step on the top of the stepladder. She already had a house full of rooms she didn't know what to do with. What on earth did she need a guest house for? And shouldn't she find something more worthwhile to do with her life than prettying up her own house?

'Louise!'

That was Ben's voice. A second later, he appeared in the stable door, breathless and dishevelled.

'Up here,' she called, her skin cold and tingling as she peered into the dingy interior. He spotted her and ran to the bottom of the ladder. How was she going to tell him? How could she prepare him for the poisonous taste of her world? Just when she thought things were finally going right, all her old choices—the kind of life she'd led, the kind of man she'd married—came back to bite her on the arse.

He wanted stability for Jas and as much as she thought he liked her, she guessed he would back away now, hunker down and protect his daughter. And she wouldn't blame him one bit. If she could escape all this, she would.

'What are you doing…? Never mind.' He held a hand out and she used it to steady herself as she descended the ladder. He looked unusually pale and serious, his mouth a thin line. Her heart began to stammer.

'What is it? Is everything okay?' she asked.

'No! Everything is not bloody okay!' He pulled away from her, then marched to the door.

'Ben!'

He pulled a folded newspaper from his back pocket. 'It's Megan. She's outdone herself this time and I am so, so, sorry… I could happily throttle her!'

'Ben?'

'I just went into the newsagents this morning and…well, there it was…and the whole village staring…'

She tried to get eye contact but he was talking to himself, reliving some memory, more than he was talking to her. 'Ben!'

'And we were trying to keep it secret, for the kids…'

She grabbed him by the shoulder. 'Ben!'

He stopped mid-sentence and stared at her.

'I know.'

He blinked, then looked down at the paper in his hands.

'Toby's agent sent me an email. He has a press agency that deals with all his cuttings…' She shrugged and gave him what she hoped was an encouraging smile. 'Seems the cat is out of the bag.'

The frown lines on his forehead deepened. 'How can you be so blasé about it? Don't you know what she said about you…about me? Don't you know how she made it sound?'

Yes, she knew. She knew Megan had told the papers that she and Ben were on the verge of a reconciliation when nasty old Louise had slunk up and stolen her man away. People would believe it. Even after it had come out that Toby had been unfaithful, the public had forgiven him and, somehow, there seemed to be an undercurrent of opinion that it had been her fault. She was too cold, too remote. Couldn't give him what he needed. Never mind that she'd given and given and given, and it still hadn't been enough.

Well, they were right about that. What Toby really needed was a good kick in the pants. And she'd have loved to have been the one to dish it out, but she wasn't about to generate even more column inches by doing so. She only cared about the smudged print on the paper if it affected how Ben felt, whether it was going to change things between them. Anything else was irrelevant.

'Forget it,' she said.

He stared at the paper again, then hurled it into the nearest stall. 'I can't!'

Louise thought back to her first really awful press story. It had hurt, cut deep. Nowadays she just usually ignored them. But Ben wasn't used to this. In one fell swoop, his ordered, stable little universe had been set on its head.

Silently, she walked over to him and put her arms round him. He was shaking with rage. She kissed him gently on the cheek, on the nose, on the lips, until he wound his arms round her and kissed her back.

It didn't matter what anyone else thought. He'd understand that eventually.

'Ben,' she whispered in his ear. 'It doesn't matter. I don't care.'

He pulled back and his frown deepened. 'What are we going to do?'

'Do? Nothing.'

'Nothing.' He repeated the word as if he didn't understand its meaning. 'What do you mean "nothing"?

She shrugged. 'As far as the press is concerned, we just don't comment. Any response from us will just keep the story running.'

'But I don't want people to think those things about you. It's not the truth!'

She silenced him with a kiss. He was so sweet for being worried about her, rather than fuming on his own behalf. 'The reporters don't care about truth. They care about the story—what's juiciest, what's going to sell more papers. The people who read that trash might think I'm a man-eating witch, but I don't care. What we think matters—what *we* believe about ourselves.'

'That doesn't seem fair.'

'But that's how it is and we've just got to deal with it.' She exhaled long and hard. 'You might want to take Jas away for a few days, just in case people turn up

wanting an interview or a picture. You've seen for yourself what some of them can be like.'

He nodded. 'I could ring up my sister in Exeter.
She's back home now and could certainly have us until
Jas starts school again, but you'll be here…all on your
own.'

She took him by the hand and they walked out into
the bright winter morning, the sun so low in the sky
it hadn't risen above the tops of the bare trees. 'This
isn't nice, but it's 'normal' in my world. I can deal with
this—I have done for more than a decade. It's Jas who
matters at the moment.'

He nodded. 'She's with a friend in the village
right now. I'd better go and tell her we're off on an
impromptu visit to Aunty Tammy's.'

Much as he'd like to wring Megan's neck right that
very second, there were some important issues they
needed to discuss. He jabbed at the doorbell of her flat
for a third time and left his thumb on the button so it
rang loud and long.

Nothing. And any calls he made to her mobile were
going straight through to voicemail.

Why? Why had she done this? Had she not thought
what sort of effect this would have on Jasmine?

No, of course she hadn't. Megan always thought of
herself first and everyone else second. It had been her
decision to end their marriage, her decision to leave

Jasmine with him—saying she needed to learn to be a whole person herself before she could be a truly devoted mother—and now that he'd finally picked himself up and was moving on with his life, she was trying to sabotage that too.

Perhaps it was just as well he hadn't caught up with her, he thought as he climbed into his car and slammed the door. Choosing to hurt Louise had been cowardly; she was an easy target.

He put the car into gear and made the thirty-minute drive back to Lower Hadwell. By the time he got back to his cottage it was almost two o'clock and he was supposed to be packing to go to his sister's before picking Jasmine up at three. It wasn't until he'd parked his car and walked round to the front of his cottage that he noticed the figure on his doorstep. Megan was sat on the low step, her face buried in her knees, drawing in jerky breaths.

Uh-oh. That damsel-in-distress thing inside him kicked to life again, robbing him of the nice head of anger he'd got going. How messed up must she be to think that selling her story to the papers would cause anything but a headache? For everyone—including her.

She stopped sniffing when she heard him walking towards her and raised her head to look at him. Her eyes were pink and her face was blotchy and puffy. He might feel sorry for her, but that didn't mean he was going to let her off the hook completely.

'Why, Megan?'

Her face crumpled, then she sniffed loudly again and wiped her nose with a crushed tissue. 'I spent the last two years following my heart, trying to work out what would make me happy, what would make me feel like a whole person...' She patted her palm against her chest.

Ben put his hands in his pockets. 'Well, maybe you did the right thing in leaving me. You obviously weren't happy, living here with me and Jasmine.'

She shook her head and rearranged the almost disintegrated tissue so she could use it for one last blow. 'No, I was happy—sort of. But it wasn't enough. I wanted more.' She fixed him with her clear, blue eyes. 'Only, I don't seem to be able to work out what *more* is.'

Welcome to the human race, honey.

He nearly always had a small packet of tissues in his pocket—required kit with a child in tow. He fished a packet out of his jacket and offered them to Megan, but her eyes were glazed and she was staring off into the distance.

'And then I realised—oh, about a month ago—that not only was I not any happier than I had been when we were together, but that I was *less* happy. The grass truly wasn't greener on the other side of the fence.' Spotting the tissues, she reached up and but instead of taking them from him, she clasped on to his hand. 'You're a good man, Ben. And I was too blind to see that.'

She looked at him with large blue eyes and her breath

caught in her throat. Oh, no. He had a feeling he knew what was coming next and he willed her not to say it. He pulled his hand away and stuffed the packet of tissues into her fingers.

'Megan, we can't go back. You don't love me that way any more, not really. And I don't want to be with you by default, because you can't find anything or anyone you like better. I deserve *more* too.'

She pressed her lips together and nodded and a fresh batch of tears ran down her face. She squeezed his hand. 'Yes, you do. And I'm sorry for what I did. I suppose I got into a real state because I was...' she struggled getting the next word out '... jealous.' She gave him a weak smile. 'It was pretty obvious, you know. The pair if you couldn't keep your eyes off each other. Just... don't let her hurt you, Ben. I see that same ache in her that I have inside me.'

No. Megan was wrong about that. Louise was stronger than she was. But he wasn't going to stand on his own doorstep and discuss that right now. He reached for Megan's hand and pulled her up to stand.

Sometimes his ex-wife could seem like a force of nature—a cyclone—twisting her way through other people's lives and leaving destruction in her wake but, right now, she looked more like a frightened child.

He put his arms around her and gave her a brotherly hug. 'We both deserve more, Meg. Don't you forget that.'

She nodded and kissed him softly on the cheek. 'Thanks, Ben. Jasmine is lucky to have a dad like you. And, I think—' she paused to take a shuddering sniff '—she ought to stay with you for the time being. I reckon I have a few things to sort out first.'

Relief washed through him. That had to be the most mature and sensible decision Megan had made in a long time. Perhaps there was hope for her yet.

CHAPTER TWENTY-SIX

With Ben away, Louise spent more time working her way through Laura's diary. She made good on her plans to divorce Alex, and Louise wasn't sure how she felt about that. Mainly, she was just sad for both of them.

Maybe it was the diary, or maybe it was the relentless grey of the winter that made her feel this way, but Louise felt bleak and empty. Maybe it was just that reading about Laura and Alex's split and the resulting fallout was too close to home, especially as her solicitor had let her know just before Christmas that the finalising of her divorce should happen in the new year sometime.

Or maybe she was just missing Ben.

She felt better when he was around—like there wasn't a hole inside, one that gnawed at its own edges, trying to increase its perimeter.

It would be better when he was back from his sister's. She would start to feel herself again. Maybe she would even feel more like the version of herself she was in her daydreams, the woman who was perfect for Ben, who didn't have a past that kept knocking down their attempts to build something more than friendship.

So, when Laura's divorce made her feel too maudlin, sometimes she skipped and skimmed the entries. She really didn't need the details, did she? She was living it herself.

But then, one evening, an entry made her stop dead in her tracks:

3rd March, 1956

I've just received the most awful, awful news. Jean Blake killed herself last night. I was walking past the news stand on my way into town to lunch with a friend and I saw the headline.

I felt so sick I couldn't even buy a copy, but when I arrived at the Savoy, it was all Brenda could talk about. How shocking it was, how sudden. How devastated poor, poor Dominic must be... (Not that she actually knows him.) And the poor, precious child, only just a toddler, now left without a mother. How could a woman leave a child like that? What must have driven her to it?

I sank down in my seat and ate my lunch, nodding and murmuring in all the right places. Even though I've had no contact with Dominic or Jean in almost two years, I had the horrible feeling I could answer Brenda's questions.

What had driven poor, unstable Jean Blake to take her own life?

I had the horrible feeling the answer might be that I had.

How feelings and fact line up, I don't know, because it shouldn't be that way, shouldn't be that way at all. I was the one left alone and grieving. She won, she had him. He chose her.

But then I thought maybe he didn't choose her. Maybe Jean had worked out that he chose the child, Caroline, instead. I've always wondered whether Jean got pregnant to keep him with her, because Dominic had always said they'd decided to wait a few years, until his hectic work schedule calmed down, but it had happened early. Maybe Jean woke up one day and realised she'd made herself a prison.

I feel wretched, even though I did the right thing. And then, underneath that sticky, heavy guilt is something else...

Something warmer, like the sun coming out, and I despise myself for feeling this way.

Part of me is happy.

Even though a husband has lost his wife, even though a child has lost her mother. Am I monster? Or am I merely human—and all that means: weak, broken, selfish?

Because, once the initial shock has worn off, all I can think of is that Dominic is now free and our time will come soon.

CHAPTER TWENTY-SEVEN

Louise frowned when she heard the knocker on the front door rap four times in sharp succession. The journalists roaming the Lower Hadwell area at present had not yet had the front to march up to her door and ask for a comment, but that didn't mean one foolhardy soul wouldn't try. She walked quickly and silently across the hall and entered the study, where she could get a better view of whoever it was at the door.

Making sure she was in the shadows as much as she could, she leaned in close to the window and squinted.

No middle-aged newshound with a beer belly, this one. It was a woman. She had her hand up to shield her eyes while she tried to peer the wrong way through the spyhole. And stylish too. She was wearing a pencil skirt and really cute boots and her long blonde hair was caught in a loose ponytail that curled into loose ringlets down her back.

It was only when she grimaced in frustration and stood up to rap the knocker a second time that Louise realised this was no journalist. There was a reason why those boots were so cute—it was Tara.

Louise knocked on the study window to get her attention and Tara whipped round so fast on those heels she almost lost her balance. When she saw Louise her eyes widened, and then she shouted, 'Open the bloody door, Lou! It's freezing out here!'

Louise was too shocked to do anything but comply. When she opened the glossy black front door, Tara had recovered herself. 'Surprise!' she said, grinning and throwing her arms wide, reminding Louise of a hostess on an old-fashioned glitzy game show.

When Louise didn't move, her mouth still slightly open, Tara stepped over the threshold and air-kissed her as if they'd lunched together last Thursday. 'You've been moaning for ages that I should visit,' she said brightly, 'and I thought you might be feeling a bit miserable over Christmas—I heard about Toby and Lapland...'

'Thanks,' Louise said quietly, pleased but slightly nonplussed. This was stunningly thoughtful behaviour for her friend. 'Welcome to Whitehaven.'

Tara took a quick and critical survey of the entrance hall. 'Love what you've done with the place,' she said, nodding. 'Very...homey.'

Louise glanced at the pale aubergine walls and off-white paintwork, the comfy tapestried armchair that sat in the corner near the hat and umbrella stand.

It wasn't all silver-patterned wallpaper and mirrored furnishings, like Tara's London pad, so she supposed in comparison it did look rather rustic.

'Come through to the kitchen,' she said, 'I've just finished a batch of white chocolate brownies.'

'Oh, Lord,' Tara moaned, as she followed Louise down the passageway. 'I'm not sure I'm as happy about piling on the pounds as you obviously are, but maybe you need the extra padding in a draughty old house like this.'

Louise rolled her eyes while Tara couldn't see her. Whitehaven definitely wasn't draughty. The workmen who'd been in before Christmas had replaced all the windows and made sure of that. But Tara could be very fixed in her ideas. If she'd decided Whitehaven was chilly, she'd be feeling phantom draughts for the duration of her visit.

'So…to what do I owe the pleasure?' she asked Tara as she put the kettle on the Aga, and motioned for her to take a seat at the old oak table in the centre of the room. 'Not that I'm not pleased to see you, you understand…'

Tara blinked away her question and gave her a smile that didn't quite reach her eyes. 'Like I said, I decided to check up on you, make sure you were okay.'

Louise smiled back. 'That's very kind of you.' But she'd seen that same smile on the other woman a hundred times before. It was the one Tara wore when she

lied through her teeth during interviews. Louise wasn't
going to push it, though. Tara wouldn't be able to sit
on her real reason for coming long; her habit for brutal
honesty would make sure of that.

'So, *are* you okay?' Tara asked, leaning forward a
little, and for the first time showing a hint of genuine
concern.

Louise rested back in her chair and looked at the
ceiling while she considered her friend's question.
Christmas had been a bit of a roller coaster, to be sure,
but when she checked deep down inside herself, she
discovered she was feeling more than okay.

She smiled at Tara, properly this time. 'Yes, I really
am. I'm missing Jack, of course, but life is…' she
wouldn't exactly call it 'good' at the moment, but it was
improving '…getting better.'

Tara nodded. She didn't look convinced. 'And what
about that story in the papers the other day? Please tell
me it's just the usual load of rubbish, cobbled together
from a few tiny grains of truth.'

Louise inhaled. She didn't want to tell Tara about
Ben. Especially as she wasn't sure just how much contact her friend had had with Toby over recent months.
Now, Toby would have no sensible reason to object to
her having a new man in her life—especially after his
behaviour—but when had Toby ever been sensible?

'There was plenty in that article that was complete
fabrication,' she said truthfully. 'But I do know the man.

His firm is landscaping the gardens for me and he's been to the house numerous times.'

Tara did a silly little laugh and pressed her palm to her breastbone. 'Thank goodness for that! For one second, I thought you'd made good on your threat to have a tawdry little fling with a muddy local.'

Louise was saved from answering by the whistling of the kettle. 'Coffee?' she asked through slightly clenched teeth as she went to take it off the Aga.

Tara leaned back in the wooden chair and stretched her long legs out. 'Gasping for one,' she said. 'I'll admit the view is stupendous, but it felt like I took a trip through several time zones—and possibly back a couple of decades—to get here. I don't know how you haven't gone cuckoo living this far away from civilisation.'

Louise made the coffee and held her tongue. Those viper-filled parties and competitions to see who could get the most column inches in a week were civilisation, were they? If that was the case, she was quite happy moving to the dark ages and staying here.

Louise carefully slid the loaf tin containing a pale yellow Madeira cake batter into the Aga and closed the door. Soon, the kitchen would be filled with the scent of lemon zest and eggs and butter. Heavenly.

She wondered if her house guest would try some? Probably not. Although Tara was as stick-thin as Louise had once been, and one slice wouldn't hurt, she also had an iron will. Tara wouldn't be Mrs Gareth Adams otherwise. It had taken a steely determination to beat all the other contenders for the role off and convince the footballer she was the only one for him.

Which led Louise to pondering, with brownies and mini-muffins in the cake tin already, why she was making yet another cake. Not that she was scared of cake any more, and would definitely enjoy some, but it was far too much for her to eat on her own. The chief cake-eating culprits—Jack and Ben—were far away. It would probably go hard in the tin.

She poured herself a cup of tea from the old brown pot and sat down at her kitchen table. Although the rest of the house had been transformed, the kitchen still remained its old-fashioned, orange pine self. She'd get a designer in after Christmas, maybe. Or the spring. Although it was ugly, something about this room felt like home to Louise. Always had, ever since she'd first walked into it.

Home. That had been where she'd perfected her baking skills. Family life had been full of noise and love, but it had also been tough. Baking had been a cheap way to cheer her brothers and sisters up when Dad wasn't doing so well. It hadn't just been about eggs and flour and sugar. It had been about love, about taking care.

She'd have baked for Toby if he'd have let her, but

he'd been unusually snobby about having the private chef do everything. But now and again, when Jack had come along, Louise had slipped into the kitchen and baked with her son. She and the chef had an understanding. And Toby had never known the chocolate fudge cake he'd loved so much had been made by his wife's fair hand.

Louise walked over to the cake tin, chose an apple and cinnamon mini-muffin and carefully peeled it from its case as she sat back down with her cup of tea. She didn't eat it in one bit but savoured it, and as she was swallowing the moist crumbs, a truth hit her.

She was baking for herself. To comfort. To take care.

The urge had just risen up from within and would not be quashed. But that was good, wasn't it? Ben had told her she needed to stop always looking after other people, that she should take some time for herself.

Louise frowned. But if she was trying to make herself feel better, did that mean she was unhappy?

No. She had Jack with her—most of the time. She had Ben, and whatever it was they were starting. She had this wonderful old house and the new life she'd dreamed of. How could she be unhappy? Everything was fine.

Maybe it was just because Jack was away. She was lonely. Or possibly she was baking for him in his absence. Madeira cake was one of his favourites.

Tara, who'd gone upstairs to have a shower and 'feel

more human again' after her distressing journey to the outer wilds of Great Britain, walked through the kitchen door, looking as glossy and as polished as always, even in her designer jeans and soft cashmere jumper.

But looks were deceiving. Louise knew that. And, as she studied her friend carefully, she wondered if she was baking for Tara too.

But Tara never let anyone close, never let anyone see the chinks in her armour. Except, maybe, by coming to Whitehaven. Because Louise knew she wasn't altruistic enough to have come all this way just to see her. Something was up. And it might just be something big.

They chatted about fashion and gossiped about acquaintances as Louise prepared a simple roast chicken salad for supper. When it was ready, she filled two glasses with Pinot Grigio—nothing more fancy was available at the local shop, but Tara wasn't much of a wine connoisseur, so she probably wouldn't notice—and sat down at the table.

When they were halfway through their salads, Louse leaned back in her chair and took a sip of wine. 'So, what's *really* up with you?'

Tara's knife and fork went still. She didn't look up. Then, slowly, she began to carve the piece of chicken again and only when it had been carefully dissected and chewed did she put her cutlery down and meet Louise's gaze.

'Who says anything's up?' She blinked and smiled, but Louise wasn't fooled for a second. She'd seen that same smile in the mirror many a time. Of course something was up. And as much as Tara drove her crazy sometimes, she wanted to help her.

'I do.' She reached across the table and laid a hand on top of Tara's. The pair of them had never been ones to share hugs or be very touchy-feely with each other, but somehow it felt right. Needed. 'You can tell me… And you know I won't tell anyone.' She let out a dry laugh. 'Ninety percent of my friends have conveniently forgotten I exist, anyway. Unless you mind the sheep round here knowing, there's no one else I can confide in.'

For the first time ever Louise saw a crack of hesitation, of self-doubt in Tara's eyes. Then she looked back at her plate.

'It's Gareth… I think he might be… I think he's…'

Louise squeezed Tara's hand. She knew just what that was like, how that felt. 'Do you just suspect, or do you know for sure…?'

Tara got up and walked over to the handbag she'd left on the counter earlier. She returned holding a mobile phone. But not Tara's bright pink, custom-made smart phone, one that looked entirely more masculine. She fired it up and scrolled through the menus until she showed a text to Louise.

'Tomorrow @ 11 The Hilton. C u then, G x'

Louise blinked. 'This is Gareth's phone? You took Gareth's phone and drove three hundred miles away with it? Isn't he going to go nuts?'

'Don't care,' Tara said, her mouth thinner than those lip injections should let it be.

Louise shook her head and looked at the screen again. 'It seems fairly innocent,' she said. 'Are you sure he's up to something?'

Tara's jaw clenched. 'He told me he was meeting one of his team mates for lunch—but at The Ivy. That's in a different part of town altogether. And I just have this…feeling.'

Louise knew all about the feeling. And her mistake with Toby had been not paying attention to it sooner.

'I'm so sorry,' she told Tara. 'What are you going to do?'

Tara took a great gulp of her wine. 'I don't know. I didn't even really plan to come and see you. I threw some stuff into an overnight bag and just got in the car and started driving. Somehow, when I saw the sign on the M25 for the West Country, I decided to take the exit.'

Ah, now *that* sounded like the Tara she knew and loved. Well, the don't-mind-if-I-inconvenience-you bit. Driving off without telling anyone where she was going, doing something unpredictable and unplanned, now that wasn't typical Tara behaviour at all.

So, whatever their ups and down had been in the

past, no matter how smug Tara had been about her perfectly devoted husband while trying to comfort Louise when she'd split with Toby, Louise decided she would do whatever she could to help. Everyone needed a friend when their carefully constructed life started to fall apart, and she had the funny feeling she might be the closest thing to a friend Tara had.

Louise was glad she'd brought Laura's diary up from the boathouse earlier that afternoon, because now she couldn't sleep. Maybe it had something to do with having another person in the house. She couldn't quite get past how jarring it was to have someone from what she now mentally referred to as her 'old' life here, trespassing on the new, making the edges blur together.

For some reason she'd waited until Tara had disappeared to have a nap before she'd hurried down to the boathouse to get the diary. She could have easily asked Tara to come for a walk with her, she supposed, but she hadn't wanted to. The boathouse was too special to her. Private. And she hadn't wanted to see Tara cast her assessing eye over her favourite place in the world and find it wanting. She didn't want to see the boathouse through Tara's jaded eyes.

She plumped up an extra feather pillow and tucked it behind her head as she leaned over to the bedside table for Laura's diary.

***

2nd July, 1956

Finally, after so many months of bleakness I have had some good news. Glorious news. I wish I could say that it was that Dominic had replied to the card I sent him after Jean's death, but it's still only been three months. I don't think he's ready, and even—oh, how my heart jumps just at the thought—even if the way was open to us to go forward , it would look a little hasty if we took up together now.

I can be patient. Loving Dominic has taught me that, because I always seem to be waiting for him.

Anyway, I had a telephone call from the Forbes-Hamiltons today, the owners of Whitehaven. It seems that neither of their sons wishes to take it on and they're feeling it's too big for them now they're getting older. I'd jokingly mentioned when I visited that if I ever they thought of selling they should contact me first, and it seems they took me seriously.

Thank heavens they did. Maybe this is what I've been waiting for—a turn in my fortune, something going right for a change. Maybe this will be the first part of my dream to come true.

I haven't said yes yet, but of course I will. I had to make the right noises about coming down to see it myself before I made up my mind. So, I'm booked on the 9.35 from Paddington tomorrow.

Please, if you're up there, God, don't take this from me too. Let me have Whitehaven. That house is special.

It can heal people; it can bring love. And if you give me this one thing, I promise I'll do my best to make sure I'm not the only one who benefits from it.

Louise looked up. There had been a noise outside her door. She waited, but all was silent. Just another of the strange creaks of an old house, she supposed.

Still, Laura was right about Whitehaven. It was special. She didn't know if it was in the air or the earth, but somehow this house did heal. She just had to pray that it worked for her and Jack. And even for poor Tara, asleep in one of the guest rooms.

But there was something in what Laura had written—her promise. She'd been right about that too. The person who owned such a place shouldn't be selfish with it. There had to be a way to share what she had.

This time it was a floorboard that creaked outside her door. A second later the doorknob turned and it opened a few inches. Tara poked an unusually dishevelled head into the room.

'I saw a light under your door,' she said quietly.

Louise smiled. 'Can't sleep?'

Tara shook her head. And just for a second Louise saw the ordinary girl, full of insecurities and issues, who had once been in the place where the focused and driven Tara Adams now stood. She patted the bed beside her. 'Me neither. I seem to have become a bit of a nocturnal creature since I split with Toby.'

Tara just nodded and settled herself on the bed, propping a pillow up behind herself. 'I'm not splitting with Gareth.'

Louise mentally kicked herself in the shins. 'No. Of course. You're not even sure there's any reason to yet.'

Apart from The Feeling.

Had Tara forgotten that already? Louise still dreaded its icy clawing, its jittery squeezing. Just as well she was shot of Toby and didn't have to worry about it any more.

Tara looked at her, wide-eyed. 'If I was sure... If he had...' She looked down at her hands clasped in her lap then met Louise's eyes again. 'I don't know if I could do what you've done.'

Louise leaned over and put an arm round Tara. 'Brain working overtime. That's one of the symptoms. Listen, you don't have to decide anything yet. You don't have to make any plans. You need to find out the truth first.'

Tara nodded, but Louise could tell that her brain was whirring away inside her skull. Tara planned. She always had, always would. But the problem was that all her platinum-plated plans had revolved around being Mrs Gareth Adams. The thought of tearing all of that down and starting again must be terrifying.

'Good book?' Tara asked, nodding at the open diary in Louise's lap.

Louise closed it and carefully replaced it on the bed-side table. She didn't want to share that with Tara, either.

But that was selfish, wasn't it? Hadn't she just been thinking about how Whitehaven healed, about how she should share that gift somehow? It was time she learned to stop shutting people out, to be more open and giving like Laura had been.

'Actually, it's the diary of the former owner.'

Tara pulled a face and sneered. 'Riveting stuff then...all counting sheep and walking in the hills? No wonder you read it when insomnia hits.'

Louise shook her head. 'No. Ever heard of Laura Hastings, the film star?'

Tara's eyes grew wide.

'Well, she lived here for forty years. I found this hid-den away and forgotten.'

And she began to tell Tara Laura's story, hoping that whatever her friend was feeling at that moment, that she'd realise she was probably better off than poor tragic Laura. '...and I've just read the bit where she decides to buy this house,' she said.

'OMG that's an amazing story!'

Louise nodded. She had the feeling she had things to learn from Laura's journey, that if only she could think about it hard enough it might contain the answers to some of her present struggles. It was a surprise and a joy to know the other woman felt the same.

'You could make a fortune selling them,' Tara said, her eyes glazing. 'Or maybe you could publish them yourself, write a foreword, add some stuff in about the house today…'

Louise opened her mouth to speak, but Tara was on a roll. She clapped her hands and sat up off the pillow.

'I know! You could do a book tour… Do all the chat shows… Don't you see, Lou? This old lady's diary could get you back in the game! You've found buried treasure.'

Louise felt nauseous. 'I don't think…'

But Tara wasn't listening. Off in her head, she was making plans. But not plans for herself—since those were on hold—but plans for Louise.

Louise supposed she should be grateful. It was actually a step up for Tara that she was trying to be help someone else, rather than just criticising their decisions. But these were Tara-type plans, and they might—just might—have fit Louise when she'd first told Toby she was leaving, but now they were big and baggy and unflattering. Not what she wanted at all.

She faked a yawn. 'Actually, I am feeling a bit sleepy now. I might try and doze off again, if you don't mind?'

Tara shrugged, then she eyed up the brown leather notebook on the bedside table. 'Can I have a read, then? It might work for me too.'

Louise picked it up and clutched it to her chest, shaking her head softly. 'I…I haven't finished it yet. I'd better keep it in case I wake up again.'

'Another time, then,' Tara said and pushed herself up off the bed and walked toward the door.

Over my dead body, thought Louise.

CHAPTER TWENTY-EIGHT

How Ben had volunteered to take Jas and her two younger cousins shopping he couldn't quite remember. His sister was subtle like that. Dangerous. Especially when the twin nephews in question were at that in-between age when they were too big for a pushchair, but too young to behave themselves in crowded shops. He supposed it was his penance for foisting himself on Tammy like this.

One slippery little hand wriggled free from his and one small boy was suddenly running into the busy crowds in the shopping mall. He yelled for Jas to follow him, scooped the other boy up into his arms and gave chase.

Thankfully, Peter—the tearaway—was stopped in his tracks by a rather fed-up-looking man in a furry turkey costume. Confronted with over seven feet of slightly disgruntled bird, he began to cry.

Angus, who was fidgeting frantically in Ben's arms, saw that his brother was in distress and started to howl too. Great. The end to a perfect shopping trip.

Tammy was going to wonder what sort of ordeal he'd put them through when he got back to her house.

He was now in grabbing distance of Peter and he hauled him up to join his brother. The turkey guy gave him a dismissive look.

'Ought to watch out where them kids are going,' he said, and waddled off.

Ben found he couldn't resist a parting shot. 'Aren't you past your sell-by date? Christmas was almost a week ago!'

Jas giggled beside him.

Great. What a great example he was being to all three kids. It was just that hiding away like this, keeping away from Louise, felt like he was hiding something. Lying, almost. He puffed air out through his lips and turned to his daughter. 'Remind me what else is on the list, Jas.'

She gave him a self-satisfied grin. 'A magazine for me and colouring books for the boys.'

Ben hefted the twins, who had obviously been overdosing on Christmas pudding, under his arms and set off back to the other end of the mall. One of the large chains of newsagents had a shop up that way and he could kill two birds with one stone.

As he walked into the magazine and newspaper section at the front of the shop, something very much like *déjà vu* made his skin pop into goose pimples. Although he was sure it was just tiredness, he took a quick look around the shop.

Jas was heading over to look at the magazines and, in one swift action, he grabbed her arm and steered her in the opposite direction. 'Why don't you go and look over there,' he said, pointing to the slightly older teenage magazines.

'Cool!' Jas didn't need to be told twice.

He was probably going to hate himself for buying her one of those later, but it was a far better option than letting her see the front page of one of the newspapers on the other display stand.

There, in full colour, was a picture of Megan kissing him on the cheek accompanied by the heading: 'LOUISE FOILED IN LOVE AGAIN'. There wasn't much text, but he could make out another small picture of Louise. She seemed to be sneering.

Of course, the main photo looked much worse than the actual event—like an intimate moment between lovers.

Hell.

He couldn't let Jas see that. For all kinds of reasons. Surreptitiously, he wandered over to the display and pulled another paper across to hide the offending article. Then he accepted the magazine that Jas was waving at him, stopped by a pile of colouring books, grabbed a couple and headed for the till.

His blood was one degree off boiling temperature.

After paying he grabbed a twin in each hand and bustled Jas out of the shop so fast she gave him one of her 'madam' looks.

Problem one dealt with.

Problem two? How was he going to explain this to Louise?

Tara marched into the kitchen, where Louise was making breakfast and trying to stop herself planning another baking session this afternoon. Surely there were better ways to pamper oneself? A bubble bath or something?

'I thought you said it was all lies!' Tara said in a crisp voice. Louise turned to find her standing with her hands on her hips. She hadn't seen her since their midnight chat the night before, but the uncertain, off-kilter Tara was gone, replaced by a harder and glossier version of the original. Even though it was barely past eight and the only plans for the day was a quiet pub lunch in Lower Hadwell, Tara was in full make-up and high heels. The one concession to their country location was a fur trim at the top of each exquisitely-crafted Italian boot.

'What was lies?' Louise asked, sensing she wasn't going to like where this conversation was going. Tara seemed to have the hump with her. Maybe it was something to do with letting Louise seeing her so vulnerable. Tara Adams didn't *do* vulnerable.

Tara walked up to Louise and presented her with her iPad, showing a newspaper website. The headline made her eyes pop. The photo beneath it made them sting.

'I didn't say it was all lies,' she said, folding her arms across her chest. 'I just said some of it was lies, and that was the truth.'

Tara's mouth dropped open. 'Some friend you are! There's me spilling my guts and all the time you're hiding stuff from me, keeping secrets.'

She really didn't have an answer for that. She *had* kept Ben a secret from Tara. It had seemed the right thing to do at the time. 'I'm sorry,' she said, 'We haven't told anyone.' She smiled a weak smile at her friend. 'And you know what it's like in our world... New romances are tabloid fodder, but once the media has eaten them up and spat them out again, they don't always survive.'

Tara's nose wrinkled. '*Romance?* Seriously? With a gardener?'

Louise lifted her chin. 'He makes me happy.'

The other woman closed her eyes. 'It's worse than I thought. A hot, dirty fling is one thing, but you can't seriously be falling for this guy?'

Louise stopped breathing.

Was she? Was she falling for Ben?

'Oh, God, you are, aren't you?' Tara let her hands drop. 'Are you nuts?'

Louise shook her head. No. In fact, she felt the sanest she'd ever done since she'd moved to Whitehaven.

Tara pulled one of the chairs from round the table out and motioned for Louise to sit down while she sat opposite her. She placed the iPad on the table in front of them. 'It's never going to work, Lou. Can't you see that?'

Louise sat in the chair. Tara was wrong, and she was going to tell her exactly why. 'Why can't it work? He's a nice man. He's kind and caring and….everything Toby isn't.'

Tara's nose creased again. Louise was starting to find that really irritating. 'Nice? What a description! Since when have women like you and me ever wanted *nice*?'

Since Toby, actually. Cool and dashing were seriously overrated. And Ben was way more than just nice, but Louise didn't have Tara's gift with words, especially when she was put on the spot.

'You make that sound like it's a bad thing,' she said. 'But I'll take decent and honest over filthy rich and adulterous any day!'

Tara swung the iPad round so it was up the right way for Louise. 'Yup. Honest and decent. What a catch.'

Louise shook her head. There could be any one of a hundred reasons for a photo like that. Okay, ninety-eight of them were making The Feeling creep up her arms and chill her stomach, but the remaining two were still a possibility.

'Ben's not like that,' she said stubbornly. 'You know how they can make things look.'

Tara stopped glaring and her posture softened. 'Okay, maybe I do know that, but it doesn't change anything. A relationship with a civilian spells disaster, you know that.'

Louise's knee jiggled under the table. In her dreams it had worked, and so far her wishes had been coming true. Why couldn't this one?

She stared at her friend, and realised there was a self-satisfied gleam in Tara's eyes. In some twisted way she was enjoying this, enjoying that she was the one in control, who knew what to do, and Louise—as always—was the one who needed rescuing.

'I'm a "civilian" too, now,' she said quietly. She'd always hated the way Tara used that term.

Tara shook her head. 'And that's why your picture is plastered all over the front of the *Daily News,* is it? Ted and Marjorie from their council flat in Wapping get that kind of attention when Ted strays, do they? Don't kid yourself, Lou. You're famous, whether you want to be or not, and there's no going back. You can't undo it.'

She stared at the swirling grain of the wooden table, at a big knot in front of her, a perfect circle.

Tara reached across and laid her hand on top of Louise's, just Louise had done to her the night before. Her fingers felt cold and bony. 'Women like us need a certain kind of man,' she said calmly and far too reasonably. 'He can't possibly give you what you need, you know that.'

Something inside Louise's stomach started to flutter. No, that was wrong. So far Ben had given her everything she'd needed and more. He had to be the one for her. Had to be.

She pulled her hand away from under Tara's and placed it in her lap, out of reach. 'You're wrong.'

Tara's lips pursed. 'I don't think so.'

'I've been nothing but nice to you,' she said, narrowing her eyes. 'Why are you being so…so…critical, so unsupportive?'

Tara pulled face that said she was shocked and hurt to be considered anything of the sort. Never mind the constant nitpicking, the endless flow of 'advice' Louise had had to put up with over the years.

And then it hit her. She knew exactly why Tara was being this way.

'You're jealous,' she said, and folded her arms again.

Tara did a very passable impression of outraged hilarity, letting out a tiny bark of a laugh and pulling her lips into a shape that was half-smile, half-sneer. She pushed her chair back from the table and stood up. 'And you're deluded.'

Louise stood up too, shaking her head. 'You're just scared. You're too invested in the whole WAG thing to leave it behind, to do what I've done, even though your husband is cheating on you, so you just want to rain on my parade instead, to make yourself feel better.'

'My husband is *not* cheating on me!'

Louise just raised her eyebrows.

'He's not!' Tara said. 'I spoke with him this morning and he explained it all. I'm driving back after lunch so we can sort it out. It was just a silly mix up!'

'Sure.' Louise nodded. 'And Toby is the patron saint of faithful husbands…'

'You bitch!' Tara said, almost spitting the words out. 'I always knew you had a nasty side, Louise Thornton, but I put up with it because I knew you needed a friend. But if you want to moulder away in this draughty old house, wasting your life, then it's your choice. I can see there's no point in trying any more. My first assessment of the situation was definitely the right one: you're nuts!'

Her heel squeaked as the turned and marched out the kitchen. A moment later Louise heard her heading up the stairs.

She didn't know whether to rant and rage, sit down and have a good cry or just burst out laughing. *She* was nuts? Louise wasn't the one about to go back to her obviously cheating husband.

Tara *was* jealous. But not in that girls' school, mean-to-you-because-you're-prettier-than-I-am-way. She was scared, and Louise supposed she could understand that. She'd spent half her marriage feeling the same way. And Tara had invested in the whole WAG thing way more than Louise had done. If she admitted Louise had done the right thing by leaving Toby, by moving away and trying to have a normal life, then Tara's life would collapse around her like a house of cards.

She emerged from the kitchen to find Tara winging her way down the stairs, case in hand. She ignored Louise, stalked out the front door—leaving it open—then jumped in her sports car and zoomed away. Louise watched her go, a heavy feeling growing inside her.

Whitehaven hadn't worked for Tara. But then Tara hadn't let it. She was still too stuck in her old fears, rooted in her old ways.

Maybe she'd be back one day... When the next text message, or phone call, or front page news story came. Because Gareth would do it again if he thought he'd got away with it this time. He was every bit as clever as his wife, and he probably knew he held all the power, that she wouldn't leave until pushed to her absolute limit.

And if Tara let him do it? If she let him carry on like that in front of her, make a fool of her like that...? Well, sadly, Louise thought she might just deserve him.

Ben lugged his holdall through the front door and kicked it closed with his foot. He'd had to come back to see Louise after finding that article, even though he'd planned to be away another day or so. Thankfully, his sister had been understanding and had agreed to keep Jas until after new year. It meant he could deal with whatever cropped up in Lower Hadwell over the next few days without having to worry about her.

No sooner had he dropped his bag on the floor than there was a knock at the door. He paused and frowned. He wasn't expecting anyone, and no one—save his sister—knew he was back. Did this mean it had started already? That there were journalists camped out spying on his house?

His first thought was to open the front door and give them a piece of his mind. But then he remembered what Louise had said about unflattering pictures when a person was in mid-rant. And that last photographer had managed to make something innocuous seem seedy; he certainly didn't want to give them any more ammunition.

Whoever it was wasn't standing on the step, but back a bit, so he had to creep close to the door to try and get a look.

'Mr Oliver?'

It was a woman's voice. Sharp and slightly acerbic. She certainly didn't sound as if she wanted to butter him up to get an interview out of him. Not like the others who'd called his mobile while he'd been away.

'Yes,' he said through the door.

'I'm Tara Adams—a friend of Louise's.'

Undoubtedly, Jas would know whether that was true. She kept up with all the celebrity gossip via her mother, but Ben had no clue. He turned the lock and cracked the door open slightly. One look told him she was far too well dressed to be a journalist. He opened the door wider and looked around. Anyone could be out there. And the last thing he needed was another photograph that needed explaining.

'You'd better come in,' he said warily, and opened the door wider.

Tara Adams didn't seem to want to be here any more than he wanted her here. She looked down her nose and marched into his house.

'Would you like to come into the kitchen? Have a coffee?'

She shook her head and looked around the panelled hallway of his cottage. 'No. This will do fine.'

He folded his arms. 'How can I help you, Ms Adams?'

She blinked slowly and a slight smile spread across her lips. 'Actually, it's how I can help you—and Louise, of course.'

His lids lowered slightly. 'Go on.'

She inhaled. 'I thought I'd better warn you that you're heading for trouble by seeing her.'

Ben nodded. After the last few days, he knew exactly what kind of trouble being with Louise could bring.

'I know,' he said. 'The paparazzi have already done a hatchet job on me, but I can handle it.'

She stared at him for a moment. 'I wasn't talking about them.' She looked away and then back at him. 'You know she's coming to you on the rebound, right? Lou falls hard and I'd say she bounces hard too. It's not going to last.'

He hadn't warmed to this Tara the moment he'd clapped eyes on her, and she was endearing herself to him less and less. 'I'd say that's for Louise to decide.'

She laughed. An irritating, high little laugh that got right under his skin.

'You know, we joked about her having a hot and dirty little fling with a local yokel before she came down here. I think you're it.'

Ben clenched his teeth together. He didn't want to give any credence to what this woman said, but he was remembering how tempting it had been when he'd been freshly split from Megan, how he'd itched to do something similar. It was only the presence of Jasmine in his house, of how confused she'd already been, that had stopped him. But Louise wasn't like that. Was she?

Tara stood up tall and looked him in the eye. 'You can't give her what she needs,' she said airily, 'and the sooner you realise that the better. Like I said, you'll both end up getting hurt. You'd be better off leaving her alone and going back to that wife of yours.'

And then she just turned and walked back down the

hallway and let herself out, leaving Ben staring behind her.

Cow, he thought.

He found it hard to believe Louise was using him for sex, seeing as they hadn't actually made it into the bedroom yet, but...

She had wanted to that first night. It was because he'd thought she was vulnerable that he'd stopped her.

No. Don't be ridiculous. Louise isn't like that. You've known her for months. If she'd wanted to use you that way, she'd have pinned you up against the greenhouse wall and had her wicked way with you ages ago.

Ben took a moment to imagine what that would be like, but then shook himself. Focus. This wasn't the time.

The Louise Thornton the tabloids had created, the frigid snob who looked down her nose at everyone might have acted that way, but not his Louise. The real Louise was warm and giving and complicated, and just didn't know how to *take* like that. As soon as that thought dropped into place, he knew for certain that Tara was wrong.

But he had to admit, she might have something with the 'rebound' thing. It was a fairly common response after all, and Louise might be doing it without realising it. She desperately needed a confidence boost after what her ex had put her through.

He didn't want that. He didn't want to be her rebound guy. He didn't want to be the one she bounced to then bounced away from. He wanted to be the one she stuck with.

He went very still.

He wanted to be the one she stuck with.

For ever.

CHAPTER TWENTY-NINE

Louise tried phoning Ben after Tara had left, but she kept getting his voicemail. She didn't really have anything pertinent to discuss; she just wanted to hear his voice, know that he still felt the same way he had a couple of days ago. She needed him.

Since talking to him wasn't an option, she settled into one of her current daydreams…

She and Ben were living in his little cottage, and she had never been famous. No one ever knocked on their door wanting an interview. No one ever snapped their picture as they left the house looking a mess. No, they'd been teenage sweethearts, married since their early twenties, and everyone left them alone to live their lives and be happy.

But the strange thing was that the Louise in these daydreams had started to look different. Prettier. Thinner. More like the other mums at the school gate. She wore wellies instead of designer shoes and had her hair cut by a girl who came to the house.

And the more Louise crafted the fantasy version of

herself into Ben's perfect woman, the more she looked like…not someone else, exactly. But not quite like Louise, either. She tried time and time again to paste her face over the imaginary woman's one, but it kept slipping back into what it had been before. In the end, Louise got so frustrated, she went to the study to find something else to do.

After Tara's grand ideas about publication and syndication of Laura's diary last night, Louise had decided to lock it in the desk in the study, just in case. She retrieved it from its secure hiding place and sat down in a winged leather armchair to read.

5th September, 1956

The sun is high, the sky is blue. I can hear a wood pigeon cooing at the edge of the woods. Down below the Dart sparkles and dances, and now and then the geometric shape of a white or a red sail floats past a gap in the trees.

I am home. At Whitehaven. And it is mine.

It's been six months now since Jean's death. Still too soon, I know, but at least now everything is ready. I am here. Whitehaven is here. All we are missing is Dominic.

I walked down to the boathouse this morning. It's looking much better. After I moved in, I decided to get rid of all the shelves and ropes and cans of varnish and make it more like a summer house. I've moved my little writing desk down there and a few wicker chairs, even a picnic set.

I imagine us building fires on the stony beach at low tide and cooking sausages, or sitting on the veranda soaking up the sun. Making love inside in the shade of the afternoon.

And then I think that maybe it'll be different with Dominic. Maybe I'll be able to bear him sons and daughters. I know it's a long shot, but I find I can't quite give up that hope. I also think of that precious little girl of his and how she needs a mother.

Would Jean mind if I brought up her child? I don't know. Sometimes I think it'd make her jealous. Other times I think it would be the best thing I could do to make amends.

So...I am ready. The house is ready. Even the boat-house is just about ready.

All we are waiting for now is Dominic.

And one day he will be ready, I know it.

There was a crunch of boots on the gravel outside the study window. Louise jumped up from the chair and Laura's diary fell of her lap and onto the floor. Her heart pounded as if the noise had been a gun-shot.

She walked towards the long sash window. Was she seeing things right, or had she merely wished him here? For there was Ben staring back at her from the other side of the glass, looking very serious indeed. He was supposed to be in Exeter.

She flattened a palm against the window, wanting to reach out to him, but glad the barrier was in place. She stood motionless as he raised his hand and pressed it against the outside of the window, covering the outline of her hand completely.

Believe me, his eyes said, and the last bit of doubt about that photo of him and Megan evaporated. Ben was no Toby. He would never, *ever* be like Toby.

She glanced down at their hands, joined yet not joined, close but not touching, and then she looked back up at him. She must have been speaking without words too, because his expression changed, became less serious...warmer. The eyes spoke again. *Let me in*, they said.

Wordlessly, she peeled her hand away and moved towards the study door. Ben mirrored her, and when she opened the heavy, panelled front door, he was standing there, waiting. Now, with no transparent barrier between them, they both hesitated. It was Ben who broke the silence.

'I can explain.'

She almost didn't need the words. His face told her everything she needed to know. The pain etched there broke her heart and she wrapped her arms around his neck and pulled him to her. He gave no resistance and walked into her arms, burying his face in the hollow of her neck. 'I'm sorry,' he whispered against her skin. 'She came to apologise. I was careless.'

She nodded, her chin butting into his shoulder. 'Why are you here? Where's Jas?'

He took a step back and steadied himself—or was it her?—by placing a hand on each of her shoulders.

'She's with my sister. Believe me, I'm heavily in debt in the babysitting stakes. But I had to see you, to know you were okay.'

He smoothed the hair away from her face with such tenderness. Her eyes began to tingle and fill. 'I'm okay. We're okay. It just…shook me for a moment.'

'You're sure? Because if you want me to go away I will. If you need space, you've got it. You know that, Louise, anything you need…'

She shook her head and her lip quavered. Nothing like Toby at all, this man. 'No. I don't want you to go,' she said quietly. 'I want you right here.'

Colour that she hadn't realised had been missing returned to his face and his whole body seemed to exhale. It was as if that simple question had been about a whole lot more than whether he came inside or not. She didn't understand why, but she seemed to have given him the right answer. She tried a shaky smile and it seemed to work.

'Come on,' she said. 'Let's do something normal. How about a walk?' Although the forecast had warned rain, it was still dry with bright clouds blocking out the sun. 'We can catch up as we go.'

'First things first,' Ben said, his mouth hitching in a lopsided smile, and then he stepped in and kissed her as he'd never kissed her before. It wasn't just lips and breath that mingled; there was longing and fulfilment, passion and tenderness, giving and taking. This was the Technicolor ® kiss of her daydreams.

When he pulled away, Louise swayed towards him a little, eyes still half shut.

'Come,' he said, tugging her hand, and Louise took a few moments to work out what he meant. Oh, yes. The walk.

'I have something to ask you,' he said as he set off in the direction of the top lawns, pulling her with him.

'What?' she replied, finding her voice a little unsteady.

Ben walked in silence for a few moments, looking straight ahead, and then he began to talk. 'I didn't mention it before, because we were keeping things quiet and then I expected to be at my sister's for New Year, but now I'm here and...'

'Ben,' Louise said, squeezing his hand, 'try making some sense, please?'

He turned and smiled at her. 'Sorry. Guess I'm a little nervous. It's been a long time since I've asked a woman out on a date.'

'A date?' she asked, her eyes wide. 'Like dinner and a movie kind of a date?'

'Not quite,' he said slowly. 'Perhaps it was fate that this all came out in the press. I'd wanted to ask you, but I didn't think we'd be going out in public for a while.' He paused. 'Lord Batterham is having a New Year's Ball at his home tonight and he sent me an invitation. I'd very much like it if you'd come with me.'

Oh.

'A ball...? But there'll be lots of people there... They'll see us!'

Ben gave her a wry smile. 'Half the country knows our secret anyway,' he said, 'and we've got nothing to be ashamed about. Maybe by just going out, by just being honest about what's going on, we can stop all the madness. We can't hide away at Whitehaven for ever.'

Hiding. Yes, she'd done lots of that since her split with Toby. Hadn't she already reprimanded herself for the same thing? Hadn't she told herself to be more outward-facing than inward-looking?

Ben stopped and turned, looking very serious. 'I don't want to be your dirty little secret, Louise. I don't want to have to hide away. I want to be the man who everyone knows is by your side—the man who wants to *stay* by your side.'

Who wouldn't weaken at such words, at that intense look he was giving her? She drew her bottom lip in under her teeth and released it again before grabbing his hand and walking past him back towards the house. He didn't budge when their arms stretched to the limit. Louise turned and found him looking very confused.

'No time for a walk,' she said with an apologetic smile. 'Do you know how long it takes a woman like me to get ready?'

Ben slowed his car to a crawl in the narrow lane that led him to Whitehaven. He'd jumped back in his dinghy a few hours ago, rushed home to change, and was now heading back to Louise in a suitable mode of transport. In places only an ancient stone wall separated the road from a steep hill that fell away into the river. Tall pines and beeches towered overhead and, even if the moon had deigned to glimpse from behind a cloud, it wouldn't have illuminated much.

The road dipped halfway down the hill, signalling the descent that led to Whitehaven's main gate, and Ben's stomach dipped with it. The last week had been an emotional roller coaster ride, yet those seven short days now felt like a lifetime.

Cold swirled around him—not from the vents; they were blasting warm air. It was just the physical reaction he seemed to have every time he thought about how those stories in the paper might have ruined things for him and Louise. He never wanted to feel that way again.

In the drive from Exeter to see her, he'd felt completely unhitched from any point in reality. She turned him inside out and upside down. And, a couple of months ago, he would have thought that a bad thing.

Perhaps he was going insane. That would certainly account for the small, satin-covered box in his pocket. It would make sense of the square-cut diamond nestled within. Just like a magpie, he hadn't been able to resist it when he'd seen it in the jeweller's window. Not that he was going to do anything with it yet. It was far too soon. It was just with him for safekeeping. For luck.

Amidst the shifting shapes of the wind-blown branches, his headlights fell upon the thick, vertical posts of Whitehaven's gates. The level drive traversed the hill with only a slight curve. He squeezed his foot on the accelerator. Not that he was late; just because he needed to.

He parked right outside the front door. The gravel drive was probably murder to negotiate in high heels. Feeling as nervous as a sixteen-year-old on his first proper date, he eased himself from the car and rang the bell. No one came. It was only as he reached for it a second time that he noticed the small note taped underneath it. '*Come inside. L x.*'

Now his heart really started to race. He entered the flagstone hallway and paused. 'Louise?'

'Up here.' Her voice drifted down through the crystals in the hanging chandelier. 'I'll be one more minute.'

Now, the untrained observer would have expected a woman like Louise to keep him waiting, but it didn't surprise him in the least when, almost exactly sixty seconds later, he heard a door open upstairs and the swish of expensive fabric on the landing.

At first he couldn't see her properly. The glittering crystals in the chandelier distorted his view. But, as she reached the top of the stairs and started to descend, he got the whole picture.

He couldn't say anything. He couldn't smile. He couldn't even breathe.

The dress was long—the shade of midnight—in some heavy, shiny fabric that flared slightly as it fell to her ankles. And her hair…it was held in glossy waves and pinned up in the back, just like a nineteen-twenties silent movie star.

'You look stunning,' he managed to mutter as she reached the foot of the stairs and smiled at him. Just as well he got that out before she turned round and revealed the impossibly low back.

Unfortunately, he needed to go to this party to keep Lord Batterham sweet, otherwise he'd have been tempted to see if that satin was a soft as it looked, if it would fall off her shoulders easily and ripple as it slid to her feet.

She gave him a sweet, sexy smile as she wound a wrap around her shoulders. She walked towards him and picked up a little bag from the hall table. 'And you don't look too bad yourself, either. I must say, for the gardener, you scrub up pretty good.'

Pretty good? He'd show her.

Before she could back away, he caught her in his arms, pressed his lips to hers and showed her just how *good* he could be.

That horrible, scratchy feeling that had plagued her since the argument with Tara had finally disappeared. She hadn't noticed when it had subsided, all she knew was that standing here, in the grand ballroom of Batterham Hall, with Ben at her side, and the magic was alive and spinning again.

As the minute hand on the ridiculously ornate clock crept towards midnight, she felt as if she'd emerged from under a huge cloud. Finally, the past was behind her and she could look forward again. And not just to tomorrow, but beyond and beyond and beyond.

She'd been quite relieved to discover that half of Lord Batterham's guests had no idea who she was. Apparently, *Buzz* magazine wasn't popular reading amongst the upper crust. And, although she'd thought she'd find some of the guests stuffy and aloof, she'd warmed to many of the people she'd met.

And there was Ben. Always there. Always anticipating what she needed before she opened her mouth to express it. Not in the annoying, sycophantic way some people did, but just in his own unique, matter-of-fact, *I knew you needed it, so I got it* kind of a way. His impeccable manners were making him a huge hit—she half-suspected there were a couple of elderly countesses who were plotting to steal him away.

The small orchestra finished their piece and paused while the master of ceremonies announced a waltz to take them up to midnight, now only five minutes away.

Ben, who had cleverly managed to be otherwise engaged for most of the dancing, now swung her into his arms and struck the appropriate pose.

'Ben, I know you're wonderful, but do mind this dress with those great feet of yours. It's vintage Chanel.'

'My feet will behave themselves impeccably,' he said without a trace of irony, even though he'd managed to stamp on her toes at least ten times already this evening. Gardening, yes. Dancing, no. But somehow that just made him all the more adorable.

'I've been practising this one,' he said proudly. 'I wanted to learn more but Gaby, Luke's wife, refused to teach me anything else. She said this was all I'd be able to handle.'

God bless Gaby, thought Louise, as they started to move around the floor.

But, as they continued to move, he surprised her. Okay, he wouldn't win any competitions, but she stopped being terrified for her dress and started to enjoy herself. Round and round they went, circling the vast ballroom. Is this what it felt like—to have all your dreams come true? Because right at this moment she was living in a fairy tale.

The music began to fade and it took her a couple of seconds to realise that the musicians were actually ending the waltz, not that everything was melting away into a dream world but Ben and herself.

The first shout made her jump. 'Ten…'

She looked at Ben, who was grinning at her, looking very pleased about something.

'Nine…eight…' the chant around them continued.

'What?' she asked, starting to smile back.

'Seven…six…five…'

He nodded upwards and bent his head back to look towards the ceiling. They were standing directly underneath a large display of greenery, dripping with bright white lights and, tied at the bottom with a sumptuous red bow, was a generous sprig of mistletoe.

She laughed, then silenced quickly as a very serious look appeared in Ben's eyes—one that made her knees tremble and her heart rate double.

'Four…three…two…'

'One,' he said, then delivered a kiss that shook her to the toes of her sparkly shoes. The cheering and clapping and congratulating carried on around them, but it was if she and Ben were in their own separate bubble.

Were you allowed to make wishes at New Year, or

was that only on birthdays and when stars fell? Because she wished that it could always be like this—total perfection, just like her dreams.

When Ben ended the kiss, she couldn't bear to open her eyes. Instead, she threw her arms around his neck and hugged him tight enough to make her arm muscles shake. Pressed right up against his chest, she could feel his heart beating, racing even faster than her own.

He kissed the tip of her earlobe and a shudder ran through her. Then he whispered in her ear. 'I love you, Louise.'

She froze. All around her the dream began to splinter. And she had no idea why, because those words should have been the perfect prelude to a happy ever after. She only knew she this was *too* real, *too*...much.

'Louise?' There was a shake in his voice and she hated the fact that she'd put it there. She pulled away from him and smoothed down the antique satin of her dress. 'I think we should leave,' she said, unable to look at him. She was angry with herself for hurting him and, perhaps a little unreasonably, angry with him, too.

Ben ran after her as she marched off to the cloakroom and retrieved her wrap. She could tell he was itching to talk to her, but there were too many people around. And, coward that she was, she was glad.

Within five minutes they were in the warm of his car, pulling out of the gates of Batterham Hall and weaving down the country lanes back towards home.

'It's too fast, isn't it?' Ben finally said grimly. 'I got carried away.'

'Are you saying you didn't mean it?'

'No! I mean…no' he said in a quieter tone. 'I would never play with your feelings that way.'

Not intentionally. But men were apt to promise the world when they were swept up in the first flush of love. Toby had been the same. It didn't mean it was going to last a lifetime. Just at the hint of the possibility it wouldn't, her stomach turned to ice. Oh, she really didn't understand what was going on inside her head this evening!

She did her best to explain it to Ben, staring at her lap mostly and only risking the odd glance across at him as he drove. 'It's all so new. How can we possibly tell what we are really feeling? We're riding the first wave of infatuation and we need to leave ourselves time to get past it.' There. That sounded much more reasonable.

He took his eyes off the road and turned his head sharply to look at her. 'You think I'm just infatuated with you?'

She'd made him angry. That hadn't been her intention at all. He glared at her for a hard second, then returned his attention to the road. An instant denial should have popped out of her mouth by now, shouldn't it?

'No,' she said slowly.

'I'm not infatuated with you, Louise.'

Suddenly, he swung into a passing place on the narrow road and wrenched the handbrake on. He reached upwards and flicked a switch for a small light in the ceiling of the car. She swallowed. She'd always sensed that beneath the down-to-earth, practical exterior, Ben was a man who cared passionately and felt deeply. She just hadn't expected it all to burst to the surface tonight.

He turned to stare out of the windscreen. 'Okay, maybe I am a little bit infatuated, if I think that everything about you is amazing, if I want to be with you all the time, if all I want to do is make you happy...'

Unshed tears clogged her throat. They were wonderful words, but if she picked them apart just a little...

Everything about her definitely wasn't amazing, and that told her she was more right than she wanted to be. They *did* need more time. Why couldn't he see that?

He turned just his head to face her, and his eyes were burning. 'It's more than that, Louise.'

She shook her head. 'You can't know that for sure. Not yet.'

His mouth settled into a grim line. 'You're wrong. I know what I feel, what I want. I've never been more certain. It's *you* who doesn't know for sure.'

How could she know? Real life wasn't like daydreams or the movies when it all became obvious in a blinding split-second. She'd felt this way before and she'd been spectacularly wrong. Of course she wasn't sure!

'I suppose the lack of a reply tells me exactly where I stand,' he said grimly as he put the car into gear and drove away.

CHAPTER THIRTY

Ben felt as if he'd been kicked in the chest. This wasn't the reaction he'd hoped for when he'd leaned in close and whispered in Louise's ear. In that moment, everything had finally been going right for them, but now Louise was pushing him away as hard as she could and he couldn't help thinking it had been his own stupid fault. Something he'd said or done had triggered Louise's panic button. He needed to find out what—and why.

When they arrived at her house, he insisted on accompanying her inside, sure that if he left it now, she would retreat inside her shell. He had to talk to her now, while it was all brimming on the surface.

She wasn't pleased about him being there. An air of irritation hung about her as she led him into the drawing room and poured him a miserly brandy. He took a seat across the room from her as she perched on a dark purple velvet sofa.

He did his best to keep the irritation from his tone, but his ego was still smarting a little from being

so very firmly rebuffed. How had he got things so
wrong?

'Talk to me.'

She took a deep breath and he saw her shutters rise.
For five long minutes she did nothing but stare into the
cold fireplace. Then, still keeping her gaze locked on it,
she said, 'I'm scared, Ben. I so want it to be real, but I
don't know how to trust if it is or not. How do you tell?'

He crossed the room and sat down beside her. He
knew she was scarred, that the wounds went deep, but
she'd seemed so different recently: happier, freer...

She leaned against him, but still continued to stare
into the empty fireplace. He placed an arm lightly round
her shoulders and stroked the soft skin of her upper arm
with his fingers. She didn't push him away. With great
difficulty he pushed aside his own need for an answer,
for resolution, and waited.

When she spoke, her voice was so soft he had to
strain to hear it. 'Right from when I was very young, life
was about putting other people first—which isn't a bad
thing. Don't get me wrong. But even when I didn't want
to, I had no choice. So, I used to daydream about the life
I couldn't have while I was being mother to my younger
brothers and sisters and taking care of my father.' She
turned to look at him and his heart broke to see her eyes
full of such pain. 'I suppose it was my survival mecha-
nism.'

'We all have those,' he said quietly.

She turned back and he guessed she found it easier not to look him.

'Well, one day,' she continued, 'someone walked up to me and offered me all my dreams wrapped up in a sparkly box with a big bow—fame, success, recognition, enough money so I'd never have to worry about not having any clothes except my school uniform, enough money so I wouldn't see the little ones' eyes when I served up beans on toast for tea again...and love. I thought I'd found love.'

He sighed. Louise had had the kind of childhood he worked his hardest to protect Jasmine from. He thought of this brave woman, not much older than his daughter, running a household, studying, caring for a sick relative. Who would blame her for reaching for the dream?

'And so I was selfish. I chose something for myself.' She buried her face in her hands and the tears came thick and fast. Ben hugged her tight and kissed the top of her head. He knew exactly who would blame her for such a thing—she blamed herself. One by one the puzzle pieces clicked into place, fragments of things she'd told him that suddenly made sense—her relationship with Toby, her father, why she continued to push people away and punish herself.

'You can't blame yourself for your father's death.'

Louise broke down completely. She cried so hard she could scarcely breathe, let alone speak. Years of guilt and pain, of grieving she had never allowed herself to do, came spilling out in one go. He hugged her fiercely, as if he could protect her from it by sheer strength.

Through the sobs she croaked, 'But I...shouldn't have...left him!'

People thought she'd stuck with Toby all those years because she wanted the glitz and glamour more than she wanted her self-respect. How wrong they were. It came to him with crystal clarity: Louise had stayed with Toby because she believed she'd deserved him.

Tobias Thornton had been her penance.

Louise opened one eye. Stark light sliced through the windows, bearing testimony to the fact that she'd been too exhausted to remember to draw the curtains when she'd crawled upstairs in the small hours of the morning.

Her eyes, her head, even her throat ached. Nerves tickled her tummy. She had that awful sick feeling in her stomach. Too many emotions, too many tears. She wanted to call it all back and pretend it hadn't happened. What must Ben think of her now?

At the thought of him, she raised herself on one elbow. Last time she'd seen him he was curling up on the sofa with a blanket—which was completely ridiculous, seeing as she had at least ten empty bedrooms—but he'd insisted.

She got out of bed and her foot met something slippery and incredibly smooth. Her dress lay in a heap where she'd let it drop before falling into bed. She picked it up and draped it over a low, upholstered chair in the corner before wandering into her bathroom and having a shower.

There was no noise from downstairs when she emerged. Yesterday morning, she'd have been rushing downstairs to meet Ben. Today she wasn't even sure she wanted to see him.

She pressed her forehead against the cold glass of the bathroom mirror and let her breath obscure her reflection. Wishes and dreams were all very well when they stayed inside your head, but once they crossed the threshold into the real world, they were fragile, vulnerable—like the thin glass of the baubles on a Christmas tree.

What was wrong with her? Hadn't she been aching to hear those words from his lips? And the reality had been even better than the fantasy. Hadn't she wanted someone to look at her the way Ben looked at her? To see right inside her?

But there was her problem. Daydream Louise had been her better self, her angel. When Real Louise looked deep down to see what Ben saw, it wasn't comfortable at all. No sugar, no spice, no all things nice. Just fear and loneliness and broken parts of the person she'd once been that she didn't know how to fix. And if Ben couldn't see all that, maybe he wasn't *really* seeing her after all.

She walked to the dressing table and picked up a comb and untangled her hair with unforgiving strokes.

She reasoned that it was far too early to go and wake him, that she'd be better off finding something to do up here until a more sociable hour, so she flopped back down on her bed in her towel and reached for Laura's diary.

Maybe Laura had the answers. Maybe she'd found a way to have her happy ending with Dominic and that would give Louise hope.

14th April, 1957

Dominic finally answered my letter—a year and a month after his wife passed away. I was so thrilled when I recognised his handwriting on the envelope, but less thrilled when I read the note inside.

It wasn't that it was rude or dismissive, or even unkind. It was just...short. And ambiguous. He said he needed to speak with me face to face, that he was coming down to Devon to visit an old school friend and wanted to drop in on me. He'd heard I'd bought Whitehaven and was interested in seeing it again.

It all seemed positive, yet...

I don't know. Perhaps I'm just having trouble believing happiness is now within my grasp. I've been in limbo for so long.

Louise looked up and stared out the window. Maybe

that was her problem too? Maybe she'd forgotten how to hope, just like Laura?

Anyway, the day came. I can't tell you how many times I changed my dress or how my stomach fluttered so. And then he was finally knocking at the door. I ran to it, threw it wide and…stopped.

It wasn't just Dominic standing there, but Caroline too. She was holding his hand and looking up at me with her dark curls and her mother's eyes. I smiled anyway. I greeted them and invited them inside. I produced tea and cakes and scones. We sat in the drawing room and made small talk.

I'd imagined that when Dominic and I could finally be together we'd be making love, not drinking tea and minding crumbs and talking about the weather.

Finally, I suggested a walk in the garden—up on the top lawn, where the child could run and play safely within the walled garden—and Dominic and I would be able to talk.

That connection we had right from the beginning was still there. I could feel it tugging at me, drawing me to him. Just one look in his eyes told me he felt it too. I began to feel lighter, more hopeful… I started to ignore the sadness that now lingered round him. I blinded myself to the lines under his eyes and the tightness of his shoulders.

'Thank you for coming,' I said, as we both walked

our eyes on Caroline as she circled one of the small apple trees again and again and again. 'It's been too long... I've missed you so much.'

And then, bothersome woman that I am, I began to cry. And I couldn't stop. Dominic put his arm round me and I felt him take a big shuddering breath too. Eventually, Caroline got curious, and came to give me a leaf she'd found. I smiled and thanked her, even though I couldn't even see what it was, and she ran off smiling. That only made me cry more.

I turned to face him, looked him in the eye. 'I love you, Dominic. I will always love you. But I need to know if you feel the same way still. I need to know if there's hope.'

His eyes told me all I could wish to know.

Yes, he loved me still. Yes, there was hope.

I leaned forward and pressed my lips to his. The sensation—one I'd waited for and dreamed about for so long—actually made me giddy. But after meeting me gently, kissing me tenderly but briefly, he pulled away and focused on his daughter.

I think that's when I knew it was all going to turn to dust, that my dreams were only ashes and my wishes only curses.

'I love you too,' he whispered. 'But I can't... we can't...' He turned to look at me and shook his head. 'I'm sorry. Too much has happened. Too much I can't undo.'

I tried to argue, to reason with him, but he wouldn't have it. I told him to wait a while, that maybe he wasn't ready, that maybe it was too soon, that we'd tried to go too fast, but he just shook his head and called for his daughter.

'I came here today to say goodbye, Laura,' he said, and then he closed his eyes and kissed me on the cheek, kissed me like he was breathing me in and saving me up for himself, and then he took Caroline's hand and walked out of my garden and out of my life. I know I'll never see him again.

Louise dropped the book on the bed, unable to see any more, her eyes were so blurry with tears. That was the second to last entry. She couldn't bear to turn the final page. There was no more story left to tell. Laura had wasted her life on a lie, trusted the dream to solidify and become real and it never had.

Or had it? Who was the man mentioned in that documentary years ago? Had Dominic finally come round or had she found happiness with someone else? She really needed to know. And when she'd had the inevitable conversation with Ben this morning, she'd get on the internet and find out. She'd strung this thing along too far already.

She wiped her eyes and sat on her bed staring at the wall. There was nothing else to do. She'd finished her paperback and her phone and laptop were downstairs.

Quarter of an hour more. That would be a sensible time to go downstairs, she reasoned. But she left it half an hour, and then fifteen minutes more.

When she could delay it no longer she padded down the sweeping staircase, dressed in a grey tracksuit and large pink slippers. The echoing silence made it seem colder than it really was and she crossed her arms across her chest and hugged herself.

She found a note in the kitchen: '*Be back soon. Something I have to sort out. Ben.*'

That just flipped her switch from sad to angry again. Just as she'd finally worked up the nerve to face him, he'd upped and disappeared? Besides, she liked anger better. It blocked out that nasty cold sensation that was trying to creep up on her. She'd thought The Feeling only applied to cheating husbands, but it seemed it made itself known when any relationship was going down the pan, like an icy prophet.

Stoking her irritation, she scrunched Ben's note into a little ball and threw it in the bin. Then, while the kettle boiled, she rehearsed the coming argument in her head. Who had given him the job of deciding what she needed? *She* ought to be what she needed, and she certainly didn't need some man to step into the slot Toby had left and take over her life. Okay, Ben wasn't the same. He was full of concern rather than apathy, but that didn't make her feel any less overruled, overshadowed.

She was losing herself again, and that wasn't good. Remember how she'd been when he'd been at his sister's? Feeling as if nothing was right if he wasn't by her side, telling herself she needed him. And what had all those cosy little domestic fantasies been about? Why had she been trying to change herself into something she wasn't?

She'd become the WAG for Toby; it would be just as dangerous to become the mousy little housewife for Ben.

As she drained the last of her cup of tea, she heard a knock at the back door and turned to see him standing there, his face grim. Outside, she might have looked as if she didn't care if he was there or not. Inside, she was seething. She walked over, opened the door, then walked away again before he could touch her.

'Is this how it's going to be from now on? You backing away every time I come near you?' His voice rose in volume. 'And what exactly did I do that was so awful? I told you I loved you!'

Joy and pain stabbed Louise straight in the heart. She knew he thought he was telling her the truth. But she was scared. Scared that the shiny gift he was offering her, the one that promised to be all she'd ever wished for, would turn out to be fake once again.

'I know you're scared,' Ben said, and the stabbing sensation came again, this time in her stomach. She didn't like it when he looked into her head like that. It made her feel transparent, vulnerable.

'We can do this,' he was saying, but Louise was only half-listening. 'If you'd just let me help you—help *us*. I can believe for both of us until you're strong enough. If you need space, you've got it. If you need time, then take it. Whatever you need for the conditions to be right for our relationship to grow. The rest will follow.'

Louise's ears pricked up. That was just how he'd talked about those hibernating little scrubby plants in the greenhouse all those months ago. And she wasn't weak. She wasn't. She was strong. A survivor. Once again, he was seeing her all wrong.

Ben was still talking, oblivious to her growing frown. 'What we've got could flourish into something amazing, something that could last a lifetime.'

She backed away, still shaking her head. 'I'm not one of your stupid plants, you know, something to be trained or cultivated. You can't fix me, Ben. I don't want to be your next project. I don't want you to love me for who I can be when you've finished with me. If you're going to love me, love who I am now—with all my hang-ups and damage—not the perfect vision of a Louise that may never be. And if you can't then perhaps I don't need you at all.'

Ben stopped walking and stared at her. How could he convince her? Of course he loved her—all of her—but she was refusing to accept that for some reason. She was finding excuses to bat him away.

'I know I messed up, Louise. And I know I jumped in too fast, but that's only because…I've never felt this way about anyone else—ever. It excites me, confuses me, scares the life out of me. I don't want to lose you.'

Her shutters fell again, and this time they were clamped down and double-bolted. With an increasing sick feeling in his gut, he realised that this was the kick-back from last night. She was too raw, and she was protecting herself the only way she knew how. It was easier to be this way than to let herself deal with any of the other things last night's conversation had brought up. And he wasn't going to get anywhere by pushing.

But he was going to leave her in no doubt as to how he felt about her before he gave her the space she needed. She had to believe him about that. Knowing she would just retreat if he approached her, he stayed rooted to the spot, and hoped the truth of his words could pierce her shield.

He wanted to say something, beautiful, elegant, poetic—something to reflect just a tiny bit of what he felt for her, but his mind was blank. No flowery words seemed to measure up. So he spoke it with his eyes, his body, his whole being, and finally, he simply said, 'I love you. That's all. No expectations, no requirements, no pressure. What you do with that is up to you.'

The shield around her buckled just enough for him to

see a deep yearning ache behind the fire in her eyes. She wanted to believe him, but she was too scared, and he tried to pinpoint why that was. What was the overriding factor here?

Guilt.

The word popped into his head as if someone had whispered it in his ear.

The irony of it all hit him like a blow in the solar plexus. Once again, he was offering all he had—his heart, his life, his love—to a woman, and it wasn't enough. While she nursed her guilt anything he could give her, even if he wrapped the whole universe up and put it in a silver box, would never be enough.

Until she believed she deserved the happy ever after she yearned for so desperately, it would always be out of her reach. Until she understood she was worth being loved, she would always doubt him. Always. And that tiny speck of doubt, like a grain of sand would irritate and irritate until she couldn't stand it any more. Even if he could talk her round now, their relationship would die from a slow-acting poison.

He had to let her go. Just the thought of that made his nose burn and his eyes sting. He coughed the sensation away.

Louise was looking at him with a strange mix of irritation and confusion on her face. It took all his strength not to reach for her, not to kiss her one last time. His feet felt heavy as he made his way to the kitchen door.

He opened it, stepped through, then turned to take one last look.

'You win,' he said. 'Maybe I'm not what you need. But I could be—if only you'd let me.' He shook his head. 'Goodbye, Louise. You know where I am when you're ready to come and find me.' Then he closed the door behind him and walked away.

CHAPTER THIRTY-ONE

Louise became more of a hermit than ever. She didn't want to risk crossing the river into Lower Hadwell and running into Ben. She didn't want to run into *anyone*. There had been plenty of people who'd seen them together on New Year's Eve and there was bound to be talk. The fact there was nothing more to talk about now would just make things worse.

He'd left her. He'd walked away and left her, the one thing she'd never thought he would do.

It didn't help that she knew she'd pushed him away, given him the first shove. She'd thought a man like Ben would stay anyway. He hadn't seemed the leaving kind.

Had she been testing him? Pushing him away to see what he'd do? She wasn't sure. Whatever her motivation, he'd failed the test. Maybe their lives were too different after all. Maybe, like Dominic and Laura, their time was brief and magical but would never translate into a proper future.

So Louise didn't dream about Ben any more. She

didn't wish for him. She didn't wish for anything—
except that the minutes would go faster until Jack came
home.

In the meantime she cleaned up the house, investiga-
ted the stables to see if they really would be a good restoration project, and she finally gave her curiosity over
Laura Hastings full rein and researched her life and
career.

It turned out that Laura had stayed at Whitehaven on
her own. There were no more husbands. Rumours of a
couple of romances, but nothing that lasted. But she'd
got very involved in wildlife preservation and children's charities. There was even a picture in one biogra-
phy showing a large picnic on Whitehaven's front lawn.
Laura had paid for almost a hundred inner-city children
to come and spend the day at her home, giving them a
break from the relentless greyness of their urban lives.
There was even a hint she'd planned to continue the tra-
dition, but her health had prevented it.

It seemed Alex had become seriously ill a few years
after their split, and Laura had invited him to come
and stay with her when the doctors said nothing more
could be done. Alex's presence at Whitehaven for those
tragic six months explained why Louise remembered a
husband being mentioned in connection with the place.
Alex and Laura might not have reconciled, but they'd
forgiven each other and moved on. Healed.

Laura had known this house could help with that. She

just hadn't predicted correctly who and what it would help. Laura had been holding Alex's hand when he died and, apparently, there was a small memorial to him somewhere in Louise's woods. She decided she would find it and look after it, because she was sure Laura would have done so as long as she could.

Dominic also never remarried. His career had petered out after Jean's death. Somehow he just hadn't had the verve and energy cinema-going audiences had loved about him any more. But he and his daughter had been comfortably off and Dominic had founded an acting school that still ran to this day. Toby had even been kicked out of it when he was younger, although Louise had no idea there'd been a connection until she'd started digging into Laura's past.

Caroline, of course, had followed in her mother's footsteps and grown up to be a singer and had a string of hits in the late seventies and early eighties. She now lived in Italy with her aristocratic husband and a gaggle of beautiful children—one of whom Louise had met, as she'd been the hottest supermodel of the day when Louise had been working. Strange, how her and Laura's lives touched so much, even though they'd never met.

After reading the diary, Louise felt as if she'd met her, so she didn't take up Tara's suggestion to sell the story and make a shedload of money. No, Laura had hidden that diary to keep it secret, and Louise understood the need for privacy, the need to at least keep some things for yourself. She was sure Laura wouldn't have wanted it all to come out. Not once in any of the film clips, interviews or books Louise had trawled through had she mentioned Dominic, so Louise too would keep her silence.

She placed her folder of research, now complete, into the drawer of the little desk in the boathouse, along with the diary, locked it and then let it all be at peace, safely tucked out of the way from prying eyes.

And she decided to start her own diary. It had helped Laura, hadn't it? Helped her to get her feelings out on paper and sort things out in her head. Louise could do with a bit of that herself.

So she ordered a nearly identical notebook from an online stationery company, and also a nice fountain pen. Her round, schoolgirlish scrawl was nowhere as elegant as Laura's had been, though. Never mind. Maybe that was something she could learn.

After letting her nib hover over the page for a good minute, she lowered it and began to write:

Dear Laura,
You don't know me, but I feel as if I know you. I found your diary in the fireplace in the boathouse. I wasn't stealing or prying—just cleaning. I own Whitehaven now. I think it called me, just like it called you. I hope you're right about its being special, because I could really do with some 'special' in my life right now. My

marriage is over, the man I thought was going to be The One has walked away...

But you know all about that, don't you? You understand.

Anyway, I wanted you to know that I'm going to start the picnics up again. A charity that helps kids who have to act as carers for their parents called up the other day, asking me if I'd like to get involved in a more practical way, to become a patron. I said yes, of course. And the first thing that came to mind was that lovely photo of the lawn filled with children eating sausage rolls and drinking lemonade.

I thought Easter would be a good time. Very symbolic. A time of new life and fresh starts. Everyone can do with some of that (especially me). We're going to start small—just twenty kids at first—and then build up from there. We'll see...

I'd really like to see firsthand what this house can do.

Best wishes,

Louise.

The day before school started up again, Toby brought Jack back to Whitehaven. Louise was waiting on the driveway for the sound of a car and when Toby parked and Jack flew out of the back passenger door, Louise ran towards him and scooped him and hugged him close until he squirmed and moaned and begged to be let down. Even then she hung onto him for a couple more seconds.

'Just wait till I tell Jas where I've been!' he said. 'Is she coming round this afternoon? It's Sunday!'

Louise shook her head. 'Sorry, sweetheart. She and…her dad…are doing something else today.' She didn't know exactly what, but she'd bet they wouldn't be making an appearance at Whitehaven today, so they had to be somewhere doing something. Anyway, Jack would probably see Jas in the village over the next couple of weeks. They could catch up then.

Her son seemed satisfied with her reply, because he said, 'Is there cake, Mum?'

Louise couldn't help smiling. 'What do you think?'

Jack just grinned and ran off in the direction of the kitchen.

'There's peanut butter cookies and chocolate muffins and lemon poppyseed cake!' she called over her shoulder. When she straightened, she found Toby standing in front of her, looking as every bit as gorgeous as the day she'd first met him. How was that fair?

'Did I hear something about cake?' he asked, smiling that smile of his—the one he used to charm people into getting what he wanted.

Louise was about to tell him exactly where he could stuff the cake when she remembered Laura and Alex, how they'd managed to put the past behind them and find some peace. Maybe she should do that with Toby.

It would be better for Jack in the long run, even if a little carbohydrate-related assault might be fun in the short term.

'Of course,' she said. 'Come inside.'

Jack had already attacked the chocolate muffins, leaving the lid off the tin, and had run off again by the time they reached the kitchen. Louise nudged the tin in her very-soon-to-be ex-husband's direction. 'Knock yourself out.'

Toby took one and bit into it. He closed his eyes and murmured his appreciation. Louise should have been pleased, she supposed, but she couldn't help thinking of another man in this kitchen doing the same thing, and she was doing her level best not to think about him at all.

'How have you been?' Toby asked, sitting on the edge of her kitchen table.

'Fine.' She was fine. *Feeling* fine would come later.

He put the cake down and walked towards her, stopping when he was close but not too close. 'I've missed you, Lulu,' he said. His eyes were warm and clear and Louise very nearly believed him. Her heart kicked in her chest. She must have been looking wide-eyed and approachable, because Toby stepped closer, placed his palm on the side of her face and leaned in for a soft, gentle kiss.

Louise felt the tingle right down to her toes. But chemistry had never been a problem between her and

Toby. It was what had kept them going when everything else had crumbled. It was what had kept Louise with him, believing it must prove something about how he felt for her.

She didn't push him away. She should have done, but she didn't. It was just that she'd been so lonely...

Toby pulled back and she stepped away and looked at the ground, shook his hand away from her face. He moved it, but only to rest it on her shoulder. When he didn't say anything, Louise glanced up at him.

'Do we really have to go through with this divorce thing?' he whispered. 'It's not too late, you know. We could stop it any time we want.'

For a crazy moment, Louise swayed towards doing just that. Wouldn't it be easier? To be Mrs Thornton again? To know Jack had both of his parents together and wasn't going to be messed up and in rehab in five years' time? To not have to wonder about who she was and what she could be? She knew who she was with Toby. It would be like slipping on a favourite, very comfortable pair of shoes.

But there was a nasty great stone in that shoe. It was twenty years old and blonde and had legs up to its earlobes. Louise shrugged his hand away.

'What about Miranda. Remember her?'

Toby stopped smiling and looked a little uncomfortable. 'Miranda was a mistake, Miranda is... Actually, Miranda's history.'

Her eyebrows rose. Really?

'She's nothing compared to you. I still love you, Lulu. Give me another chance?' His voice had that soft, gravelly tone that used to turn her insides to mush. 'Please?'

Louise was speechless. This was exactly what she'd been desperate to hear for years. If Toby had looked at her like this just once in the run up to their split…

She shook her head and backed away, folding her arms across her middle. 'Sorry, Toby. I can't. Not now.'

Not now she knew just how love should be. How it should be equal, not one person giving and the other person taking. How it should make you feel like you could fly, not like you were something crushed under someone else's boot.

Oh, hell. And how exactly did she know these things? The only man she'd ever loved was Toby. Wasn't it? She wasn't supposed to be able to make comparisons.

'Don't be like that, hon,' he said, a hint of hardness in his tone, even though the eyes remained soft and inviting. 'We need each other. You know that…'

And then it all came sharply into focus. Poor little Miranda probably hadn't realised what hard work a movie star fifteen years her senior would be. And Toby was a movie star who'd grown used to having absolutely everything his own way from most of that time.

Guilt washed over her. That was partly her fault.

She'd let him get away with murder, had fooled herself she'd been doing at out of love, when really she'd just been scared he see through her glamorous exterior and reject her if she wasn't everything he wanted.

Well, he had. And she'd survived.

'No, Toby. I don't want to go back. I can't.'

When his smile dropped and he started looking a little sulky, Louise reached for him and laid a hand on his leather jacket. 'But I hope we can find a way to be friends—for Jack's sake.'

Right on cue, Jack rushed back into the kitchen, heading straight for the muffin tin. Toby pounced on him before he could snaffle another one, threw him over his shoulder and tickled him. Pretty soon father and son were a tangled mess of limbs and giggles on the kitchen floor.

Louise couldn't help smiling. Toby might be a lot of things, but he was a good father. She'd give him that much.

But that's all he would be from now on to her—Jack's father. Because no way was Mr Tobias Thornton talking her into being his doormat again. She'd finally moved on.

Ben stood on the jetty at Lower Hadwell and looked across the river. Just one corner of Whitehaven's roof was visible from here. In fact, because it was so hilly and the roads didn't run along the shoreline, this was the only place one could see Whitehaven from on this side of the river. And even from a boat you could only catch tantalising glimpses, never the whole thing.

A bit like its owner in that respect. Just when he'd thought he had her figured out, she turned around, showed another facet of herself and either amazed or confused him.

He turned and called for his daughter, who was busy trying to shake a crab off her fishing line into an already overflowing bucket. 'One more catch, Jas, then you'll have to put them back. Your mum's coming to pick you up soon.'

At least he hoped it would be soon.

He sighed and wandered over to Jas, who was now very carefully plopping the crabs back into the murky water. What was it with him and high-maintenance women? Was he a magnet for them, or something? Then he sighed again, because that really wasn't being fair—to Louise, especially.

It wasn't that she was self-centred or insensitive. She was just…broken. Life had broken her. And she was right. He hadn't been able to fix her, just like he hadn't been able to fix Megan.

He helped Jas collect together her bucket and line and they wandered back through the lanes to the cottage. Much to his surprise, his ex-wife turned up at six on the dot to collect their daughter. Jas hadn't even got herself ready yet, so he invited Megan inside.

'Actually,' he said, steeling himself for a torrent of you're-trying-to-sabotage-my-renaissance abuse, 'I was wondering if I could pick Jas up half an hour later on Sunday? I've got a client who wants me to meet him in Brixham earlier in the afternoon and I might be a little late getting back.'

Megan surprised him again by nodding. 'That's fine. No problem.'

Blinking, he smiled at her. 'Thanks. I appreciate it.'

She looked at him, and that hard, shiny shell that seemed to have hardened over her in the last couple of years flickered and dissolved. Just for a moment, she looked very much like the teenage girl he'd had a crush on all those years ago.

'I wanted to say again…how sorry I am about the whole newspaper thing again,' she said. 'I don't know what came over me.'

'Thank you,' he said again and then he pressed his lips together while he thought through his next words. 'There's no reason why we can't get on, why we have to keep the fights going. We were friends once, Meg…' At the start of their marriage, and even farther back— before the crush. They'd walked home from school together every day until he'd started to notice she was a girl. 'Can't we be that way again?'

Megan nodded. 'We can try,' she said, her voice a little hoarse. 'I want to try.'

Jas clumped down the stairs and banged her way into

the kitchen, her overnight bag slung over her shoulder.
'Dad, I can't find my iPod.'

'Try the floor in the living room. I almost stepped on
it earlier on.'

Jas raced off and Megan made her way towards the
door. 'See you both Sunday,' he said as he closed it
behind them.

And Ben was on his own again.

He hadn't used to mind his own company, but nowadays he seemed to have too much time to think. He sat
down on the sofa in the living room and flicked the television on, deciding to watch a game show. One of the
questions caught his attention.

What three things do plants need to grow?

Easy.

Water. Sunlight. Food. Next question, please.

But he never even heard if the contestant got it right,
because his brain started spinning.

I'm not one of your stupid plants, you know...

Louise's words from the previous week echoed
inside his skull. And then he was reminded of another
conversation he'd had with her. Months ago, way back
when they'd first met.

'You can't control the plants,' he'd told her. ' You just
tend them, give them what they need until they become
what they should.'

The sun couldn't give a plant water, and the clouds
couldn't give it food, just as the soil couldn't give it

warmth or light. And maybe…maybe…the reason he hadn't been able to fix the women in his life was because he'd tried to do everything for them, instead of just doing his bit.

Megan was starting to grow finally, starting to change. He'd just given her room, and she was getting through the hard seed stage and was starting to shoot. But it was something inside *her* that had started the metamorphosis. It had had to come from Megan.

And maybe that was that Louise needed as well. Time. Room to grow. A chance to discover whatever it was she needed inside herself. Of course, there were no guarantees. It might never happen. She might never blossom the way he knew she could, but he had to give her the chance to do it herself.

He reached over for the remote and turned the TV off and sat in the silence, processing this revelation. What Louise needed from him now was patience. Because he wasn't giving up on her. He'd meant what he'd told her—he loved her. He'd never loved anyone the way he'd loved her. Forget first love. It was second love that was the killer.

It was winter still, and the river was grey and the trees were bare, but spring would come. And until it did he'd satisfy himself with a glimpse of the white house on the top of the hill every now and then.

But he wouldn't forget. He'd be waiting for Louise to be ready.

CHAPTER THIRTY-TWO

5th April

I hope I'm continuing to fulfil the promise you made, Laura. You told God that if He gave your Whitehaven, that you'd do your best to make sure you weren't the only person who benefited from it. You also said Whitehaven should be filled with the noise of children, so I know you would have loved what we did at the picnic today.

Someone must have been smiling down on us, because it was warm enough to be June and the sun shone all day long. We had twenty teenagers, ranging from thirteen to eighteen, all of them carers for sick or elderly relatives. They don't get much fun in their lives. I know that from experience, but that's a long story...

I baked my best chocolate fudge cake and scones and banana and toffee muffins and we ate crusty rolls with cheese and ham and drank pink lemonade. I always loved the idea of pink lemonade, ever since I was little. Something about it just makes me smile.

Anyway, after lunch we had a game of rounders on

the lawn. We would have played for longer, but one of the boys was such a good hitter that the ball ended up halfway down to the river. Two of the other kids wanted to go and look for it but, as you know, that hill's rather steep and they were all a tad over-excited.

I couldn't help thinking about who wasn't there, though. I found myself staring across the river and just sighing. I wanted him to see all of it. I wanted to be able to tell him what I'd done. I miss him so much it hurts, Laura. I try to tell myself I don't think of him at all, but that's a lie. He's there in the background of every day, a presence I just can't shake. Is that how you felt about Dominic? If so, I can tell why you pined for him.

But I was horrible and hurtful and I made him go away. I know he said I should go and find him, but I can't. And it's not pride that stops me. Quite the reverse.

I don't know why I'm telling you all this. I hadn't meant to. But maybe I need to tell someone. I lied, Laura. I told him I didn't need him, but I do. Oh, how I do. That's not the problem, though. The real problem is that I don't think he needs me. Not in the sense that he doesn't want me, but in the sense that I'm no good for him. And I'm not sure I can change that.

I'm being very depressing, aren't I? But I thought, of all people, you'd understand. You knew how to pine and yearn too. I only wish I could move past it, as you did, but it doesn't seem to want to let me go.

Enough. I haven't finished telling you about the day

yet. And what happened next was probably the most important bit. After games on the lawn we just let the kids explore. I chatted with Sue, the lady from Relief who had helped me organise the day. She was so appreciative, and I kept having to tell her that, really, it was my pleasure. I don't think she believed me. She asked if we could do it again in the summer, but I didn't answer straight away because we'd ended up near the stable blocks.

I'm renovating them. The plans were for a guest house—a separate apartment entirely, with its own bathroom and kitchen and living space. It's where I would have put my mother-in-law if I still had one. That woman never liked me.

Anyway, as we stood there, looking at the scaffolding and builders' debris, an idea hit me. I don't know why I didn't think of it before. I turned to Sue and said, "Yes, of course," and then I told her I had something else I wanted to discuss with her. I'm hoping that while she's in a good mood, she'll say yes.

Ben drove up to Whitehaven's gates the Tuesday after the Easter bank holiday. He'd have much rather come his usual way, via the river, but he sensed that wouldn't be quite right. Things were back the way they were right at the start; he'd be a trespasser.

He felt a little like that now, but his team had been here for a week, doing some planting and finishing up some paving that couldn't be done when the ground had been waterlogged in winter. Any communication he'd had from Louise on the matter had been through curt email. Eventually, he'd let his second-in-command liaise with her instead.

His heart thumped inside his chest like the hammer on one of those old-fashioned fire bells—relentless and impossible to ignore. Loud.

He hadn't seen Louise since New Year's Day, and every second of the last few months had dragged its heels like a truculent teenager. Had it been long enough? Her divorce must be final now. Would that have changed things?

He didn't even know if he was going to see her. He'd decided to let fate decide. He'd go and survey the work, talk to his men—and the one woman on his team—and then he'd leave. If he came across Louise in the meantime then maybe it would be a sign.

But he didn't come across Louise.

In fact, her absence seemed…deliberate. It was as if he could sense her presence at the darkened windows of the house but never saw her. He tried not to look too often, but sometimes he couldn't help himself.

Right at the last moment, as he'd opened the door to his car and was climbing inside he glanced over his shoulder. He saw half a face in the study window. Just one eye. One gorgeous eye. And the swish of dark hair as she moved away.

He turned back towards his car and lowered himself carefully into the driving seat.

She wasn't ready. Even though spring was in full riot. But he supposed humans had different seasons to plants.

He put his car into gear and drove out of Whitehaven's gates without looking back. How long this winter of Louise's would last was anyone's guess. He knew some people who'd made it last a lifetime.

The bluebells had been an gone and summer was in full swing by the time the work on the old stable block was completed. The garden was looking fabulous too, although that always made her feel a little sad. Ben's men had done a grand job. She hadn't seen him again, really, since New Year's Day. Only that one time she hadn't been able to stop herself spying on him. Usually she was stronger. Usually she kept away from the village and shopped in the nearby towns. She never took the ferry any more, but drove the long way round if she wanted to get to the other side of the river.

How could she face him? After all those awful things she'd said to him? She'd had a chance and she'd blown it. More than that. She'd blasted it to smithereens with dynamite. She couldn't put it all back together again now, even though she wanted to more than anything.

At least by fulfilling Laura's promise she'd found something to do to take her mind off it all. There had been a lot of years when she'd been alone in this house. A lot of years when she might have forgotten her promise and kept Whitehaven to herself. Louise had the feeling that Laura might have been sad she hadn't done more.

Since Easter she'd spent a lot of time unpacking her feelings about her childhood. Writing in her diary helped. For some reason, she always addressed the entries to Laura. It had started off for a reason, but now it had become habit. Even though she'd never known the old lady, she felt like a friend. And talking to a friend seemed easier than just filling blank page after blank page.

When Louise looked back at her life now she saw it differently. In her teenage years she'd just soldiered on, doing the best she could. But now, looking back on her past with the eyes of a mother, she wondered why there hadn't been more help. Social services had been all very keen to let them know when things weren't up to scratch, but nobody had ever offered to step in and help. Not really. Not in any lasting or sensible way.

A break—just a week away from it now and then—might have made all the difference. She'd have gone back refreshed, ready to carry on. And she'd have been less susceptible to impossible fairy tales and knights. Not knights in shining armour, but in black leather—wolves' clothing. She sighed. Maybe that was being unfair to Toby. He wasn't the devil incarnate; he was just immature and weak. Spoiled.

Louise picked up her bunch of keys and headed out towards the stables. It was time for one last look around before her guests arrived.

In the small cobbled courtyard in front of the stables, there was now a fountain and bright flowers in pots, benches to sun oneself on. Inside was even better. She'd torn up the original plans for the interior and started again, driving her contractor nuts. Thankfully, a promise of a hefty bonus if it was ready in time for the school holidays had put a smile back on his face.

Sue had said yes to her idea. A joyful and unequivocal yes. Relief were apparently desperate for more respite holiday centres to send the kids they supported, places they could rest, unwind and meet others in the same boat. On site would be a cook and general den-mother, so the guests didn't have to do chores like they did at home, and a child psychologist would be making regular visits. Activities were on hand for those who wanted them, from sailing to pony trekking to lounging on a beach with nothing to do but smile.

Louise opened the front door and stepped inside. The lounge area, with large U-shaped sectional sofa and all the toys and game consoles a teenager could ask for, filled one end of what had once been the stalls. The other end housed a kitchen and eating area. Beyond that was a smaller sitting room better for private chats and an office where Louise was taking care of the admin herself. After organising Toby's life for more than ten years, she'd discovered she was rather good at it.

Upstairs were six bedrooms for the young people who were coming to visit, and a room for the live-in youth worker who'd be here in any and all of the school holidays—except Christmas. No matter who your family were, you always needed to be home at Christmas.

Louise took one last look around the apartments, checking everything was perfect. Three girls and a boy were due to arrive from London in the next hour. They'd decided to start at less than full capacity to iron out the kinks. Each group would stay for ten days. By the end of the summer, twenty teenagers would have had holidays here. She wished it could be more.

Looking round one last time, she made her way to the door, stopping to plump a cushion on the sofa. She'd chosen everything herself. She'd even done most of the painting herself. Apart from the woodwork. She'd left that to the experts.

As she walked out she felt a lump rise in her throat. Silly, she knew, but she was pleased the reality of the Laura Hastings Retreat lived up to what she'd seen in her imagination, what she'd wished for them. She just wanted these kids to have the best. They deserved it.

***

It was a long time before Louise unlocked the drawer in the boathouse desk again. She lost the key. But as she was hunting for a business card of a local café owner who'd said he'd be amenable to giving pizza-making lessons to the teenagers at the retreat, she found it in a basket in the kitchen. Lost items had a habit of turning up where you least expected them. Like the diary itself, she supposed.

That same afternoon she strolled down to the boathouse and opened the drawer. She pulled the diary out ran her fingertips over the smooth leather surface, then she picked it book up and flicked through it. It was only as she neared the back she realised she'd never read the final entry, the one after Dominic had left Laura standing in the garden. She'd been too upset to read any more at that point and after she'd done all her research to find out how the story ended, she'd forgotten all about it.

Carefully, she leafed through the pages one last time. There were a dozen or so creamy blank pages at the back of the book, so it felt as if this last entry, which was only a page long, wasn't so much a running out of room, but having nothing further to say.

She took a deep breath to still her fluttering heart and began to read:

1st May, 1957
I should have seen it coming. But hope, like love, is

blind. It sees what it wants to see, and I didn't want to see Dominic walking away from me one last time.

He feels so guilty about Jean, you see. He feels her unhappiness was his fault. And I suppose part of it was, but not all of it, and she should have appreciated the man who sacrificed himself to keep her happy, not leave him in the most cruel way, having to explain everything to their child.

He was too good for her and, unfortunately, too good for me.

And a noble heart like that feels its mistakes keenly. He couldn't get past the guilt. Couldn't forgive himself, even though it was only his heart that wandered and never his body, and he did his best to put it right and leave it behind.

Months ago now I heard that Jean had problems with drink, that it had run in her family and that her mother's sister has spent the last fifteen years in a sanatorium. Dominic aside, I think Jean had other, much more powerful demons to wrestle, but I don't think he'll ever let himself believe that. So, even if we'd taken our chance, his guilt would have poisoned it in the end.

Perhaps it is better to think of him as the perfect soul I could never have than the man who grew to hate me more and more each day. I've already made one of those and one is enough.

No, Dominic will never be mine, I understand that now. He won't ever let himself be truly happy again, because he doesn't believe he deserves to be, and he and I are the casualties of that lie. I don't want to accept it, but I have no choice, and I refuse to send myself mad pining for what can't be. It's time to find a new dream, a new future. It's time to close this chapter of my life and move on.

It's time to stop waiting.

Louise put the diary down and cried. For Laura. For Dominic. For poor loyal Alex. For Caroline, who'd never known her mother's love. And for herself.

She'd blown it, hadn't she? With Ben.

He'd offered her all she'd ever wanted and she'd been too scared to reach out and take the gift. Just as Dominic hadn't been able to allow himself happiness with Laura.

Could she go to him now? He'd said she could. But that had been six months ago. Had his offer had an expiry date? And even if it hadn't, what would she say, what could she bring to him in return? She was still the same damaged Louise who didn't know a good thing when it happened to her. What if she hurt him again?

The problem was, Ben really didn't deserve *her*, and she didn't know how to change that.

CHAPTER THIRTY-THREE

By the end of the week, the occupants of the new apartments had stopped staring every time they saw Louise and were much more ready to beg for cake or tease her. Jack was really enjoying having the company too. He and Kate, the den mother, had taken three of their 'guests'—James, Letitia and Rebecca—across to Lower Hadwell to go crabbing off the jetty. Jack was eager to show his expertise with a bit of string and some bacon rind, apparently.

Only Molly had remained behind. She was a quiet, mousy girl, who had only hovered on the fringes of the group all week. Louise found her in the stable court-yard when she went to collect a cake tin she'd left in the kitchen.

'Hey, Molly! How's it going?'

Molly dipped her head and looked at Louise through her thick, dark blonde hair. 'Okay.'

'Have you been having a good time?'

Molly grimaced. 'Yes.' She fidgeted. 'I can't get a

signal on my crappy mobile here. Can I use the office to phone home?'

Louise sat down next to her. The spring air was sweet and fresh and the sun was beautifully warm on her skin in the sheltered courtyard. 'Of course, you can. But I thought you already called this morning.'

Molly nodded and looked away.

'They're okay, you know, your family. They'll do fine while you're here. Relief will have sent some excellent staff to help with all your usual tasks while you're away.'

Molly looked unconvinced. 'They might not do things right. I need to check.'

Louise dearly wanted to put her arm round the girl, but she wasn't sure it would be welcomed. Only fourteen, and already she carried the responsibility for her two disabled parents. The psychologist had warned her that some of the children might be like this, and she had vague memories of not being able to switch off herself.

'How would you like something to do?'

At this, Molly brightened. Just as Louise had guessed, she would feel less uncomfortable…less guilty…if she had a job.

'You lot are eating cakes faster than I can bake them. I was planning to do a chocolate one today and I could do with an extra pair of hands.'

For the first time that week, Molly smiled. 'Sure. I can help.'

As they measured and mixed and washed up back in Whitehaven's kitchen, Molly began to relax a little. Louise took the opportunity to dispense a little wisdom.

'It's okay to enjoy yourself, Molly.'

Molly frowned. 'I know that.'

Hoping that this would be the right time, she walked over to her and put an arm gently round her shoulders. 'You don't have to feel guilty for being here. It's what the scheme is all about.'

Molly sniffed. 'I know that. It's just that I feel bad leaving Mum and Dad alone while I get to stay in a beautiful place like this…and with you. It's too nice.'

One-handed, Louise tore a piece of kitchen towel off the roll on the table and passed it to the girl. 'Molly…' Oh, blast, she was tearing up too. She grabbed a piece for herself as well. 'You work hard all year round. Much harder than other kids your age. You deserve this, you really do. And your parents would want you to enjoy yourself while you're here, not spend the whole time worrying about them or feeling guilty.'

As she hugged Molly, she suddenly could picture her own father's face the day she'd run home from the supermarket and told him about the modelling scout. He'd been so proud of her. And never once had he said anything to make her feel as if she was abandoning him. He'd been such a special man.

And yet, for all these years, she'd held onto the same feeling that was eating Molly alive. The girl beside her started to tremble and Louise pulled her close for a proper hug. 'Is it really okay?' Molly whispered.

'Yes.' The kitchen distorted and became all blurry. Louise's lip began to wobble. 'Yes, it really is.'

Ben walked into Mrs Green's shop on a bright July morning to get his usual paper. She'd been as meek as a lamb with him since that incident at Christmas. Louise now had a most loyal supporter in her. And that was good. For Louise. The tide of opinion might turn one person at a time, but it was still turning in the right direction.

Thoughts of Louise led to thoughts of Whitehaven and its luscious gardens. He would have loved to have seen how they looked now in full summer, with all the borders in bloom. He wanted to know if they matched the vision in his head when he'd drawn up the plans.

He reached the counter and Mrs Green just handed him a paper without asking which one. Then she handed him a glossy women's magazine, not one of the cheap, gossipy ones, but one of the high-fashion mags that also ran articles on serious subjects.

'A bit old for Jas, Mrs Green,' he said, without looking at it, and handed it back to her.

She shook her head. 'I thought you might be interested.'

Him? He started to chuckle, but a glimpse of a pair of dark and stormy eyes on the cover made him look a little closer. Louise. She'd done an interview. He moved out of the way of the counter so the person behind him could pay and scrabbled through the pages until he found the article he was looking for. It was a long one.

He read it as he walked down the hill back to the cottage. He was working from home today. More than once he stopped in the middle of the road and shook his head. Especially when he'd realised he'd forgotten to pay Mrs Green. But she'd understand. And she'd know he'd settle up tomorrow.

Then, as he reached his front gate he started to smile, even though the ache in his chest that he thought had dulled a little in the last few months began to quietly throb again.

Amazing. He'd always said so. And here she was believing it. Living it.

Not only had she done something amazing at Whitehaven with her new respite centre, she was doing the interview to raise the profile of the charity she was now patron of. Relief were lobbying the government for new funding for child carers, not just respite care, but proper practical help on a day-to-day basis.

And Louise Thornton, the woman who would rather cut off her right arm rather than talk to a journalist, had not only given an interview—and let the photographers into the new apartments at Whitehaven—but had opened up about her own childhood, her own lack of education, in an effort to prevent more children to have to live through the same things. He felt his chest expand as he read that she was planning to study part-time for a degree in child psychology.

He reached his front door and misjudged putting the key in the lock, because he just couldn't stop reading. He flicked the magazine closed so he could stare at the cover. The eyes were the same perfect almond shape with their dark lashes, and, yes, they still held the same dark intensity, but there was something new there.

Some people might call it confidence. Some might call it resilience. But Ben knew what it was that he saw there.

He saw not just Spring, but Summer.

This could be the stupidest thing he'd ever done. Except, maybe, that time when his sister had convinced him to fly off the shed roof with a pillow case for a Batman cape and he'd ended up with two broken arms for his trouble. Ben tied his dinghy onto the iron ring outside Louise's boathouse and wondered whether he should just sail straight back across the river, because, actually he'd been right the first time. This *was* the stupidest thing he'd ever done.

It was just past noon and the most glorious summer day. He stood for a moment on the jetty and considered his next move. Where was Louise likely to be at this time? Up at the retreat centre? In her kitchen? Up in London visiting friends?

He didn't have a clue, and it saddened him that he didn't know, that her life had changed so much since he'd last seen her. But at the same time he was immensely proud of her. He'd seen all that potential inside of her, knew she had the ability to do something with it, but it had taken strength of character and guts to turn that into something real.

Something flashed up on the boathouse balcony and he immediately craned his neck to see what it was. The sun had bounced off the glass part of the door as it had opened and out stepped…Louise.

She was wearing a faint smile and her long chocolate-brown hair glowed chestnut in the sunshine. He couldn't move. Despite all his carefully rehearsed speeches, suddenly he didn't know what to say. If it was possible, he'd forgotten how beautiful she was—or maybe she had just got more beautiful, because there was something different about her.

She rested her hands on the edge of the balcony and leaned forward, breathing in the salty river air.

And then she saw him and stiffened in surprise. He couldn't hear her from where he was standing, but he was sure he saw her mouth his name. The lapping of the river, the constant shrieking of the seagulls all died away as they both stood frozen to the spot, staring at each other.

And then she smiled.

He wasn't sure how he got there, but suddenly he was

at the top of the jetty, then running up the steps to the boathouse's upper room. He made himself stop when he got to the door that led onto the narrow balcony, half-worried she would disappear into thin air if he got too close.

She was leaning against the rail, her back to the river. The breeze tugged at the hem of her long, frilly-edged skirt.

'Ben,' she said again. Her smile was soft and warm with a hint of sadness. 'It's good to see you again.'

He nodded. Nothing sensible was going to come out of his mouth unless he got his act together. 'You too.'

'I've been meaning to come and see you,' she said, 'but I just haven't…' She trailed off, leaving the rest unsaid, but Ben didn't care. The fact she'd been considering making the first move was all that he needed.

His heart started to pound in his chest as he crossed the threshold onto the balcony. He was close enough to touch her now, but he wouldn't—not yet.

'I saw the article in the magazine.'

Okay. If this was as smooth as he was going to get, he might just as well jump back into his dinghy right now.

She nodded. 'I'm going to be in the spotlight whether I like it or not, so I might as well get to choose where it shines.' She looked at her feet, then back up at him. 'So, Ben Oliver, why are you trespassing on my land again after all this time?'

It was a joke and he was supposed to laugh, but he seemed to have lost the knack.

'I…um…forgot to give you something.'

She frowned and her eyebrows arched in the middle. 'We haven't seen each other for months. What do you mean? Is there another invoice I haven't paid, because—'

'It's not so much *what* I didn't give you, but *when.*'

'When…?' she repeated frowning.

He nodded. 'Christmas.'

His heart slunk into his boots. On the way over here this had seemed clever, now it just seemed…lame.

'Christmas was a long time ago.'

He reached into his pocket and his fingers closed around the palm-sized box hidden there. 'I know. But some gifts have their own seasons. This one was a little premature back then.'

She bit her lip. 'Am I going to like this gift?'

It was now or never. And he was shaking in his sensible boots. He looped the little ribbon holding the box closed round his finger and used it to pull the silver parcel out of his pocket. Then he dropped it in her hands.

'I really don't know. And I'm not sure it's in season even now, but sometimes, you can just wait too long…'

It didn't seem to matter that he wasn't making any sense, because she was staring so hard at the little package he sensed she wasn't taking it in anyway. With excruciating slowness, she tugged the velvet bow and let it fall to the floor. Then she took the lid off the box.

'Oh.'

Oh? Was that a good *oh* or a bad *oh*?

'Oh, Ben!'

A good *oh*. Warmth began to spread upwards from his toes.

Her nose crinkled in confusion. 'Mistletoe? But it's almost summer!' Gently, she reached into the box and pulled the sprig out to look at it. A thin white ribbon looped round the top and was tied in an elaborate bow. 'It's not even plastic! It's…'

'…the real deal,' he finished for her.

She stepped close enough for him to smell her perfume. 'How did you…?'

He shrugged. 'I have my sources.'

She twiddled the mistletoe between finger and thumb and suddenly grew more serious. 'What does this mean, Ben?'

'Isn't it obvious?'

She bit her lip and looked away. 'You want to…kiss me?'

Always. Forever. But he'd promised himself he wouldn't until she'd given him the answer he wanted to hear. 'I told you I knew what I felt and I still feel the same way.'

Louise shook her head. 'After all the things I said to you! The way I behaved… I don't deserve it!'

He couldn't use his hands to make her look at him, so he concentrated on just pulling her gaze to his by the force of his will-power. 'Yes, you do.'

Six months ago, he would have seen the doubt in her eyes, but the woman standing before him looked deep into his eyes and he saw the light of recognition and understanding flicker on. Slowly, she raised her arm so the little green sprig dangled above her head and, taking a deep breath, she closed her eyes.

This was it. Now or never. He thought perhaps he was going to hyperventilate, but managed to pull himself together. Louise was still poised, ready for the kiss, her lips soft and slightly parted. When he didn't respond straight away, she lifted one eyelid, making the other scrunch up.

Her whisper of uncertainty only made his fingers shake all the more. 'Ben?'

He nodded up to the little green sprig with its cluster of white berries above their heads. 'Look a little closer.'

With his fingers as deft as a bunch of bananas, he tugged her hand downward so the mistletoe rested at eye level and she could see the diamond ring held fast by the white velvet bow.

'Marry me?'

Louise's eyes snapped all the way open and she dropped the sprig on the floor, then her hands flew to her chest and stayed there.

He bent down and gently rescued both mistletoe and

ring before he trampled it with his boots. Louise looked as if she was in a trance. Taking a chance, because she wasn't slapping him in the face or running up the hill, he twirled the mistletoe above their heads once more.

'Will you…?'

'Yes! Oh, Ben, yes!' She threw herself at him and almost sent him flying over the edge of the balcony. And then she was kissing him on his face, his neck, his lips… He particularly liked the bit when she got to his lips. But eventually he pulled away, peeled her hand off him and guided them so she could pull gently at the ribbon to release the ring. It dropped into his waiting hand.

She looked up at him, laughing and shaking her head, her eyes shining. 'Are you for real, Ben Oliver?'

He nodded and lowered his head, then brushed his mouth across hers, savouring the moment, and slid the ring onto her left hand. Even though it was high summer, he had one last wish to bestow upon her.

'Merry Christmas, Louise,' he whispered against her lips before wrapping her in his arms and pulling her into the cool darkness of the boathouse.

CHAPTER THIRTY-FOUR

2nd September

I don't know if you ever saw a wedding at Whitehaven, Laura, but it was a beautiful thing. I wanted to have it at Christmas, but it turned out we just couldn't wait. In the end we were married in the church in Lower Hadwell and then the whole wedding party made its way in little boats across the river and up the hill to have the reception at Whitehaven.

There was a marquee on the top lawn and fairy lights in the trees and magic in the air. I set a place for you, because I thought you would have enjoyed the party. Ben told me you liked a good tune and a dance.

I did what you wanted: I filled Whitehaven with children—and children who really need it. You should see how they change while they're here, how they look when they leave. And I'm hoping to fill it with more of my own too.

I know you didn't have your first choice happy ending here, but from what Ben tells me about you, I don't think you'd begrudge mine. He said you always had soft spot for him and nagged him mercilessly to find a nice girl and get married again. I'm not sure I'm who you'd have picked, but I promise you this, Laura: I love him so, so much, and I will take the very best care of him. I don't know who to thank for bringing him to me—you or Whitehaven—but I'm very grateful. When he looks at me, I know I'm not an empty shell, and I know that I have plenty to give him too.

Oh… One last thing: I'm putting your diary back where you left it in the fireplace, and I'm adding this one too. I've only kept it about six months, but it's full, and there's a lot of living and a lot of thinking in it. Maybe they'll both stay there undiscovered until they rot, but maybe they won't. One day, someone who needs them might find them. I hope so. Because then Whitehaven's magic will start again.

Thank you, Laura, and goodbye. I hope you are as peaceful and happy where you are as I am at this moment.

Lots of love,
Louise Oliver

***

Feeling peckish after reading about Louise's delicious cakes? Don't worry, here is Fiona Harper's yummy recipe for Madeira cake, so that you can make your own.

Happy baking…and Merry Christmas!

Madeira Cake

I can't resist the unfussy, dense golden taste of a good Madeira cake. Once you've made your own, you'll never want to buy it from the supermarket again.

240g/8½oz softened butter
200g/7oz golden caster sugar, plus a little extra for dusting
210g/7oz self-raising flour
90g/3oz plain flour
3 eggs
Grated zest and juice of 1 lemon
Few drops vanilla extract

1. Pre-heat the oven to 170C/Gas 3 and butter and line a 450g/1lb loaf tin.
2. Cream the butter and the sugar together, then add the lemon zest and vanilla extract.
3. Add the eggs one at a time, along with a tablespoon of flour, and mix in well.
4. Mix in the rest of the flour and then the lemon juice.
5. Spoon into the loaf tin and smooth the mixture into the corners with the back of a spoon. Sprinkle the top with a couple of tablespoons of sugar.
6. Bake for one hour, or until a cake tester comes out clean. Let it stand on a wire rack in the tin until cool, then turn out. *(If you're impatient, like me, and don't wait until it's cool you'll end up cracking the cake. Of course, this also works as an excuse to hoover up the broken bits while they're still warm. It's up to you if you want to confess this to the family or pretend it was all a horrible accident.)*

Sparkling Christmas kisses!

Bryony's daughter, Lizzie, wants was a *dad* for Christmas
and Bryony's determined to fulfil this Christmas wish.
But when every date ends in disaster, Bryony fears she'll
need a miracle. But she only needs a man for
Christmas, not for love…right?

Unlike Bryony, the last thing Helen needs is a man! In her
eyes, all men are *Trouble*! Of course, it doesn't help that as
soon as she arrives in the snow-covered mountains, she
meets Mr Tall, Dark and Handsome *Trouble*!

www.millsandboon.co.uk